The Struggle

By: Suz Armstrong

The Struggle
Copyright ©2020 by Suz Armstrong

All rights reserved. Printed in the United States of America.

No part of this book may be used or reproduced in any manner whatsoever without the express written permission of the author.

This is a work of fiction. Names, characters, places and incidents are either the product of the author's imagination or are used fictitiously, and any resemblance to any actual persons, living or dead, events, or locales are entirely coincidental.

Published by CLC Publishing, LLC, Mustang, OK.

ISBN: 9798582419723

Fiction/Christian/Romance
Fiction/Romance/Western

Prologue

She looked up as she heard footsteps coming close to her. She turned just as a good-looking man approached the front of the truck. "Vehicle trouble?" He asked, grinning at her. Carlie blushed.

"I'm really not crazy." She sputtered, a bit embarrassed about her sudden outrage on 'Ole Blue. "Just been a rough morning." The man grinned at her. "Ma'am, mind if I take a look?" He offered.

Carlie nodded. She took him in. Tall. Dark hair. Just enough of the five-o-clock shadow to makehim look genuine. Cowboy boots and hat. Wrangler jeans that looked really good on his slim, but muscular, cowboy-type figure. The man looked like he just hopped out of one of those cowboy movies.

Clint Eastowood on his best days, had nothing on this good-looking guy standing before her. She sucked in a deep breath. "Thanks." She said. "I did the usual stuff. You know, checked the fluids and the spark plugs,thinking it might be the fuel pump." She supplied. The handsome man nodded. He is really cute, she thought to herself. Then, just as quickly, she reprimanded herself. But why should she not look?

Chapter 1

Joe Welsh stared out the window of his office in the high rise in Cincinnati. He was pondering his life, his marriage. At age 40, he was every bit in the shape he had been in high school when he played on the school's baseball team. Joe stood exactly 6'. He was well built and could still get the ladies' attention. He had married his high school crush and had two children, but he had not been happy in his marriage for a while now. When the boredom had settled in, Joe couldn't be sure, but it was there. He had gone to college to become an architect and loved his job. Currently he was working on a remodeling project for one of the top modeling agencies in Cincinnati. His work often took him to places like California and New York. He did his job well and thought he had the perfect life. That's the way it looked on the outside anyway. He was married to Carlie Michaels Welsh and thought he loved her. However, loving someone and being *in* love with someone were two different things.

He was the worship leader at the church he and his family attended. Joe often made quite large contributions to local charities and their causes to fight cancer or to feed hungry children. He liked his wife to stay home and tend to the house and kids. He worked hard and had become a very successful architect. He used to love coming home to his wife and kids after a long day's hard work. His family had given him a sense of security. Sure, he loved his kids, but even the kids made him feel tied down.

Joe had always been the adventurous type. When he married Carlie, he had imagined a totally different life with her. He had imagined traveling the world with her. Then, Carlie became pregnant with their first child, a girl. A few years later, they had their surprise baby, a little boy. Of course, Joe had been happy at the time, but now the kids were getting older and didn't need him as much. At least that's what he thought. He still loved his kids, but he needed to do other things. He loved that his job let him travel. He loved that he didn't have to be home at a certain time.

Joe used to look forward to quiet romantic time with Carlie. He had loved Carlie since the first time he had laid eyes on her.

She had been a cheerleader for the football team, while his affections were for baseball. That had been twenty some years ago.

Although Carlie was still beautiful and had maintained her strong, slim cheerleading figure, Joe could feel himself becoming bored with the daily "family man" routine. He had been feeling restless for the last couple of months. Carlie had become boring to him. She played the good house wife, the good church girl, and good mom to the T just as he asked her to. So he couldn't exactly blame her for feeling bored and restless in their marriage.

He could blame it on a mid-life crisis like so many other men his age seemed to do these days. Had he fallen out of love with Carlie? Was that even possible to do? Wasn't true love supposed to be forever? When had Carlie lost her vivaciousness, her love for life? These were the thoughts that went through his mind as he sat at his desk with the plans for the modeling agency. The phone rang, jolting him out of his thoughts.

"Joe, Katrina from La Bonita Modeling Agency is on the phone for you." His secretary informed him. Joe felt himself sitting up a little straighter as he picked up the phone. A smile played at the corner of his mouth. Katrina Pickard was the owner of La *Bonita*. She was the one who screened and hired the models, although she could have easily been a model herself. She had flirted with Joe on several occasions, when they had worked together on the new plans for the agency. She definitely had his affections. In fact, Joe had fantasized about being with Katrina and what it would be like. "This is Joe Welsh." He said into the receiver. "Joe, Kat." He could hear her smiling through the wires that carried his voice to her pretty little ear. *Stop it, Joe! You are married to a beautiful woman.* He silently reminded himself. Then, as if to counteract the thought, *Beautiful, yes, but she is becoming a bore.* "I am just confirming our meeting in your office this afternoon at 3." Joe cleared his throat and checked his day planner. "Yes, it's on my calendar." He confirmed. "Good, I'll bring the coffee. See you at 3." Katrina said.

Joe hung up the phone and checked his watch. It was p.m. He subconsciously straightened his tie and ran his fingers through his hair. He sprayed on some extra cologne and straightened up his desk. He mentally ran through Carlie's schedule. She had some kind of activity to attend at their son's school and would not be home with the kids until late. Maybe he could invite Katrina to the house for a glass of wine. He could make up some excuse about the plans being in his home office. He smiled as he tucked the plans into his briefcase. Carlie usually took the kids out for a treat after any school activity and would not be expected home until 10 or so. Yes, he decided, tonight would be the night with Kat.

At exactly p.m., Kat waltzed into his office wearing a short, tight red dress with a small gold belt that accentuated her perfect waist line. The dress plunged just enough for a man to wonder what was underneath. Her long auburn hair flowed down her slender back. Her matching high heels accentuated her long, slender legs that went on forever. Joe stood and pulled a chair up to the desk for Kat. He started to sit, then snapped his fingers. "Oh, would you mind if we went to my house to do this? I picked up the wrong plans. I grabbed the plans for a building I'm constructing in Manhattan instead. The plans for *La Bonita* are on my desk."

Kat grinned. "That would be fine. I thought I was going to be late so I passed on the coffee." Joe laughed with her as he grabbed his briefcase, opened the door for her, and locked it behind him. He led her to the elevator, where it was all he could to do to not grab her and kiss her right then and there. The elevator took them to the parking garage and he led Kat to his car. The hour drive was tense as Joe felt like he would explode if he didn't at least touch the woman next to him. Kat was twenty-two and gorgeous. She talked his head off about the remodeling, the new models she was screening next week, and all the new outfits she had ordered from local designers for the new models to wear. Joe politely smiled and made a few comments here and there. He could not wait to get her to his house, where he could pour glasses of red wine and see where things went.

Joe could imagine running hot soapy water in the tub that was luxuriously made to easily fit two people. He had it designed for that purpose. That was where he and Carlie had spent their romantic evenings....before he got bored with being a family man. He pushed the fact that he was married out of his mind. He could picture Kat smelling wonderful in lavender or coconut. Finally, he pulled the car into the driveway. He smiled as he led Kat into the house. He locked the door behind them.

After seating her in his office, he retrieved the wine and wine glasses from the kitchen, which also had been designed with Carlie in mind. He pushed his wife out of his mind. Tonight he was going to be with a gorgeous, sexy woman. Tomorrow he would worry about the consequences.

Chapter 2

One Year Later

The wind and rain beat fiercely against the brick house. The heavens let go with all their anger as the thunder roared and lightning bolted through the dark sky. The trees swayed and their branches bent underneath the weight of the storm. The two-story brick house could stand against the bold weather, it was those inside the house who were experiencing their own stormy weather in life.

A family whose lives had been turned upside down over the last year were struggling to put the pieces back together. Circumstances had left Carlie Michaels a single mom with two kids to raise. The first few months had been as if Carlie and her two children were living a nightmare.

Carlie had struggled with so many emotions for the first couple of months of the affair and ultimately, the divorce. She had spent a month applying for several positions here in Wilmington, Ohio, but with no luck. Finally, the local grocery store had called her and hired her as a cashier.

The pay wasn't much, but Carlie took it as she needed some kind of income to keep her bills paid. She at least was able to get in forty hours a week. It kept the bills paid and food on the table, but not much for any extras. The house itself, thankfully, was paid for, as it had belonged to Carlie's parents. Carlie had not understood at the time, the sudden turn of events. She still didn't, but she had to make a choice to either to move on with her life or to sink in self-pity and depression.

She chose the former. She had to be strong for her two children, Roxanne and Josh. Roxanne had just turned thirteen and was going through the normal and expected changes of becoming a teenage girl, mood swings and attitude included. Josh was quite a bit younger than Roxanne. He was just seven. He had been a surprise baby, but nonetheless, Carlie loved him just as much. It was one year ago today that their lives came crashing down on them. One year ago today Joe Welsh had decided that he no longer wanted his family or the life and responsibility that went with a family.

He had become more interested in his girlfriend that he had met on a job. It was that day that had sent Carlie and the kids into a spiraling hurricane of a new struggle and a new life that they had to rebuild on their own.

The crashing sounds woke Carlie with a jolt. She looked over at her alarm clock. It read 5:00 a.m. She longed to stay snuggled under the safety of her big comforter that her grandmother had quilted for her. Carlie had been in her senior year at Wilmington High when her grandmother had quilted the black and orange quilt in honor of Carlie being Valedictorian. The quilt didn't exactly match the elaborately decorated bedroom, but Carlie loved and treasured the quilt more than anything. Joe had not liked the quilt. So, Carlie had put it in her hope chest and only brought it out on nights that Joe had to work late. Now, she slept underneath it every night.

Her grandmother passed away the year before she and Joe had split. Carlie missed her grandmother greatly. She wanted to stay under the quilt now and sleep for a few more hours, but she knew she should get up and get her day started. . She dreaded these kinds of mornings. She really preferred to stay in bed with a good book over getting up on stormy days like this one. However, responsibility called and she had to answer. She would have to wake up her daughter in an hour to get her ready for school. Her son, being only in the second grade, could sleep in a little longer than his sister. Usually however, Josh was up with Roxanne.

Carlie let him stay in bed though and watch whatever happened to be on *Nickelodeon*. Carlie slowly rolled out of bed, letting her feet land on the soft, plush, maroon carpet of her bedroom floor. She grabbed her robe and slid on her slippers before padding down the hall to the bathroom. She let the water get hot before stepping into the shower stall. She was thankful to have the shower separate from the tub, a convenience her ex-husband had built into the bathroom before he ran off with his model girlfriend last year.

Normally, Carlie enjoyed taking relaxing bubble baths in the tub late at night when the kids were asleep. She remembered how she and Joe would pour glasses of sparkling wine and sit in the tub together enfolded in each other's arms, the way bonded, happy married couples should be. That was until she came home from a school activity with the kids and had found Joe and his model girlfriend wrapped up in each other's arms in the tub. As if that had not been bad enough, they had bathed in Carlie's favorite scented soap.

After that incident, *incident,* was that what she had called it? More like an *affair.* At any rate, Carlie had scrubbed and bleached the darn tub until her fingers turned white, but she still could not bring herself to sit in it. Images of Joe and his perfect, model girlfriend kept creeping up in Carlie's mind. Well, ok, so she wasn't *exactly* a model. She was more of the owner of a modeling company, a company that Carlie's ex had been working with on a remodeling project.

Kat, short for Katrina, was a five-foot-eight-inch brunette with hair like silk and legs that went on forever. She had enticed and flirted with Joe until he had given into her, fell in love, and ran off. So the story goes. Carlie and her two children had tried to move on with their lives, but it had been a tough year for all of them since the divorce.

Ironically, the divorce had not taken that long to finalize. Joe had actually admitted to having the affair and Carlie got the divorce. She had gone back to her maiden name of Michaels as she no longer wished to be known as Mrs. Joe Welsh. However, child support and alimony were still tied up in the court system as Joe had been fired, well *supposedly* had been fired. Carlie had her suspicions that Joe had actually quit his job in order to avoid having to pay the owed child support and alimony. However, Carlie also knew, from conversing with her attorney, that if Joe and Kat married, then Kat could be made to pay the child support. So much for wishful thinking.

Carlie had taken a job at the local grocery store. It didn't pay much. She could barely pay the bills, but it was a job and with the child support still being held up in court, she had to work as many hours as she could to make ends meet. Carlie shook her head as she stepped into the shower and let the hot beads wash over her.

Once showered, Carlie stepped out of the stall onto the cream-colored, plush bath mat. The softness of the mat felt like heaven underneath her feet. She dried off and wrapped a towel in turban style around her wet hair. She put on her robe and slippers and went back down the hall to her room to dress.

How many times had she and Joe lovingly and playfully roamed down this hall after their romantic soaks in the tub? Carlie sighed deeply as she went to her dresser and pulled out her favorite jeans and a teal sweater with a cowl neck. Once dressed, she returned to the bathroom to blow dry her hair and apply a light coat of make-up. Today was her day off, but she had to go pay bills and go to the grocery store for their weekly food supply. Carlie stood before the full length mirror of the bathroom door.

At thirty-eight years old, she was still a beautiful woman. Her chestnut hair hung half-way down her back in waves. She still had the slim figure she had in high school where she was the captain of the cheerleading squad for the school's football team and where she had met Joe.

Joe had not been on the football team. He had spent his time playing for the school's baseball team. But he had regularly attended the football games and set his affections and attention on one, Carlie Michaels. They had dated all through high school. Joe had gone off to college where he studied architecture while Carlie stayed to help with the family business, an interior decorating shop her mother had started.

They married shortly after Joe received his degree in architecture and business. A couple of years later, they had Roxanne, whom Carlie nicknamed, Roxy. Roxy had been a beautiful baby girl with curly blonde hair and sea-blue eyes. Seven years ago, Josh, a brown-haired, brown-eyed, handsome baby boy, was born. A year ago, Joe had thrown it all away. Carlie couldn't help but wonder what Joe would do if Kat got tired of him, or had to move away in order to discover new models, or even left him for someone younger, more her own age. After all, Joe is forty and Kat just twenty-three.

Carlie, satisfied with her appearance, crept down the spiral staircase into the kitchen to set the coffee to brew. There was nothing like a fresh cup of java to start her morning with, especially on rainy, stormy ones like this one. She grabbed a bagel and slid it into the toaster. After it was done, she spread cream cheese on it and ate it slowly while waiting for the coffee to finish brewing. She checked the clock. 5:30. She had half an hour to relax with her morning coffee before heading back up the stairs to wake Roxy for school. She dug out her favorite mug from the oak cabinet and poured her coffee, adding cream and sugar. She sat down at the table and drank it slowly, relishing in the hot drink's ability to soothe her soul.

Carlie finished her coffee and got up to set out the bowls and spoons for the kids' morning cereal. She made her way across the living room and back up the stairs to wake up Roxy. She knocked on the door to Roxy's room before slowly opening it. "Roxy, it's time to get up." She said. Roxy yawned and stretched. "Can't I skip school today?" She inquired of her mother. Carlie sat on the edge of her daughter's purple canopy bed. "No, Roxy, you cannot skip school today. You have that big test in History. Remember? Besides, Thanksgiving break is coming up soon and you will have a couple of days to sleep in then," Carlie reminded her. Roxy stretched again. "Ok, fine. I'm up." Carlie stood and waited to make sure Roxy was up and headed to the shower before proceeding down the hall to check on Josh.

She slowly opened the door to her son's room. "Come in Mommy, I'm awake." A small boyish voice called out. Carlie smiled at Josh as she entered his room. He had already flipped on his T.V. and was watching a *SpongeBob Squarepants* episode. She sat on his bed and tussled his sandy-brown hair. He sat up and hugged her tightly. "Storm woke me up, Mommy," Josh stated matter-of-factly. Carlie nodded. "It did me too." Then added, "Do you want to come on downstairs or do you want to lay up here for a while?" Josh smiled his boyish grin at her. "I'll hang here for a while, Mommy." Carlie smiled and nodded. "Ok. I am going to get Roxy off to school and then I will be back to get you up and ready. Ok?" Josh smiled. "K."

Carlie paused momentarily at the top of the stair well to listen for the shower running. It was. Satisfied that Roxy was indeed up and showering for school, Carlie went back to the kitchen and waited for her daughter to come down. After what seemed like an eternity, Roxy finally entered the kitchen. She was sporting a mini skirt and a low-cut sweater, too low-cut for her mother's liking. Carlie shook her head. "No. You are not wearing that to school. You go up and put on something more appropriate, young lady." "But, Mom...." Roxy started to protest. "No, but mom about it. You are not dressing like that!" She paused. "Oh and by the way, my name is not 'But Mom'." Carlie teased cocking her head to one side. Roxy rolled her eyes. "Pleeeasssee, Mom. Your jokes really need some work." Carlie just smiled as she watched her daughter turn to obediently go change.

A few minutes later, Roxy emerged wearing jeans and a more appropriate cream-colored sweater and boots. "Much better." Carlie noted as she took down the box of Frosted Flakes. She poured the cereal into a bowl and smothered it with milk. She handed the bowl and spoon to Roxy who took it and sat down to eat. Roxy preferred bacon and pancakes, but she knew that kind of breakfast was reserved on the weekends when her mom didn't have to work. She pushed the cereal around in her bowl. She really didn't want to eat, but she knew better than to waste food.

Since her dad had left, money was tight. Roxy knew that her mother did the best she could, but still it was frustrating and totally unfair. Roxy had taken up smoking cigarettes with her friends. What her mother didn't know wouldn't kill her. She had to have *something* she could do and hide from her mother. After all, with money being so tight, they never got to go out and do anything.

Roxy longed to go to the mall with her friends and shop, like their family used to before her father left them. They used to do a lot of things, like going out to eat once a week, going to the amusement park in the summer, and going swimming. But those days were gone. Roxy hated her father. She blamed her mother. And Josh, well Josh was just plain annoying. Not that she didn't love both her mother and little brother, but it wasn't fair that she had to be stuck inside these four walls with them all the time.

Her mother worked, but worked earlier shifts now so that she could be home when they got home from school. *That* annoyed Roxy the most, the fact that she felt like she didn't have any freedom. Oh they had internet and cable. At least Roxy could close the door to her room and watch T.V. However, the family computer was a desktop that sat on the desk in the living room. That way her mother could see everything she and her brother did on the internet. That wasn't really fair either,but Roxy knew better than to try to argue with her mother. After all, maybe her mom was just trying to protect them. Still....still it wasn't fair and it made Roxy so aggravated. Sometimes she felt like she was suffocating. Oh, her mother wasn't all that bad. She did let Roxy hang out with her friends after school for an hour or two, but was very strict about her being home in time for supper. Roxy guessed she couldn't blame her mom for that.

However, she cherished that hour or two after school. That was when she could let loose and smoke with her friends. She liked being a different person with them than who she was at home. It gave her some satisfaction that she could have a little bit of fun. Roxy finally finished her cereal. The bus pulled up and honked. She quickly threw her jacket on and grabbed her book bag. "Bye, Mom. Love ya." She called as she raced out the door. "Love you too, honey!" Carlie returned.

Carlie watched the bus drive away before turning back to the kitchen. She placed the cereal bowl in the sink before calling up the stairs to (tell?) Josh to get dressed for school. Josh, who was already dressed, came bounding down the stairs in his jeans and favorite *Undertaker* shirt with his matching book bag slung over his shoulder. He scurried into the kitchen and sat down at the table and waited for Carlie to pour his cereal and juice. Carlie smiled at him as he slurped the milk out of the bowl and wiped his mouth on his sleeve. *Oh how I miss Roxy being little and innocent like this.* She thought to herself.

She cleaned up Josh's breakfast dishes and helped him with his coat. A few short minutes later, his bus pulled up. Carlie hugged her son and sent him off to school. She closed the door and turned back to the kitchen. After washing the breakfast dishes, she poured a second cup of coffee and grabbed the bills off the counter, along with her coupon book. Oh how she dreaded going through the stack of bills and deciding which ones she should pay immediately and which ones could wait until her next paycheck.

Carlie sighed. She squared her shoulders and attacked the stack of bills looming before her. She decided to make two piles. One pile would consist of "must pay immediately" while the other pile would be labeled as "can wait." Carlie picked up the electric bill first. It wasn't due for another two weeks. She placed it in the "can wait" pile. Next was the water bill. $95.46. It had to be paid immediately, along with the heat bill. She picked up the cable bill next and sighed. If she was lucky, she could possibly manage to keep the cable and internet on for another month. Carlie doubted it though. She knew how companies worked. She was already two months behind on the bill and knew that the probability of the cable company cutting her off was very high. She knew how disappointed the kids would be, but what could she do? They had to eat after all.

Next, Carlie methodically went through the cabinets and refrigerator and made her list for the store. *How can two kids eat so much?* she wondered as she jotted down the usual items of milk, bread, eggs, and meat. She tried to make sure they had after school snacks and frozen meals to snack on for the weekends, but with her budget getting tighter and tighter, Carlie found herself having to cut back on the extras and getting only what they needed.(She tried to make sure they had after schoo snacks and frozen meals for on the weekends. Her budget was getting tighter and tighter, so Carlie found herself having to cut back on extras to get only what they needed. She reasoned that the kids could always eat peanut butter and jelly sandwiches for snacks if they were really hungry. Peanut butter and jelly wcrc good and necessary staples. Bread was cheap enough to buy. Although she knew Josh preferred bologna sandwiches, he was pretty good at not complaining. His sister on the other hand, was always griping about there never being enough food in the house.

What Roxy *really* meant, Carlie knew, was that there wasn't always what Roxy *wanted* to eat in the house. Carlie had applied for food stamps through the county, but had been denied because she made too much working her $8.00 an hour, 40 hours a week job. She scoffed at the way these agencies decided who could qualify for help and who couldn't. The drug dealers,users and the alocholic good-for-nothings down the road sure got anything they wanted. Oh what was the difference? Carlie knew she shouldn't judge or complain. She had gone to church at one time and she knew God would frown on her for grumbling about her circumstances.

Church. That was another activity that had disapeared from their lives after Joe had left. Their family used to faithfully attend church. Carlie had taught Sunday school and the children's classes. Joe was a worship leader and guitarist. But after the *incident,* Carlie couldn't bring herself to attend church and face the embarrassment of having her "spiritual" husband cheat on her and run off with another woman. Woman. Now that was laughable. Kat was still a girl.

OK. Enough of that. Carlie told herself. *Focus.* She finished writing out her list. Then sitting back down, she pulled out the coupons from her coupon book that she could use for her shopping. She loved couponing. If the sales were right, she could often get free boxes of cereal or a free gallon of milk. With prices being so high, coupons helped a great deal. Carlie shoved the list, coupons, and "must pay" bills into her purse. After double checking to make sure she had her check book, she grabbed her coat to head out. Just then the doorbell rang.

Carlie cautiously opened the door. Sure enough, it was the cable guy. Carlie crossed her arms as he greeted her and glanced over the papers on his metal clip board. "Carlie Michaels?" "Yes." She supplied. "I am Chuck, from your cable provider." Chuck cleared his throat before continuing. "It appears that you are two and a half months behind on your payment." *It appears?* Carlie wanted to laugh, but restrained herself. *Mr. Cable Man, just say it like it is. Miss Michaels you ARE two and a half months behind on your bill* is what she wanted to tell him. He looked up at her. "You currently owe \$239.67, are you able to pay that today?"

Carlie sighed. "No. I'm sorry. I can't." She told him. "Do you think you can have it paid within the next week?" Chuck asked. He was trying to be sympathetic, Carlie realized. But she was not one to sugar coat things. She had always been the type to tell it how it is, to be straight forward. "No, honestly, I probably won't be able to pay withing the week." She stated. Chuck looked down for a moment. "Well, Miss Michaels, we will have to schedule a date and time that we can come out and disconnect your service and collect the equipment." Carlie reached in her purse and dug out her schedule. "I have next Saturday off." She supplied. "Any time would be fine." Chuck nodded. "I have 3-5 open that afternoon." He told her. Carlie nodded. "That will work." Chuck jotted down the date and time and wished her a good day. Carlie stood and watched him drive away.

She sighed deeply. *Well this will be another reason for the kids to hate me.* She thought grimly. OK, so hate was too strong of a word. Disappointed they would definitely be. She shrugged. Move on. Get over it. She locked the door behind her and climbed into her trusty old baby blue pickup and headed to the store.

Chapter 3

Carlie drove through town, getting frustrated at the fact that her gas gauge was almost on empty and she was hitting every red light on the way to the store. It always seemed that whenever she was low on gas, traffic was slower and more jammed than usual. She tried to keep her mind off of the fact that the kids would hate her forever for letting the cable and internet get disconnected.

She shifted in the driver's seat and turned up the radio. What could she do? It was buy food or pay the cable and buying food was a little more important, although she doubted that her children would see it that way. Josh, well, he wouldn't care as much. He would be content with throwing in one of the million dvds Carlie owned. Roxy, on the other hand, would gripe for months about not having T.V. and internet. Carlie could hear her daughter now. *There had to be some way you could have come up with the money, Mom! This isn't fair!* And on and on and on it would go.

Carlie knew Roxy was still struggling with Joe leaving the way he did. She had been acting out some and Carlie had quite the job keeping Roxy in check. Carlie knew that her daughter was probably doing things with her friends that she shouldn't be, but Carlie also knew that she couldn't be with Roxy twenty-four-seven. Carlie had found a cigarette in the pocket of Roxy's jeans one day last week while doing laundry. She hadn't said anything as there wasn't any proof that Roxy had actually been smoking. Carlie shook her head as she sang along to the *Garth Brooks* song blaring on the country music station. She pulled into the gas station and put ten dollars' worth into the tank before going into the parking lot of the grocery store.

The old truck sputtered as she pulled into a parking spot. She knew that auto repairs was another expense she would have to come up with. The old truck was on its last leg and Carlie had to keep it going for as long as possible. She sighed as she climbed out and headed into the store.

Carlie grabbed a cart and fished out her shopping list and coupon envelope. She carefully went down the aisles, getting what she absolutely needed first while calculating the cost. After making sure she had what she needed, Carlie decided there was enough left to get a few extras for the kids. She grabbed a couple of boxes of snack cakes, a bag of chips, and four frozen meals. They would have to be satisfied with that. She got in line, picking up the latest issue of her favorite magazine and skimmed through it while she waited for the girl in front of her to finish. She unloaded the cart and pushed it through.

"Hey Carlie!" Laura, her friend and co-worker greeted her. "Hey Laura." Carlie greeted her back. Laura started scanning the items. Carlie pulled out her wallet to pay for the groceries. As she did, Laura leaned over the counter. "Hey, check your schedule before you leave today." She stated. "Why?" Carlie asked. "Because Mr. Marley changed it and he cut everyone's hours." Laura supplied. Carlie rolled her eyes. "You are kidding, right?" Laura shook her head. "Afraid not, love. I think you are down to 30 hours this week." Carlie sighed a deep sigh. "Thanks, Laura." Laura smiled at her.

After her groceries were bagged and placed back into the cart, Carlie went up to the customer service counter where the employee schedule was located. Sure enough, she had only 30 hours. *Ugh. How am I going to get the truck fixed now?* Her truck needed a lot of repairs and Carlie had been putting them off. Things were hard enough. She definitely did not need less hours. Carlie jotted down her new hours and headed out to her truck.

As Carlie unloaded the groceries into the back of her truck, she couldn't help but to wonder if she had other options. She had often thought about going back to school, but was it possible? She smiled as she climbed into the driver's side. *Yeah right Carles. I can just see myself sitting in a classroom full of eighteen-year old kids.* She dismissed the idea and turned the key in the ignition. The truck coughed and sputtered, then stalled. Carlie tried again, but this time it wouldn't even start.

She put her head on the steering wheel. *Think! Think! Think!* She knew a little about vehicles as she had watched her father work on cars in his garage. She popped the hood and climbed out. The rain had stopped and Carlie was grateful for that. At least she didn't have to be stuck in the cold, pouring rain. Was it just last week that it had been sunny and seventy degrees? Well, this was

Ohio. The weather changed in the blink of an eye. As the saying goes, if you don't like the weather, wait five minutes, it will change. She just wished mother nature would quit being bi-polar about the weather. If it was going to do anything, Carlie preferred it snowed.

Check the oil and all the fluids. Then one by one unplug the spark plugs and check them. Fuel pump? Alternator? Battery? Carlie tried to start the truck again. Cough. Sputter. Cough. Sputter. Stall. She kicked the side of the truck. "Come on!" She yelled at it, not seeing the man who was cautiously walking her way. "Start you piece of junk!" Carlie leaned her head against the door for a moment. She looked up as she heard footsteps coming close to her. She turned just as a good-looking man approached the front of the truck. "Vehicle trouble?" He asked, grinning at her. Carlie blushed. "I'm really not crazy." She sputtered, a bit embarrassed about her sudden outrage on 'Ole Blue. "Just been a rough morning." The man grinned at her. "Ma'am,(do you) mind if I take a look?" He offered. Carlie nodded.

She took him in. Tall. Dark hair. Just enough of the five-o-clock shadow to make him look genuine. Cowboy boots and hat. Wrangler jeans that looked *really* good on his slim, but muscular, cowboy-type figure. The man looked like he just hopped out of one those cowboy movies. Clint Eastwood, on his best days, had nothing on this good-looking guy standing before her. She sucked in a deep breath. "Thanks. "She said. "I did the usual stuff. You know, checked the fluids and the spark plugs. Thinking it might be the fuel pump." She supplied. The handsome man nodded. *He is really cute, Carles!* She thought to herself. Then, just as quickly, she reprimanded herself.

But why should she not look? It had been a year since Joe had taken off with his girlfriend. Why shouldn't she be allowed to look? She deserved to find someone and be happy again, didn't she? "Well, you could be right. It could be the fuel pump." The cowboy was saying. Carlie could feel the tears starting to well up in her eyes. How was she going to pay for that? She had no money for this! The man came around to the side of the truck where Carlie was leaning. He must have seen the desparation in her face.

"Listen, I can call a tow truck for you." It was then he noticed the bags of groceries in the back. He also noticed that there was no ring on the woman's finger. Single mom, no doubt. As he assessed the damsel in distress, he noticed how beautiful she was. She was tall, about five feet, eight inches. He took in her long, wavy chestnut colored hair. Country girl, no doubt. He could tell by the jeans, sweater, and boots. She had definitely not been raised in the city. Small town at the very least. "By the way, I am Colt. Colt Storm." He reached out to shake her hand. "Carlie. Carlie Michaels." She shook his hand. "Well, Carlie Michaels, why don't we get a tow truck for you. A buddy of mine runs an auto shop here in town. He can let me know what the damages are." Carlie could only nod. "Why don't we unload these grocieries into my truck and then we can call the tow truck and get you home." Carlie hesitated. "I can call a cab." She supplied. Colt smiled at her. "Nonsense. Let me give you a ride. I promise I will keep both hands on the steering wheel." Carlie laughed. "OK then, I accept."

As they waited for the towing company, Carlie learned a little more about her cowboy hero. He informed her he wasn't from Ohio. He was here visiting a friend of his. He was from Colorado and had a horse ranch there. His buddy, the one who owned the garage, had moved here to Ohio a few years ago after meeting his wife online. Carlie had to laugh at that one. "Not one for meeting people online." She said. "You never know who is out there. Your friend got pretty lucky." Colt smiled. "Yep, one out of a million." Carlie smiled at him. *Don't get too personal, Carles.* She warned herself. *He will be going back to Colorado and you will never see him again.* Yet there was something about Colt Storm that made her feel alive again and she couldn't help but to tell him about herself. It was as if she had known him for years. He was just that easy to talk to. Too bad he was going back to Colorado.

"I'm from here." She told Colt. "Grew up on a farm about twenty miles from here. My brothers run it now. I live in the house Mom and Dad bought in town several years before they retired. They left it to me when they moved up to Maine." "Maine?" Colt questioned. "That's quite a change from farm life." Carlie smiled. "Yeah. Mom had a thing for going to the East coast. She always wanted to see another side of the world besides farming." Colt nodded. "I guess I could see that." He said. "Me, I'd rather stick with horses." He paused. "So how is it that you aren't married?"

He had asked the dreaded question. The question that was painful and embarassing at the same time. Carlie took a deep breath. Colt noticed her hesitation. "I'm sorry, Carlie, if you don't want to talk about it, I understand." Carlie smiled sheepishly. "No, it's just it's hard to explain." Colt nodded, waiting to see if she would continue. "My husband and I divorced a year ago today. Joe took off with his twenty-three-year-old girlfriend he met on a job he was doing." She paused.

"He worked as an architect and was doing some work for a modeling agency. Kat, short for Katrina, set her eyes on him and I guess that was when he decided to leave." Another pause. She lowered her head. Colt waited. Carlie slowly brought her head back up. There were tears in her eyes. "I thought we were happy. He was a worship leader at our church and I didn't see it coming. I have two kids. Roxanne, my daughter, is thirteen and my son, Josh, is just seven. But that's life, ya know?"

She wiped the tears from her eyes. Just as Colt was about to say something, the tow truck pulled up. Colt slid out of his dual cab pick-up to give the towing guy a hand. "Hey Jack." Colt greeted his buddy. He glanced back at Carlie, who was watching them. "Listen," Colt said in a low voice. "I am going to take care of this, OK. But keep it between you and me. I am paying for the tow and any repairs needed." "Gotcha buddy." Jack said, shaking Colt's hand. He looked towards Colt's truck. "Is she the lady?" Colt nodded. "Yep. She's beautiful and sweet. Too bad I have to go back to Colorado in a few days or I would stick around and get to know her some more." Colt supplied.

Jack tilted his head. He tugged on his goatee. "Ya know, it might take a week or so before I can get this thing going again." He stated, gesturing towards the truck. "If ya can swing it, why don't you stay in town for a little while longer?" Colt smiled. "I might just do that ole boy." The two men shook hands and parted. Colt watched Jack drive away, Carlie's truck in tow, before climbing back into his truck.

"OK. That's taken care of. Let's get you home." Carlie nodded. Even though she didn't say it, Colt knew that Carlie was worried about the repair expense. He would tell her when it was all said and done that he would foot the bills. In the mean time, he needed to get her home and make plans to find out more about this mysterious and beautiful woman. " Go straight like you are going out of town, about three miles. First road to the right. I live in a brick house at the end of the road on the left." Carlie directed him. Colt pulled his truck into Carlie's drive-way. She unlocked the door and then hesitated. "Um...you can just set the bags on the porch. I can get them in," she stammered. Colt smiled at her. *Man! He is cute!* "Not a problem, Ma'am. If you would oblige me, I'd be happy to carry the groceries in for you." Carlie was speechless. "Um..Sure," she stammered for the second time. *Get it together, Carles! He's just offering his help. It's not like he's going to kill you or something.*

Carlie opened the door for Colt. "The kitchen is through the living room to the left." She instructed him."You can just sit them on the table." Colt did as she wished. After all the groceries were in, he stopped and removed his hat. "Listen Carlie, I'm gonna be in town for a couple of weeks. I'd love to take you out to dinner and get to know you a little better." Carlie looked at him. Suddenly she couldn't breathe. Everything had come to a stop. *What was wrong with her? She was acting like a little girl who just caught stealing candy from the candy store!* She pulled herself together.

"Sure. That would be nice." Colt smiled. "Well, since I'm not from around here, I will let you pick the place. But, I will tell ya Ma'am, I prefer a good steak house over some fancy restaurant, ya know, being from Colorado and all." Carlie smiled. "As do I. I don't go for fancy places where you can't figure out which silverware goes with what." She wrinkled her nose at him. Colt laughed as he replaced his hat. "Well Ma'am, would you mind writing your phone number down for me?" Carlie went to the desk drawer to fish out some paper and a pen. She quickly jotted down her number and handed the paper to Colt, her hand brushing his as she did. She felt a shock go through her. *It was like magic. Isn't that what Meg Ryan had said in that movie "Sleepless in Seattle"?*

Carlie placed the pen back on her desk. Colt was striding towards the door. "I will call you tomorrow, Miss Carlie. You have a good day now." Carlie smiled and thanked him for his help before shutting the door behind him. She had an urge to just grab and kiss him, but that would be way too forward. She didn't want to frighten the poor man. He had already seen and heard her kicking and yelling at Ole Blue. That's what she had called her old truck, Ole Blue. She took a moment to pull herself back together before heading into the kitchen to put the groceries away.

Wow, Carles! Way to go! She couldn't help but to feel a slight let down however, at the reminder that Colt Storm was not a native Buckeye and he would be returning to Colorado at some point. Oh well, at least she would have one nice dinner with a hot guy before returning to her boring life. Boring. Was that how she saw her life? Boring? She loved her kids and all, but more and more, Carlie was feeling like something was missing. She just wasn't getting the satisfaction she needed from working in a grocery store. She wanted more. She wanted a real job. Maybe working as a chef or a social worker or working with troubled kids...something, anything that would make her feel like her life was worth something. Maybe she should go back to school after all and maybe, just maybe, Colt Storm was the beginning of that new life. Now she was being silly.

Going back to school and making a career change was one thing. Thinking she could have something with Colt Storm, well that was practically impossible. *This isn't one of those reality shows like "The Bachelor"* Carlie reminded herself. This was real life in small town, Ohio. Romance didn't just happen like it did on T.V. and in Hollywood. Or did it? Only time would tell.

Chapter 4

Colt Storm pulled the Chevy into the empty spot in front of the entrance to the hotel. Once inside his room, he removed his hat and boots, and then stretched out on the bed. He couldn't get his mind off of Carlie Michaels. She was awfully pretty and seemed like a very well-bred, sweet young woman. He knew she was dealing with a lot of hurt still. He could read it in her eyes. As much as Carlie Michaels tried to hide behind her smile, Colt could read the stress and hurt in those brown eyes. A divorce from a cheating husband, two kids to raise alone, and a truck that was falling apart. What else was there to the chestnut haired woman? Don't get him wrong, the cheating husband would have been enough to put any woman over the edge, but from what he could tell, Carlie Michaels kept it together pretty well. Maybe it was because she had to for her two kids who no doubt were struggling with anger, fear, and hurt themselves. He had always been pretty good at assessing other people, especially women. He had been able to make quite an assessment of Carlie Michaels just within the last short hour and a half. He wondered if Carlie cried herself to sleep at night behind her bedroom door. Colt could picture her in a pair of cotton pajamas, curled up on her bed reading her favorite novel or watching her favorite movie on T.V. He could also picture her looking at a photo album of her and Joe, perhaps their wedding album, and crying herself to sleep.

He preferred to think of Carlie Michaels laughing out loud over seeing the tears that had formed in her eyes when she had told him about "cheating Joe" and the divorce. Colt knew that he shouldn't be having these types of thoughts just yet. He had only just met the woman and was already struck by her. When he had rescued the damsel in distress, Colt had read the desperation in Carlie's eyes. She had appeared to have been on the brink of a break down, yet the strength she showed said it all. He could not even begin to comprehend the strength this woman had. Carlie Michaels must be Super Woman, or at the very least, the strongest woman he had ever come across.

She had cried when she talked about the divorce and Colt knew that there was a world of hurt in her heart. Colt could not put a finger on it, but there was something appealing about Carlie that sparked his interest. He was looking forward to dinner with her. He longed to know more about her. He wanted to know what she did for fun, if she ever got to get out. He wanted to know what her interests and hobbies were. Oh heck, he knew he couldn't possibly get to know Carlie in one night over dinner, but he definitely would like to try. Then there was the fact that as soon as he got her truck paid for and made sure she had reliable transportation, he had to head back to Colorado to his horse ranch and his furniture store. Colt had felt her hand brush his when she handed him her phone number. He had felt something like a lightning bolt go through his entire being and wondered if she had felt the same thing.

Colt sat up and leaned against the headboard, crossing his feet and putting his hands behind his head as he did. He thought about the fact that Carlie mentioned that she and Joe had attended church at one time. She had mentioned that Joe had been a worship leader. Colt wondered if Carlie had been back to church since the divorce. He highly doubted it. Being a devout christian himself, Colt would find it exceptionally hard to step back into church after an embarrassing divorce. Well, it wasn't the divorce; it was the *affair* Carlie's husband had been having that was more likely the embarrassing factor. He imagined that Carlie was more hurt over the affair than the actual divorce. Really, how could she not be? Wouldn't he be if he was in her shoes?

Colt tried to stop thinking about Carlie's situation, but he couldn't get his mind off of her. Would she go to church with him if he asked her to? Probably not since he was going back home and since she barely knew him. He was lucky that she had said yes to have dinner with him. Still, he could not help but to wonder if they could make a relationship work. If it would be possible and if Carlie would be interested. Long distance relationships, he knew, often did not work. But what if it could? What if it was possible? He had been single for a long time. He had dated a girl about eight years ago, before he became a Christian. Colt had met Jenna at a local pub while having dinner with a friend. She was a 5' 7" beauty with shoulder-length auburn hair and light blue eyes. Her beauty had captured him and he had let that alone influence his feelings for her. It hadn't been long before he had agreed to let Jenna move in with him, not knowing at the time she was only interested in his money. He should have known, he should have read the signs. But once again, he had been awed by how beautiful she was. Jenna had lived with him on the ranch for a little while, but she was a partier. Although Colt had taken to drinking a beer or a shot of whiskey here and there, he did not approve of his girlfriend's lifestyle. Jenna was also more interested in shopping than she was in his ranch or furniture business. She was always trying to get him to wear suits. Colt Storm did not wear suits and ties. The only day he would actually wear a suit would be the day he would get married. Even that was stretching the idea a bit. He hoped he would find a woman that would not mind getting married country-western style with him in a long trench coat and her in a dress and cowgirl boots. He smiled at the thought. The woman he would eventually choose to be his wife would have to be a really good sport to have such a wedding, but Colt liked things simple and fun.

After about seven months of Jenna attempting to spend the family fortune, Colt had blocked his credit cards and bank accounts. He had finally told Jenna to leave. She had pouted and cried and stomped and begged him to let her stay, but Colt Storm was not influenced that easily. He had packed Jenna's suitcases for her and had sent her on her way. Being that Colt had often bragged on being a good judge of character, especially with women, he had even surprised himself when he had fallen for the seductive gold digger; a mistake he had vowed would never happen again. Colt had vowed that he would never again allow himself to be taken in by a woman's mere beauty, and he hadn't.

It was shortly after he had broken up with Jenna that his best friend invited Colt to church. Colt gave his heart to the Lord and he had remained single ever since. Oh sure, he'd had many offers from women. It seemed as though women had been lining up to date him. Women had offered to give him many gifts, anything from cooking a romantic dinner for him to sleeping with him. After all, Colt was the ultimate dream man for any woman. He often felt as if he were on the reality show, *The Bachelor.* Colt did not understand why a man would want to appear on a show like that. Sure, he understood that rich single men got lonely too, but was appearing on a show in front of millions of people the way to find someone? Maybe for those men breaking twenty-some women's hearts to find "the one" was ideal, but it certainly was not for him. Colt knew that he had broken a few women's hearts over time, but some of those women were ones who had chased him and he had denied their desires to date him. There had only been a couple whom he had seriously dated and had broken it off with, like Jenna. He had to admit that he had been tempted a few times over the last couple of years, but his promise to and faith in God had kept him from stumbling. Colt had no desire to be with another woman like Jenna who was only after his money and whatever else a man of his nature could offer her. He had been praying for God to send him a good Christian woman who shared the same interests as he did. Today he had met Carlie Michaels. Colt knew better than to jump the gun, but man, she had really made an impact on him and had sent his head spinning. Still, Colt wasn't one to get ahead of God. True, he asked Carlie to have dinner with him so he could get to know her better, but he would still take this before his Lord in prayer. If Carlie Michaels was supposed to be in his life, then Colt prayed that God would make a way. If a relationship with Carlie Michaels was not meant to be then he was happy he had been there to help her when she needed a hand.

Colt got up and slipped into his boots and grabbed his hat. He hadn't realized how hungry he was until his stomach started growling just now. He had not eaten breakfast and now he was starving. There wasn't much in this small Ohio town, but that suited him just fine. He had noticed a steak and rib place in the middle of town and decided that would be perfect for lunch. The thought of calling Carlie and asking her to have lunch with him crossed his mind, but he pushed it away as he figured she was probably busy. Then again, what could it hurt? She just lived on the edge of town and he could pick her up. He would enjoy having her company. Colt toyed with the idea before finally reaching for the phone. He dug the paper out of his pocket and dialed the number.

"Hello?" Carlie answered. *Man, does her voice sound like an angel!* What was with him? He never fell for a woman this easily. *Slow down, Colt. She is beautiful, but remember to not jump ahead of God on this. Wait.* Colt turned his attention back to the phone. "Um...Hi Carlie, it's Colt. I was heading out to get some lunch and was wondering if you would like to join me." There was a long silence on the other end. He knew she was thinking it through. A million questions were probably going through her head. Was he moving too fast? "I would love to, Colt. I just have to be home by three to get Roxy from school." Colt smiled on the inside. His heart took a wild leap inside his chest. "Great. I will be there in about fifteen minutes." He hung up the phone.

Carlie looked in the mirror. She brushed her hair and applied a light coat of lip gloss. She had changed her sweater and was wearing a baby blue, long- sleeved cotton shirt. She glanced at the clock. It was 12:00. Had it just been three hours ago since she had broken down at the grocery store? She suddenly became nervous. It was one thing for Colt to have helped her and for her to agree to have dinner with him, but now he wanted to have lunch with her just a couple of hours after they had met. Was she insane to have said yes? Could this be fate? No. Carlie Michaels did not believe in fate, Even though, she had not been in church for a year now, she still believed that God was in control of all things. She had not prayed much, either, since the affair and divorce, but she still believed that if something was meant to be, then God would allow it to happen and he would put everything in place.

Carlie slid into her fake tan leather jacket and her matching light brown boots. She waited for Colt. Within a few minutes, she heard his Chevy pull into the driveway. *He has a good memory.* Carlie thought to herself. *Then again it was just a couple of hours ago that I directed him to my house.* Carlie reasoned as she opened the door and greeted him in the drive-way. Making sure the house was properly locked up, Carlie allowed Colt to open the passenger door for her and help her up into the truck. He shut her door and climbed into the driver's side and the two headed back into town for their first date. "First date and only a couple of hours after meeting for the first time." Carlie joked as Colt turned onto the main drag. Colt grinned. "Nawww, this isn't a proper date. Now when we go to dinner, that will be a proper date."

He tilted his head just slightly and glanced at her. She looked amazing in the baby blue shirt she was wearing. Her eyes were shining and she was smiling. This was how Colt had pictured his newly found friend when he had been thinking of her back in the hotel room. They pulled into the parking lot of the restaurant and went inside.

After being seated and handed their menus, Carlie and Colt glanced over the lunch specials. "Order whatever you want, darlin'." *Darlin'. A country term of endearment.* It didn't mean that they were a couple or anything, Carlie knew. She was smart enough to understand that "Darlin'" was just an endearing term country boys often called women they knew and liked. *So now he likes me?!* Carlie mused. *Geesh, Carles! Slow down girl!* Carlie didn't know what she wanted. Nothing too messy. She didn't want to be embarrassed by having messy juices or sauces running down her chin onto her shirt. She finally decided on the grilled chicken with a Caesar salad instead of fries while Colt ordered the bbq ribs basket with fries.

They both ordered sweet teas to drink. The waitress set their drinks down on the table with promises that their food would be out shortly. Carlie took a sip of her tea. It tasted like heaven compared to the Kool Aid she and the kids had been drinking. "OK." Colt was saying. "Now that we got the ordering out of the way, I can concentrate on you, Darlin'." Carlie felt her cheeks blush. "Tell me about the infamous Carlie Michaels." Carlie chuckled. "There is not much to tell. My life is pretty boring." She supplied. Colt folded his hands under his chin and waited. Carlie sighed. "OK. As I already told you this morning, I divorced my husband a year ago today for cheating on me. I came home from a late activity with the kids at my son's school and found him and Kat wrapped in each other's arms in the tub." She cleared her throat. "He informed me that he had fallen in love with *her* and decided to move in with her. I, of course was devastated. It was really hard on the kids too. Joe hasn't bothered to try and see them. Alimony and child support are still tied up in court."

She hadn't meant to spill her guts like that. *Geesh Carles, can't you talk about anything but the affair and divorce. He wants to know YOU!* Carlie changed the subject. "As for me, I don't get out much. It's hard to find someone to watch the kids. But when I do get out, I like to go to the movies once in a while. But mostly I like to go to quaint shops and marvel at antiques. I also like to go bowling or take long walks with the person I'm with. In the summer, I am a sucker for walks at the lake and horseback riding. I love to read." She informed Colt. *Horseback riding! Walking along the lake! No shopping! She had said movies, but even I like to take in a good movie now and then.* Colt mused. Carlie was still talking. "I like to watch some T.V., but that's only been more recent. I find myself getting lonely at night now and I watch T.V. To get my mind off of it. However, my cable is being cancelled this Saturday so I will have to resort to books instead." She smiled. Their food came and it smelled wonderful. Colt bowed his head to pray. That startled Carlie momentarily, then she followed suit. He said a quick prayer over the meal, then dug into his ribs. Carlie laughed at the sauce all over his face. She reached for a napkin and found herself playfully wiping Colt's face. He grinned at her as she put the napkin down on the table. "Tell me more." Colt said. Carlie swallowed. "Well like I said, I have two children. Roxy, short for Roxanne, is thirteen and Josh is just seven. He was our surprise baby. Other than working at the grocery store and raising my kids, there isn't much more to tell. Oh, I do like to write. I used to write poems, but I kind of got out of that when everything happened." She took another bite of her salad. "Oh, and I love to read older literature from the 18 and 1900's as well. Have you ever heard of the German author, Gerhart Johann?" Colt shook his head. "Oh, well he was a German author who wrote dramatic plays and poems that were romantic and symbolic. He won a Nobel prize in 1912 for his literature." Colt was grinning at her. "Well, Carlie Michaels, I think you are a very fascinating woman."

Carlie just about choked on her salad. *Fascinating?I wouldn't call myself fascinating. What does Colt see in me that I can't see? Even Joe never told me I was fascinating! Joe used to call me practical.* Carlie did not say those words aloud.

"And I think you are a very strong woman considering all you have gone through. Roxy and Josh are the two luckiest kids in the world if you ask me." Carlie smiled. She wasn't used to all these compliments. She finished her salad, and then tackled her chicken. "Enough about me, tell me about Colt Storm." She said in between bites.

"Well I am from Colorado. Raised around horses all my life. I took over my parents' ranch. They still live on the land, but just can't do the work any more. I also own a furniture store where we handcraft furniture. I inherited a lot of money from my grandpa, but I still believe in hard work. I like to fish and hunt and of course ride horses. True cowboy ya got yaself right here." He patted his chest. "I haven't dated in eight years. My last girlfriend, Jenna, moved into the ranch house with me, but she was more interested in partying and spending my money than she was in our relationship. So one day I woke up and realized I didn't want that kind of relationship so I told her she had to go, even packed her bags for her." Colt shook his head. "Can't believe I did that. Anyway, I started going back to church shortly after the break up and came to know the Lord in a service a couple of weeks later." Carlie couldn't help but to feel a pang of guilt. She had not stepped inside a church in a year, let alone really prayed. At the same time, she was very impressed by Colt and his laid back, yet strong ways.

The couple finished their lunch and exited the restaurant. Colt opened the truck door for Carlie and once again helped her to climb in. As he took her hand, Carlie felt the same kind of shock she had felt this morning when she had handed him the piece of paper with her phone number on it. It was like a really strong electrical current that traveled throughout her entire being and she wondered if Colt felt it too. Was she imagining things, or did Colt hesitate a moment before letting go of her hand?

"Where to now, Miss Michaels?" Colt was asking her as he pulled the truck out of the parking lot. Carlie was stunned for a moment. It was supposed to be just lunch, now he wanted to take her somewhere else. "Well," Carlie said. "There really isn't much to do in this small town on a Tuesday afternoon." Colt grinned. "Well, then, how about we just take a drive." Carlie's brain turned to slush instantly. It was kind of like when you first pull a popsicle out of the freezer and don't eat it right away. It just turns slushy and starts to melt. That's how she felt now, like a slushy popsicle that was melting.

"There is a park in the middle of town." She finally suggested. It is just before the grocery store." Colt followed her directions. "Go through the park here and to the other side." Carlie pointed at the drive that circled around the park. "There is a pond there and the ducks and geese are fun to watch." Colt did as she wished. He pulled into a parking spot in front of the lake. After turning off the engine, he turned sideways as to face Carlie. She turned to face him as well. *Gosh! She is beautiful!* Colt thought.

"Every summer, the kids and I pack picnic lunches, with extra loaves of bread for feeding the ducks, and come here and hang out. Roxy doesn't find it quite as fun and exciting as Josh does, but she still likes to get out of the house." Carlie was saying. "I guess she would rather go hang out with her friends and go to the mall or something, but I prefer to keep her in town and raise her with the same small town traditions I grew up with." She stopped there and looked out the window to watch the ducks and geese make their way towards the white bridge where a few people were throwing pieces of bread out to them. Colt studied her momentarily. "I think that's great, Carlie. Someday she will appreciate it and understand all that you do for her and Josh." Carlie nodded. Then, changing the subject, she asked, "So what is Colorado like?"

Colt smiled. "It's beautiful country. Like I said before, my life is the ranch and the furniture store. I prefer to stay near a small town. After all, what do ya need a big city for? As long as ya have a grocery store,a decent diner to grab a bite and cup of coffee now and then, and movie theater, what else do ya need?" He paused. "Oh sure, we have a General store to buy groceries and such and a country store where folks can buy gear for their ranches. And we have a couple of antique shops and home deco shops, mostly country and primitive stuff. But that's about it. Then again, what more do ya need?" He supplied, smiling. "Ya know, I bet if ya could get Roxy interested in horses, she would love it. Horses have a way of, well, calming ya down and speaking to ya soul like no other animal can do." Carlie nodded. "I try to get her to go riding with me, but going to a horse farm to just ride is different than being on a ranch and actually taking care of the horses." She agreed. "But, we are in Ohio, not Colorado." Colt nodded. "Well, Darlin', ya never know. Maybe someday y'all can come out to my part of the country and visit me." Carlie smiled. "Maybe someday."

Colt checked his watch. "Well, Miss Michaels, I ought to get you home so you can get ready for your kids to come home from school." Carlie sighed. "Part of being a Mom." Colt backed the truck out of the park and headed towards Carlie's house. Once he pulled in, Carlie climbed out. "Thanks for lunch and the time out." She thanked him. Colt nodded. "My pleasure ma'am. Dinner Saturday night? Say around seven?" Carlie nodded. "It's a date." She smiled at him as she closed the door. Colt sat in the truck and watched as she went into the house. *Man! She is some woman! God, if this be your will, please make a way for us to be together.* Colt prayed silently as he backed out of the driveway.

Chapter 5

Roxy breezed through the door just a little after three. Her eyes were glazed and she seemed to be staggering. "Roxy?" Carlie addressed her daughter, taking her by the arm. "Roxy, what's the matter with you?" Roxy turned and looked at her mom. She started to laugh. It was then that Carlie noticed that Roxy was not wearing the same clothes she had left in for school this morning. Instead of the cream-colored sweater, Roxy was sporting a low-cut red halter shirt. She had also traded her jeans for a black mini skirt. A leather jacket was slung over her shoulders. Carlie could feel the rage rising up inside her. It was obvious that Roxy had put these clothes in her book bag instead of her school books this morning and that she had not gone to school. Carlie knew she had to find out where her daughter had been and where she had gotten these clothes from, or from whom. Carlie certainly had never bought these clothes for Roxy, nor would she ever buy something like this for her daughter. Carlie herself, would never even wear something like this, not even in her younger, wilder days. Roxy looked like she ready to go stand on a street corner somewhere. She certainly was not looking like the daughter Carlie knows and loves. Carlie clenched her fists at her side as she sat next to her daughter on the couch. One whiff of Roxy's breath confirmed that she had indeed been drinking. But where and how? Carlie was not ignorant of the fact that kids these days could conjure up fake identifications, especially on the internet. Yet, at the same time, neither did she want to believe that her own daughter would do something like that. Yet here she was, ready to confront Roxy about where she had been. Carlie took a deep sigh. "Roxy, now before you go and lie to me, I know you weren't at school today. That is obvious. Now, you are going to tell me where you got these clothes and where you have been and with whom." Roxy looked at her mother.

"Where in the hell do you think I've been, Mother?!" Carlie took her daughter by the arm. "You listen to me young lady, you are in some deep trouble! Now you are going to tell me who you were with and where you got these clothes! Then you are going to tell me where you have been! Do I make myself clear?" Roxy leaned back and crossed her arms. Her head was starting to hurt and she felt like the room was spinning. "Fine." She slurred. "Jackie's mom took us to the mall one day and bought us these outfits. *Her* mom is cool. She doesn't care if Jackie goes to school and learns about France or what 2 plus 5 equals. We had a history test today and Jackie's mom said she could skip it. Jackie and I skipped school and took a cab to the bus station and took the bus to Dayton. We had fake ID's made by this guy Jackie knows and we went shopping with her mom's credit card and then went to a bar. We hopped on the bus and came back." Roxy shrugged. "I forgot to change my clothes so I wouldn't get caught. But then again, I guess you would have smelled the alcohol on my breath anyway." Roxy smirked. Carlie could feel her anger rising. What she really wanted to do was to yank Roxy up and give her a good beating. But she knew that wouldn't accomplish anything.

Carlie took a deep breath. "Roxy, you know I love you. I know things have been very hard since your father left, but that is no excuse for you to be skipping school and drinking. Now, I am going to make you a cup of black coffee to help with your head, but I will not tolerate this behavior! You are to go to your room and change out of those clothes. While I am making your coffee, I will decide what punishment to give you." Roxy glared at her mother. "Whatever!" "Go now!" Carlie ordered. She was doing all she could to not yell. Roxy tossed the throw pillow to the other side of the couch. She managed to get up and stumble up the stairs. "And NO T.V. or phone!" Carlie called after her. Roxy slammed the door to her room and collapsed onto her bed.

She knew she was supposed to change her clothes, but her head was spinning and she couldn't focus. Her mother was being ridiculous! She needed to get out and have some fun! And not her mom's kind of fun either. If it was up to her mother, Roxy would be feeding the ducks at the park pond or watching corny movies under a blanket tent while eating popcorn. *Ugh. Get a clue, mom!* Roxy thought. It was then that Roxy broke down and cried. Maybe it was the alcohol. Or maybe all the hurt and anger she had been holding inside was finally surfacing. Or maybe it was the combination of both. Roxy didn't really hate her mother. She loved her mom and her brother. She hated her dad. In Roxy's opinion, there was no excuse for what her dad did. He must have just stopped loving them. And she tried to blame her mother, but knew that her mother always tried to do her best for Roxy's dad. Her father just decided one day he didn't want his family anymore and for that, Roxy hated him. She knew it wasn't fair to take it out on her mom. She just wished that her mom was cool like her friends' moms were. She wished her mom had a better job and they had money again to do things that were actually *fun*. Roxy realized that her mom was trying to please both her and Josh and that she was doing everything she could, but Roxy also knew that she needed a little bit of freedom and a little bit of a life of her own; even if she was only thirteen. She knew her mom was angry with her, but that she was also hurt. OK, so maybe she had taken things too far today. Maybe she shouldn't have taken off to Dayton with Jackie. Maybe Jackie's mom *seemed* cool, but was that coolness going to get Roxy in trouble? It had today. Roxy hadn't meant to take things this far. She was really starting to feel guilty.

Her family had gone to church at one time, and she remembered the pastor talking about forgiveness and how her youth pastor had talked about being respectful and obedient to your parents. Roxy longed to go back to youth group. Maybe not at the same church, but maybe somewhere. She could hear her mom coming up the stairs and she quickly changed into her cotton pajama pants and a t-shirt. She wiped the tears from her eyes and took a tissue to blow her nose. She didn't want her mom to know she had been crying.

The bedroom door opened and Carlie came in with a cup of hot, black coffee. "I know this won't taste very good, but it will help ease the hangover you are going to feel later." Roxy grudgingly took the mug from her mother's hand. Carlie sat down on the bed next to her daughter. "Roxy, I don't really know what to do with you right now." She took a deep breath as she watched Roxy gulp the hot steaming liquid that probably tasted putrid without the cream and sugar in it. "For now, you are grounded. You are to come home directly after school for the next two weeks. You are to bring a copy of your school work home from every class with you from school as proof that you were there. I have called

your principle and he is going to make sure you do."
"But, Mom...." Roxy started to protest. Carlie held up her finger. "You do not get to speak, young lady. I am going to be going through your room very thoroughly. If I find anything that should not be in here, there will be some even harsher consequences. Do you understand me?" Roxy nodded reluctantly. She figured her mom would do this. She had broken her trust with her mother. She knew she was rebelling against all that she believed in and knew was right. Roxy realized she was lashing out at and hurting her mom. The thing was, she wasn't even angry with her mother. The person that deserved this was her father, but of course he wasn't here. If he had been, Roxy was sure she would have yelled at him and said some not-so-nice-things to him. Carlie stood. "Now, I am going down stairs to wait for your brother to get home from school. Your homeroom teacher, Mrs. Snook, will be here to drop off your assignments you missed today. You will do them."

Carlie turned on her heels and prodded down the steps just in time to hear the bus pulling up. Carlie opened the door to the kitchen door just in time for Josh to run into the house. "I had the most amazing day at school, Mom! "He exclaimed as he tossed his back pack onto a chair. "Really? What was so exciting about your day?" She asked him. "We had a *real live* firetruck and firemen come to our school today. They gave us hats and cookies and *everything!*" Josh pulled out his red plastic fireman's hat along with coloring pages and a fake badge from out of his book bag. Carlie tussled his hair as she smiled at him. "That is great, sweetie!" She exclaimed, trying to share his excitement. Josh looked around the kitchen. "Where's Roxy?" Carlie smiled. "She's in her room." That was all she said. Josh did not need to know any more than that, although Carlie was sure he would find out sooner or later that his beloved sister was in trouble. But for now, she had pleased him with her simple answer. She placed a couple of chocolate chip cookies on his plate and poured a glass of milk.

Carlie wondered if Josh would rebel when he turned thirteen. Her heart was breaking over the impact Joe's leaving had on the kids. She was very concerned about Roxy's recent behavior. Maybe it was time she got her family back into church. Roxy had loved going to youth group. Maybe they could find a different church where they could really enjoy going as a family again, minus Joe, of course. Carlie knew she had to move on with her life, and maybe getting back into a church where her and the kids could feel welcomed and really be a part was the first step.

Chapter 6

Colt had thoroughly enjoyed his lunch with Carlie. He had been very impressed with her reference to an eighteen-hundredth century author. She was beautiful, smart, and down-to-earth. All qualities in which he looked for in a woman. He still wondered if she would ever step back inside of a church. As he drove around town, Colt wondered if Carlie listened to rumors about her family that small town people tended to spread. He wondered if she ever blamed herself. He wondered if she had any close friends who were giving her support or if she took it with a grain of salt and realized that she was not to blame. Colt wondered about Carlie's children. He couldn't help but to wonder how the affair and divorce was affecting Roxanne and Josh. Colt perceived Carlie to be strong. He guessed that she never showed weakness in front of others, especially in front of her children. He imagined her to be one of those moms who cried behind closed doors, then came out with a smile on her face. He could picture her tussling her son's hair and wrestling with him. He could almost hear Carlie having one of those famous mother-daughter talks with Roxanne. She held down a job for a year in spite of everything. She was managing to raise two children on her own and he wondered how she did it all. He had hesitated for a moment when helping her up into his truck. He had held Carlie Michaels' hand a couple of seconds longer than it took to help her up. He had secretly been studying her over lunch. He took in her deep brown eyes, her not-too-thin lips and her chestnut-colored hair. But more than that, Colt was studying her expressions that would give him any type of clue who Carlie Michaels truly was. Surely, this woman had dreams and goals beyond just merely trying to keep her bills paid and her kids in line. Colt Storm wanted to know what those dreams and goals were. He wanted to know what laid inside the heart and mind of Carlie Michaels. He wanted to know what kind of poetry she wrote. He wanted to know how she knew so much about ancient German authors. Dang it! He wanted to know *her!*

Colt found Jack's auto shop and pulled in. He wanted to see what his good buddy had found out about Carlie's truck. Jack came out of the garage as soon as he saw Colt pull in. Colt put the truck in park and climbed out to greet his friend. "Hey Jack. So what have you found out about our lady's truck?" Colt asked as the two men strode into Jack's office. Jack poured two cups of coffee. Handing one to Colt, who added cream and sugar, he motioned his buddy to have a seat. Cole sat in the leather chair and crossed his leg over his knee. Colt took a couple of sips of coffee, then setting the mug down on the desk, he looked Jack in the eye. "How is the truck?"

Jack leaned forward. "I started to replace the water pump, but didn't finish it." Jack supplied. Colt raised an eyebrow. Jack continued. "Your lady friend's truck is a lost cause, my friend. She did a really great job of keeping it maintained and all, but it's not going to be worth all the repairs. I could list everything that is wrong with it, but bottom line is she is going to have to get a new vehicle." Colt shook his head. "That's not good. She doesn't have the money for a new car, I can tell ya that right now." Colt took another sip of coffee. "I better call her and tell her the news." Jack waited while Colt completed the call.

Colt could hear Carlie's voice breaking when he told her the news. He knew that she was just on the verge of tears and was trying to hold it in. It definitely took a strong woman to not just break down and right then and there. Colt could picture Carlie sitting down and holding her head in her hands. He could see her throwing something against a wall once they hung up. He could picture her crying and his heart was breaking for her. Colt tucked his phone away and was silent. "She's crying. She didn't want me to know she is, but I could hear her voice breaking. Geesh, Jack! How much can one woman take?" The two men were silent for a moment as Colt gathered his thoughts. Jack stood. Gesturing towards the back of the office, he motioned for Colt to follow him. "Come with me, my friend. I have something out back here that I am sure would suit your lady friend jest fine." Colt obediently followed. Jack opened the door and led Colt to a silver SUV. "Now, I have spent a couple of years fixin' this beauty up. It's got a new motor, new brakes, new tires. You name it, it's pretty much new. I will give this to your lady so she will have a reliable vehicle for her and those kids." Colt shook his head. "I can't accept this for free and I am sure Carlie would not want to take charity either." Jack placed his hand on Colt's shoulder. "My friend,   the   good Lord above has blessed me beyond anything I could ever imagine. I would not do this if it wasn't in my heart to do so. No sense in you wasting any more of your money and your lady friend needs a car. The way I see it, I am blessed to be able to offer her such a gift." Colt stood thoughtful for a minute. "Jack, let me at least offer you something for it." Jack shook his head. "No can do, buddy. When God puts it in your heart to do something, you do it. I can't take anything for this. This is my gift to her and to you too."

Colt knew Jack was right about being obedient to God. He, himself, had been prompted to give to someone in need. He smiled. "Very well then, I will gladly accept your offer and we shall deliver it to her this evening." He shook Jack's hand and then turned to head back to the hotel with promises that Jack would call him as soon as the shop closed up. Colt could not wait to see the look on Carlie's face when he delivered the new car to her. Colt prayed that God would work on Carlie's heart and that she would accept the gift. He prayed that this would be a step in Carlie realizing that God does love her and cares for her.

As Colt drove back to the hotel, he debated on whether to eat out for an early dinner or stay in until Jack called him. He opted to order pizza to the room and stay in. He didn't want to watch T.V. He wanted to eat and then spend some time in prayer before God. He needed to talk to his Lord and Savior about one, Carlie Michaels, and her children. God had given Carlie a gift and Colt would pray that this would open her heart to God. He parked the Chevy and went inside. After ordering a deluxe pizza and a bottle of Pepsi, he took his Bible out of the bed table drawer and found himself reading Psalm 23. He bowed his head and prayed the Psalm over Carlie. He asked God to show her that he was with her and her children. He prayed that God would let Carlie see the love Jesus has for her and for her children and that God would open the doors for her to fulfill her dreams and goals. Deep down, Colt was starting to hope that he was a part of that plan, but he knew he needed to wait for God to heal Carlie and to open that door. For now, Colt was satisfied that he had been able to help Carlie in her time of need.

Chapter 7

After receiving the phone call from Colt with the news of her truck, Carlie plopped down onto the couch and covered her face as she let the tears fall. Sheer panic was sweeping over her entire being. Numerous questions raced through her mind. *How am I going to get to work? How am I going to go shopping? How am I going to make school appointments and other important appointments? How am I going to get Josh to his upcoming school holiday programs? What if the kids have an emergency at school?* The questions went on and on. Carlie knew she had to pull herself together. She had to be strong and face her problems head on. She could not afford another car right now and she definitely did not have the money to take a cab every day.

Carlie grabbed a tissue. She dabbed her eyes dry and wiped her nose. She felt like an emotional wreck. She sighed as got up to go into the kitchen. Carlie methodically began to prepare supper for her and the kids. It had been an emotional day between her truck breaking down and Roxy's problems that had been dealt with. She wanted to run to her room and cry. However, as she glanced over at Josh, who was sitting at the table doing his homework, she knew she couldn't do that; not now anyway. She sighed as she pulled out a box of mac and cheese that would go with the cheeseburgers. Roxy's homeroom teacher had, as promised, dropped by the assignments Roxy had missed today as well as the homework that would be due tomorrow.

Carlie looked at the stack of books and folders sitting on the kitchen counter. They would have to wait until after supper. She sighed, it was going to be another late night. Carlie longed for a quiet night where she could just relax and read the latest novel by *Susan Wiggs* or *James Patterson* or write a poem of her own. She shook her head as she prepared the salad that would accompany their supper. Just as she had drained the water and mixed in the milk, butter, and cheese, she heard a knock on the door. "Who are you?" She heard Roxy say. *Oh Roxy, don't be rude.*

Carlie silently scolded her daughter as she went to see who was at the door. Roxy stepped aside as her mother approached the door. Carlie smiled at the sight of Colt standing there. Roxy raised an eyebrow as she crossed her arms and glared at her mother. *Who is this man that Mom seems sooo happy to see?* "Hey Colt, this is a surprise. Three times in one day. To what do I owe this honor?" Carlie greeted him. Colt stepped inside the living room. "You must be Roxy." He smiled at Carlie's daughter, who was studying him. "I'm Colt. Colt Storm. I helped your mom out this morning when her truck broke down." "Oh. Hi." Was all Roxy said. Carlie glanced at Roxy.

Her look told her daughter to behave. Roxy sauntered over to the couch and plopped down, keeping her eyes on the strange man as she did. Colt cleared his throat. "Could you step out for a moment? I have some news about your truck." Carlie hesitated, but then stepped outside, closing the door behind her. It was then she noticed the rugged man who had towed her truck this morning. She shook her head. "This can't be good." She supplied. She could feel the tension building up. She rolled her neck and took a deep breath. "OK. Give it to me straight." "Well Miss Carlie, this is Jack. He is the one who towed your truck this morning." Carlie nodded. "Yes. I recognize you. How do you do?" She shook Jack's hand. "I'm fine, Ma'am. But, I am afraid I have bad news for you, regarding your truck." He paused momentarily. "Your truck isn't worth the money it's going to cost to fix. Like I told Colt here, I could run down a list of things needing replaced, but bottom line is that you are going to need a new vehicle. "Yes. I know. Colt told me on the phone." Carlie reminded him. "Right. Right." Jack said, nodding his head.

Colt could sense the tension rising up in Carlie's being. He knew she was stressing over how she was going to afford a new vehicle. He couldn't help but to grin on the inside. He glanced over at Jack who was showing just as much anticipation as Colt was about presenting Carlie with her new car. Just then, Josh came bounding out of the house. He stopped suddenly at the two strange men standing in the driveway. He moved closer to Carlie's side. "Who are they, Mommy?" He asked in a whisper. Carlie knelt down beside him. "Josh, This is Colt Storm. He helped Mommy this morning when my car broke down. And guess what?" "What?!" Josh exclaimed, as he continued to study Colt and Jack. Carlie smiled. "Colt here, is a real live cowboy! He is from

Colorado and has a ranch there." Josh's eyes lit up. "Really?" It was Colt who answered him this time. He took a step towards Josh and squatted down in front of him.

Carlie took note that Colt did not get too close to Josh. She realized that Colt was in new territory and he knew that Josh was too. She was grateful that Colt did not impose himself on Josh. "I really am." Colt supplied. "You must be Josh. Your Mom told me a little about you and your sister." He stuck out his hand. Josh reluctantly grasped Colt's hand and shook it. "My sister said she doesn't like you because you're not our dad. She said that you are going to try and take daddy's place. She said that you are going to date mommy and try to kiss her too! She told me that when Mommy came out." Carlie's head shot up. Her eyes widened, looking at Colt to see what his reaction would be. She must have had a horrified look on her face as she felt her cheeks turning a hundred different shades of red. She felt as if the world had stopped for a moment. Time just stood still for a few short seconds as she waited to see what Colt's response would be.

Leave it to Roxy to pull something like this. Carlie would deal with her daughter later. Right now, she had to deal with Josh and Colt. Colt just smiled. "Well cowboy, I'm not trying to be your dad. Right now, your mommy and I are just friends and I'm just trying to help her out. Is that OK with you?" Josh nodded. "Sure." was all he said. "Thank You." Carlie mouthed to Colt as she scooted Josh back inside the house. Once she recovered, she turned her attention back to Colt and Jack.

"OK. Now I know the two of you didn't just come here to tell me that my truck is not repairable. I mean, you already told me that on the phone. So what did I do to earn the honor of you visiting tonight?" Colt grinned. "Jack, would you like to do the honors?" Colt addressed his buddy. Jack stepped forward. "Miss Carlie, I would like to present you with a gift. Now, before I do, I just want ya to know, that I won't take anything for it." Carlie was confused as she had no idea on planet earth as to what Jack was talking about. Jack must have read the confusion on her face, for he took a step closer to Carlie. He reached in his pocket and pulled out a set of car keys and handed them to her. Carlie looked from Jack to Colt and back to Jack. She shook her head. "I don't understand."

she said.

Colt stood, smiling, but it was Jack who spoke. "Well, Ma'am, Colt here told me about you having a job and two kids. As I told you, your truck isn't repairable." He paused as he cleared his throat. "I am giving you the silver SUV sitting there on the street in front of your house." Carlie turned to where he was pointing. She gasped. She hadn't even noticed the vehicle sitting on the street. Jack's sudden announcement of giving her a new car startled her. Carlie did not know what to say, let alone how to act. She just stood in place as if her feet were cemented to the ground. She opened her mouth to speak, but nothing would come out. It was as if she had transcended into another world; another dimension. *For crying out loud, Carles! Say something!* "Ummm.. I..I...I...ummm..I don't understand." She finally managed to stammer.

"Ma'am, all I can say is that I have had this vehicle sitting at my garage for two years. The good Lord told me to give it to you and when the good Lord tells ya to do something, you just do it. I can promise ya that it will be a reliable vehicle for you. I spent a lot of time repairing it." Carlie stared at the keys in her hand. She still could not believe nor comprehend that this was happening to her. Why would two complete strangers do something like this? She looked up at Jack and then at Colt. Tears were streaming down her face. "Wow. I don't know what to say." She wiped her cheeks. "Thank you! Thank you so much! You have no idea what this means to me; to my kids!" She couldn't help herself. She threw her arms around Jack and then Colt, who both had tears in their eyes. "It's a gift from God, Ma'am." It was Colt who spoke this time, his voice so tender. Carlie nodded. "Thank you." Colt gave her another hug. "Go get those kids and take it for a spin, Miss Carlie. And I will see you Saturday night at 7, if not before." He gave her a wink as he and Jack turned to go.

Carlie stood and watched them drive away. She turned back to go into the house. Roxy had moved from the couch into the kitchen. Josh was sitting on the floor watching one of his favorite shows on television. Roxy turned at the sound of her mother coming into the kitchen. "I finished dinner, Mom." She said. "Who was that anyway?" Carlie addressed her daughter, first thanking

Roxy for finishing supper, then addressing the question of who was in the driveway. "I explained that to you when you answered the door, Roxy. But, I will tell you again. His name is Colt Storm. He was the one who helped me this morning when the truck broke down at the store. The other gentleman with Colt was Jack. He is the one who was trying to fix our truck." She stopped there to see if any curiosity had aroused in Roxy. Roxy set the plates on the table. "Oh." Carlie turned to face her daughter. "Is that all you have to say is 'Oh'?" Roxy sighed as she sat down. Carlie continued. "And for the record, Colt is just someone I met today. He is not taking your father's place. I am not going to run off with him. And he's not going to just steal me away and kiss me. Next time, young lady, you better be more careful about what you tell your brother." She paused. "Besides, Roxy, there may be a time when I *do* meet someone and when that day comes, that man will be one who will love all of us. No man can ever take the place of your father. Your dad will always be your dad, but your dad has moved on and I deserve to find someone, too. And you, young lady, will be a little more respectful to Colt and to whoever else comes to this house. Do I make myself clear?" Roxy nodded.

"Mom, look, I am really sorry about today. I don't know what is wrong with me. I know I shouldn't do what I did. I'm sorry." Carlie hugged her daughter and then sat across from her. "Roxy, I know your dad hurt you doing what he did. He hurt all of us. I know things aren't the same. I know we don't get to do what we used to be able to, but honey, that is no excuse for your behavior. I appreciate the fact that you came to me and apologized and I forgive you. However, your punishment stands." Roxy sighed. "But, this isn't fair, Mom!" "It's called accountability, Roxanne, and you need to adjust your attitude and prove to me that you are going to change your behavior!" Roxy sighed. She knew better than to argue any further with her mother. Carlie gave her daughter a moment to process what she had told her. "Now, would you like to know why those two gentlemen came here tonight?" Roxy nodded. "Well, our truck is not repairable." Carlie stood and got out the buns from the cabinet, then moved to the fridge to take out the condiments for the burgers. She turned back to Roxy. "So, Jack had an SUV sitting in his lot and decided to give it to us!" Roxy stared at her mother for a moment. Carlie smiled. She had just had that same reaction a few short minutes ago when Jack had handed her the keys. "What?! I mean, you're kidding, right?" Carlie shook her head.

"No. I'm not. Jack wanted to give it to us." She paused as she gently stroked her daughter's cheek. "Now, maybe I can go back to school and get a better job." Roxy smiled before turning and running into the living room to get Josh. "Mom has a new car, Josh!" She exclaimed as the two returned to the kitchen for dinner." Carlie grinned at Josh's jumping in the air. "Yippee!" he cried. "OK. You two, let's eat. Then we will take the car for a drive." Carlie made their plates and placed the food in front of Roxy and Josh, After getting herself a plate, she sat down. "Hang on a minute, there, sport." She said to Josh who was fixing to take a big bite of mac and cheese. "I think we need to say a prayer tonight before we eat." Josh stopped his fork in mid-air. Roxy froze, her eyes bulging as she tried to comprehend her mother's sudden need to pray. Her family had not prayed or attended church in about a year now. Both of the kids looked at her as if she had lady bugs crawling out of her ears. Carlie held her hand up. "I know. Praying sounds foreign to you, especially since we haven't been in church for a long time. But, I think we should at least give thanks for a new car." They all bowed their heads and for the first time in a what had been a very long, troubling year, Carlie led her children in a short, but meaningful prayer.

Chapter 8

Colt rode shotgun back to Jack's shop. He could not get the shocked look on Carlie's face out of his mind. Her expression when Jack handed her the keys to the SUV was forever engraved in his mind. He laughed out loud. "What's so funny?" Jack asked, stopping at the red light. "I was just thinking of the expression on Carlie Michaels' face when you handed her those keys and told her the car was a gift. I thought for a moment there she was going to have a heart attack." Jack grinned. "She certainly looked like she had just transcended into another dimension, didn't she?" Colt nodded. "It was a good deed, ole buddy." he said as he slapped Jack on the shoulder. Jack shifted gears as the light turned green. "I said it once and I'll say it again, when God tells to do somethin,you just do it. You don't ask the Sovereign One questions, you just do what He asks ya to do."

Colt couldn't agree with his friend more. Since that day eight and a half years ago, when he had given his heart to God, Colt had promised the good Lord that he would do whatever was asked of him to do. Today, that "whatever" was being able to help Carlie Michaels. He hoped that he had made a good, lasting impression on her today. He had noticed the horrified look on her face when Josh had come out to inform Carlie of his older sister's warning to take heed concerning Colt. Carlie's cheeks had turned more shades of red than a wild rose ever could. Colt knew that the prudent behavior from her children was to be expected. After all their father had just taken off and left them, giving them no explanation whatsoever other than he didn't want his family anymore. Therefore, Colt knew that Josh and Roxy would see him as trying to take their father's place as well as someone who was going to take their mom away. Colt decided that when he bowed his head tonight, he was going to pray for Carlie's children to see that he was not there to hurt them or their mother, but as a friend. He would pray that God would touch their young hearts as he was beginning to do with Carlie. Colt had seen her heart soften just a little tonight and he was hoping that he could be the one to break down the wall around her completely.

"Why are ya so quiet?" Jack's voice jarred Colt out of his

thoughts. He glanced over at Jack. "Just thinking about Carlie and her kids. Ya know friend, if this works out between Miss Carlie and I, her kids are going to be a little bit of a challenge." Jack nodded. "Yeah, but what's the story behind her being single?" Colt took a shallow breath. "Her husband became involved in another, much younger woman. Guess he decided that he didn't want his wife and kids anymore. Just told them he had found someone else and up and left." He paused momentarily. " I don't know if the kids ever see their father or not. Carlie didn't say, but I kinda have a feelin' that he doesn't come around much. Those kids have gotta be hurtin'."

Jack nodded as he pulled the truck into the shop's lot. "Yeah. You are going to look like the bad guy comin' in, stealin' their mama away and tryin' to take their daddy's place." Colt opened the door and climbed down from the truck. He came around to the front and waited for Jack to get out. "Yeah, that's what I'm afraid of, Jack. I'm gonna have to be real prayerful about this."

Another moment of silence as Colt gathered his thoughts. "Gonna have to tread lightly and win 'em over slowly. Just show them that I care about their mother and I'm not out to hurt her." Jack unlocked the door to the office. Shutting it behind them, he sat down in one of the leather chairs. Colt followed suit. "It may be a little rough at first, Colt, but I truly believe that if this is God's will, then he will bring it all together. Just tread lightly and take it slow. Don't jump ahead of God. Just take it to Him in prayer."

Colt leaned forward, folding his hands on top of his knees. "My thoughts exactly, my friend. If Carlie Michaels is meant to be, then God will bring it to pass. If not, well, I am glad I was here to help her in her time of need. And maybe, just maybe, I planted a seed in her heart and she will come back to the good Lord and realize once again that he loves her and those kids."

Colt's words got Jack's curiousity aroused. "Did they used to go to church?" Colt nodded. "Actually, yeah. Carlie told me that her husband was the worship leader at their church before he ran off with the other woman. Carlie informed me that she and the kids have not stepped inside a church since. Can't say that I blame her really. I don't know that I would be so inclined as to face my church either if something like that had happened to me. She was probably mad at God for a while anyway. I probably would be too." Jack shook his head. "She's a strong one to have gone through all of that alone." Colt couldn't agree more as checked his watch and stood.

"Well, ole buddy, time for this cowboy to go get some relaxation in before hittin(hitting) the hay." Jack stood and shook Colt's hand. "Don't worry, Colt. God will work this all out." Colt nodded.He let himself out, pausing to promise Jack that he would be in touch . Jack would want to know the details of Colt's date with Carlie. Colt promised Jack that he would fill his buddy in after his date Saturday night. Colt climbed into his Chevy and headed back to the hotel. He had a lot of thoughts going through his head as he unlocked the door to his room. Most of those thoughts were of Carlie Michaels and her children. He would definitely need to spend some time praying tonight. *God, if it's your will, let it be. Only if it's your will.* He silently prayed as he stretched out onto his bed and once again pulled his Bible out of the bed-side table's drawer. He read his favorite passage, Psalm 23, before bowing his head to pray. Colt Storm hadn't known how long he had been praying until he opened his eyes and saw that the clock read 10:00 P.M. It had been him and God for the last two hours. Colt had never felt a peace like the peace that was filling his heart now. Colt Storm knew that God was going to bring to pass what was meant to be. Whether or not that included Carlie Michaels, he was not yet sure, but he knew that either way, God was working. Working in his own life and in the lives of the Michaels' family.

As Carlie sat down to eat dinner with Roxy and Josh, she still could not comprehend the fact that she had been given a new vehicle. *Who in their right mind would hand over keys to a new car to a total stranger?* Carlie couldn't help but to wonder. Jack said the vehicle was a gift, and that was all he had said about it. Carlie knew she had to get the vehicle registered in her name and get the tags transfered from 'Ole blue to the new car. *Oh no! The tags!* She hoped that either Jack or Colt had remembered to take the plates off of the truck so that she could just transfer the plates.

After all, her birthday was in June and she didn't want to have to pay for new tags and then turn around in a few short months and pay for them all over again. Plus, it would be a lot cheaper to just have the plates transfered to the new car than to get new plates anyway. With her budget, she needed all the help she could get with saving money. She was scheduled off for tomorrow, according to her revised schedule. She silently groaned inside about that. At any rate, she would be able to make it to the DMV to take care of the tags.

Carlie had told the kids that they could take the new car for a quick spin after supper. But now, as she looked at the clock, she realized it was getting late. Both Josh and Roxy still had homework to finish and they both needed to take their showers. Carlie piled up the plates and silverware and placed them into the sink. She turned to the kids. "I know I said that we could take the new car for a spin, but it is getting late and both of you still have homework to do and showers to take." She advised them. "But, Mom...." Roxy started to protest. Carlie arched her eyebrow. "No 'buts' young lady." Then thinking for a minute, she had an idea. "Why don't I drive you guys to school tomorrow? That way, you can get to ride in the car and it will give you a break from the crowded buses. Besides, I have to go to the department of motor vehicle anyway and get the plates transferred from the truck to the SUV. " Roxy and Josh looked at each other, as if deciding if they really liked that idea or not, then looked at Carlie. "That's fair, I guess." Roxy said. "Yippeee!!! I get to be escorted to school!" Josh exclaimed. Carlie smiled. She wondered sometimes where Josh got his extensive vocabulary from. After all, there weren't too many seven year old kids, especially *boys*, who used or even knew what the word *escorted* meant. "OK. Now you two scoot and get your work done. Josh, let me know if you need help with your Math. Oh, and Roxy, you bring your workthat Mrs.Snook dropped off in here." Roxy rolled her eyes, but chose to not argue. Josh followed his sister and a few minutes later, both children were sitting at the kitchen table solving Math problems that Carlie knew they would proclaim to be "dumb and useless." She smiled as she turned back to the kitchen sink to wash the dinner dishes.

Chapter 9

Carlie managed to get both kids to school without too much difficulty. The weather was sketchy. With just a few weeks before Thanksgiving, the sky looked as if it was ready to release the ton of snow it had held in it's reservoir all summer long. Carlie didn't mind, she actually liked the snow and colder weather. Before leaving the house however, Carlie had thoroughly checked Roxy's backpack for any would-be contraband. Then, kissing her daughter on the head, had dropped Roxy off to school. She made Roxy promise to bring all her work home from school that she did throughout the day. Roxy reluctantly promised and Carlie had sent her daughter off with a warning. Josh, on the other hand, had been much more compliant in getting ready for school.

Both of the kids had enjoyed being "escorted" to school, as Josh had put it the night before. Carlie sighed as she watched Josh skip into the building and then headed for the DMV. Early this morning, when she woke up, she had called Colt about the plates from the truck. She apologized for waking him up so early. Colt had informed her that he was always up early. Colt had stated that he got up early every morning to read his Bible and pray. Another pang of guilt had seared Carlie's heart. She pushed it aside as she inquired about the plates. He told her that they were under the driver's seat. Sure enough, when Carlie had come out this morning to start her new vehicle, the plates were exactly where Colt said they would be.

Carlie's thoughts drifted from the business at hand to Colt Storm. She liked him well enough. Yesterday had been an amazing, yet emotional day for her. Colt had shown up out of nowhere to help her with the truck. Carlie had not slept much last night as she had a difficult time comprehending the events of yesterday. First, Colt had helped her get her truck to Jack's shop. Then he had asked her to have lunch with him; which she had hesitantly, but happily obliged to do. By the day's end she had a set of keys to a new car, which Jack had informed her was a "gift."

In the middle of all of this, Roxy had come home drunk and Carlie had had to deal with her daughter's issues. Carlie knew she had to pay both men back somehow. She was not accustomed to recieving something for nothing. Even when she and Joe were married and things had been good between them, Joe had never given her anything without expecting something from her in return. Carlie Michaels was not one to just take charity. She vowed that she would find a way to pay back Jack and Colt for this "gift."

Carlie pulled into the parking lot of the DMV. After locating a parking space, she opened the glove compartment to gather the registration forms. As she pulled out the forms, she noticed an envelope with her name written on the outside. She paused for a moment as she studied the mysterious envelope. She opened it slowly. Inside was a letter. She carefully unfolded the paper to read it. As she did, another piece of paper fell onto the floor. Carlie picked it up. It was a check. Carlie stared at it in amazement, then placed it under the letter as she read.

"Miss Carlie, I wanted to give you this check to help out with some of your expenses. I enclosed enough for you to keep your cable on for the next six months and to pay for the registration expenses for the car. There is also a little extra for you to take the kids out to dinner. See ya Saturday night. Your new friend, Colt Storm."

Carlie could only sit and stare at the letter. *How did he know how much my cable is? Why is he doing all of this for me?* She wondered. She did not want Colt to feel sorry for her. It was nice of him to befriend her and to help her, but Carlie knew that she could not take charity from him; and she definitely did not want her problems to be his problems. Yet at the same time, she knew that she could not return the check. She had to accept it. Carlie decided that she would make it clear to Colt Storm at dinner Saturday night that he was not to help her anymore. She was thankful for his help, but she needed him to not worry about her or the kids. After all, he was going back to Colorado, and chances were she would never see him again. Not unless some inexplicable, God-sent miracle happened that took her to Colorado or brought him back to Ohio.

Carlie did not believe in fate. And she did not believe that God would allow a man to love her only to have to let him go. She could not handle falling in love again and losing love again. Joe's abrupt affair had left her in a comatose state and had caused her and the kids more pain than anyone could ever imagine. She was just starting to get over the affair and the divorce. Now, with Roxy acting out, Carlie needed to focus on healing her kids. It would not be fair for God to make another man to fall in love with her only to lose said man. Carlie would have dinner with Colt Saturday night, but she would not allow herself to become attached.

Clearing those thoughts from her head, Carlie placed the check into her purse and stepped out of the car into the DMV. Fortunately, the line was short and Carlie was able to get in and out fairly quickly. She went back outside and put the plates on the SUV. Luckily, she had remembered to bring a screwdriver with her as the screws were fairly tight and not easy to unscrew. The temperature had significantly dropped from what yesterday's temperatures were. The colder temperatures made it even more difficult to get the screws off and back on. Carlie managed however, and went on her way.

The bank would be her next stop and then she would make the half hour drive to the nearest cable company's office to pay for her cable. She smiled as she pulled out of the parking lot. In spite of the emotional and confusing feelings Colt had manged to arouse, Carlie knew that the kids would be tickled to death to be able to go out to eat tonight. She would let them pick the place. This would be a welcome treat for all of them being that it had been a year since they had been able to eat anywhere but at home.

Just then, her cell phone rang. "Hello?" "Carlie, it's Laura. Mr. Marley wants everyone here in two hours for a store meeting." Carlie sighed. "What is he up to now?" She asked Laura. Carlie could picture Laura shrugging her shoulders. "I don't know, but be here at noon." "Will do." Carlie sat her phone down on the seat.

Mr. Marley had not been a very decent manager. In fact, Carlie and her co-workers often discussed whether or not he even was qualified to run a supermarket. Customers often complained about him, too, as he never went out of his way to help anybody. He thought his job was to sit up in the manager's office with his feet propped up on his desk and watch everyone through the tinted windows.

Carlie shook her head. She had enough time to get to the cable company, pay her bill, and get to the store meeting. She could feel butterflies in her stomach as she drove. The last time Mr. Marley called a store meeting, it had been just a week after Carlie had started working there. He had gone on a rampage and fired over ten employees for supposedly not doing their jobs. Those employees were ones with disabilities. The store had contracted with the local mental health facility and gave jobs, such as bagging groceries, to those who were high-fuctioning, mentally disbabled citizens. Carlie had enjoyed working with them and thought it unfair for Mr. Marley to have been so cruel.

Now, as she drove, Carlie couldn't help to wonder what was up "Scrooge's" sleeve now. She thought it was ironic that his name was "Mr. Marley" and everyone called him "Scrooge." She chuckled out loud at that one. "Oh, Carles, what's next?" She asked aloud. Then, just as quickly as she said the phrase, she clasped her hand over her mouth. She knew better than to say things like that. They always ended up coming true. *Please don't let me or anyone else lose their jobs this time.* Carlie prayed silently as she pulled into the cable company's parking lot.

Carlie ran inside with the money to pay the bill for the next six months. The woman behind the counter was smacking her gum and chewing her nails. Carlie dreaded the idea of this woman being the only customer service representative on the clock. "Can I help ya?" She asked Carlie. Carlie hesitated before stepping up to the counter. "Um.. yeah." She said, still unsure that this was the rep she was going to trust her money with. "I am paying my cable for the last two months and for the next six months."

The twenty-something, jet-black haired girl looked as if Carlie had just landed a space shuttle in the middle of the lobby and was climbing out of the shuttle in full astronaut gear. "I'm not sure we can do that, hun." *Please tell me that there are not just twenty- year old bimbo girls in this world who have absolutely no brains!* Carlie thought as she practically leaned over the counter. It was as if there was suddenly a whole generation of bimbos who didn't know what two plus two equalled and who had stupid names; like *Kat.*

Carlie knew that she should not be so judgemental and harsh, but seriously, this girl needed to get a clue! She definitely should not be working with people. "Can I have your name please?

And your supervisor?" Carlie demanded. "It's Candi." Carlie choked back the laugh. *Perfect name for a perfect brainless bimbo. She thought. Stop it, Carles! Just because Joe took off with a woman-child, does not mean that you have to be cruel to every twenty-something girl that crosses your path!* Carlie looked at Candi. "Can I just see a supervisor, please?" Candi nodded. "Yeah, sure." Candi stepped into the back and emerged a few seconds later with a handsome man wearing a suit and tie.

"Hi. I am Jared. Can I help you?" Carlie ignored Candi, who was irritatingly smacking her gum. Carlie really wanted to reach over and grab the gum out of the girl's mouth and give her a lesson in manners. However, she ignored the urge as she addressed Jared. "Yes. I am Carlie. Carlie Michaels. I need to pay my cable bill for the last two months and I also would like to pre-pay for the next six months. Candi here, informed that pre-paying was not possible." Jared let out a sigh. Carlie could tell that the supervisor was just as irritated with his employee as she was. "I am sorry about that Miss Michaels. I would be happy to take those payments for you." Carlie smiled. "Thank you." Jared quickly brought up Carlie's information on the computer. After a few quick clicks, Carlie was handing him the money. He entered the payment into the system, then printed out two copies of the reciept. One was for Carlie to sign and the other was her copy to keep. Carlie completed her signature and handed it to Jared. She folded and put her copy in her purse. She reached out to shake Jared's hand. " Thank you so much." She said. "No problem, Miss Michaels. We appreciate your business. You have a good day." Carlie smiled as she exited the building. As she made her way out, she could hear Jared repremanding Candi. Carlie assumed the poor girl would not have a job much longer. She climbed into the SUV and headed back to Wilmington for her store meeting, which was bound to be another frustrating venture.

As Carlie pulled into the store's lot and found her parking space in the employee parking of the massive parking lot, she couldn't help but to feel nervous. Her hours had already been cut down to thirty a week and she was hoping that Mr. Marley was not going to cut anymore off her schedule. She could not even begin to imagine or guess what was so important that he had to call a meeting today. It must be urgent, Carlie concluded as she climbed out of the SUV and locked the doors. She fished her employee I.D out of her purse and placed the lanyard around her neck. She assumed that all employees would be required to clock in for this. After all, they should get paid, especially when some of them, like herself, had to come in on their day off.

She breezed through the automatic sliding doors and clocked in. Laura spotted her and came over to walk with her to the conference room for the meeting. "Who is going to man the registers and floor while we are up here?" Carlie inquired. "The supervisors are keeping two registers open." Carlie groaned. "This must be bad. The store is packed and Mr. Marley is only going to keep two supervisors on registers?" Laura nodded. "Pretty crazy, even obscene if you ask me. But it is Mr. Marley calling the meeting and we all know he is not the best customer service person in the world." Laura stated. "Yeah, as long as he gets his paycheck, what does he care?" Carlie agreed.

The two women seated themselves at the oblong table along with the other cashiers. Carlie could feel the tension in the room. It clung to the air like thick smoke after a fire had been put out on a burning building. In other words, one could cut it with a knife. Laura and Carlie continued to whisper to one another as they waited for thier boss to come in. "I hope he is not going to fire anyone." Carlie whispered, leaning over to Laura. Laura nodded. "Yeah. We are all nervous about that." She whispered back.

After the last bout of firing employees a year ago, the store had suffered. Even though, the ones fired were the contracted mentally challenged individuals, customer service had suffered greatly. Cahiers struggled with bagging their customers' groceries. This was not an easy task to do as some customers could have up to three carts of groceries at a time, especially around the first week of the month when the food vouchers reloaded.

Carlie silently observed the other cashiers. Some were biting their nails while others had their arms wrapped around their stomachs as if they were going to vomit from nerves. Whispers encased the room. Questions begin to arise as to whether or not some of them would have a job when this was over and who the lucky ones would be to stay.

The door opened and the room suddenly became quiet, as if a great presence had entered. In a sense it had. Mr. Marley entered the conference room wearing a gray suit and tie. He was in his mid-forties with distinguished features and salt-and-pepper hair. He was feared by his employees more than he was admired by them. Another man walked in behind Mr. Marley. He was also in a suit and tie. This man appeared to be in his early fifties with gray hair and sported a mustache. Carlie leaned over and whispered in Laura's ear. "Who is that?" She asked, discreetly motioning to the older man. Laura shrugged. "I don't know." She answered. The two women fell silent as Mr. Marley cleared his voice.

"OK. Thank you all for coming up today. I know some of you were off today so thank you for making the trip in. I will make this as short as possible.: He paused. "I would like to introduce you to our district manager, Tom Clarington. Mr. Clarington would like to have a few minutes to speak to you about some of the changes our store is making. So, please give him your undivided attention." Mr. Marley sat down and gave Mr. Clarington the floor. Mr. Clarington greeted the group before pulling up a power point presentation which contained productivity charts as well as the store's yearly budget.

"Ladies and gentlemen, this is a chart of your productivity for the last year. As you can see, the productivity for the year has gone down significantly. You, as cashiers, have not been pulling your weight fully. Therefore, we are going to need to make some major adjustments." Carlie held back a snicker. *"Major adjustments"* meant firing people and hiring new people. "Now, before we get to that, let's take a look at our budget." Mr. Clarington continued.

"The good news is that you as a store, have risen in the amount of profits taken in over the last year. Which surprises me because usually productivity and profits go hand in hand, but in this case, they do not. Now, along with the extra profits, we have given some of the supervisors raises as well as a few employees." He paused again as he took a sip of his water. Carlie wished she had grabbed something to drink as the water in the glass sparkled and looked amazingly refreshing. Mr.Clarington continued.

"I know some of you have only been here just a year and

you will recieve your evaluations at the end of this meeting." He turned and fully faced the group. "The bad news is that, I regret telling you this, but due to low productivity and low-quality customer service, some of you will have to be let go. Now, in order to not embarrass you in front of your co-workers, each of you are about to recieve an envelope. When I tell you to, you can open your envelope. Inside you will either have a pink slip, meaning you have been let go, or you will have a blue slip stating you can contiunue your employment here. Before we do that, however, I need to let you know of a couple of more things. We are going to be expanding the store. I have talked to our finacial advisors and we are going to be putting in a book section as well as a corner cafe."

Gasps were heard all around the room at the announcement of the renovation that would be taking place.Yet Carlie knew that some employees, like herself, were wondering how and why Mr. Marley was opting to fire people when the store was making plans for new additions. Wouldn't he need people to man those stations? Then a thought hit Carlie. Maybe he was going to hire local college kids to run the trendy cafe and bookstore. That would make sense, excpet for the fact that he had no regard for those who might lose their jobs. Mr. Clarington motioned for Mr. Marley to stand. He handed the store manager a pile of envelopes.

"OK. Now, Mr. Marley will hand out the envelopes and you may open them as soon as everyone receives theirs." Everyone waited anxiously as the envelopes were placed down one by one in front of each cashier. Mr. Marley returned to the front of the room. Carlie held her breath as she waited for the go-ahead to open her envelope. Carlie glanced over at Laura who had already ripped open her envelope and was holding a blue slip in her hand. She could see the relief that flooded over her face. Of course, Laura had worked at the store for five years now and was considered an asset.

Carlie slowly opened her envelope. She could feel the butterflies in her stomach. She peeked in and her heart sank. A pink slip. A *pink* slip! Why? She was a good worker and she had only called off twice in the last year. Why was Mr. Marley letting her go? She fought back the tears that threatened to fall. She looked at Mr. Marley who was dismissing the group. "Please, if you have any questions, I will be happy to answer them."

Carlie definitely had questions; well one question. Why? She waited until the room cleared before approaching Mr. Marley. He looked at her without smiling. "I'm sorry Miss Michaels." He said before she even got her question out. Carlie squared her shoulders. "All I want to know is why, Mr. Marley. I have worked here a year and I have been faithful and have worked hard." Mr. Marley didn't flinch. "That's the way things fall; the way the cookies crumble, Miss Michaels. I'm sorry." He left the room, leaving Carlie with unanswered questions. She was devastated. Now what was she going to do? She didn't have any training other than running a run-down boutique shop with her mother in her college days. She stepped out into the hall where Laura was waiting. Laura waited for Carlie to speak.

"He fired me." She told the other woman. "What?! Why?!" Laura was as shocked as Carlie was. "I don't know. I asked him and all he said was 'that's the way the cookies crumble.' No explanation whatsoever." Laura put her arms around her friend. "I'm so sorry, Carles." She let go. "What are you going to do?" Carlie shook her head. "I don't know. I don't know what I'm going to tell the kids. I don't know what I am going to do. I am 38 years old and I don't have any training." Laura took Carlie's arm as they descended the stairs back onto the floor. "Listen, I need to get back to work. I will call you tonight and we will talk." Carlie smiled sheepishly. "OK" Was all she said as she exited the building. She had known Laura a little over four years now. The two had met at a school program that Roxy and Laura's daughter, Kelly, had been in together. They had bonded quickly and became fast friends. Laura had become a great friend and support for her, especially over the last year. She was just 40 with dark auburn hair that barely hung to her shoulders. She had been a fun person to have worked with too. Laura could always make Carlie laugh. Carlie just loved Laura to death.

Carlie took a deep breath as she stepped outside. *Just at the height of revalty, a bomb is suddenly dropped.* She thought as she climbed behind the wheel. She put the key in the ignition, but didn't start the car. She placed her head on the steering wheel and cried. She let the tears fall freely. She didn't understand this. None of this made sense, not the car she was given, not the way Roxy was acting, and certainly not losing her job! She wanted to throw a brick through the store window. But, she knew that would only lead to trouble. So, Carlie Michaels did what she always did; she wiped the tears from her eyes, blew her nose, fixed her make-up, and went home with a smile on her face to meet the kids when they came home from school. She would carry on the normal routine with her kids tonight. After dinner out, she would help them with their homework. Once they were settled into bed, she would watch her favorite T.V. show before going to bed while sipping on some hot tea. Tomorrow, she would make a game plan. Life was harsh. She had learned that the hard way with Joe's affair and now losing her job. There was no time to cry over spilled milk. Carlie Michaels had to face her troubles head on and find a new plan.

Chapter 10

Saturday came quickly. Carlie dressed for her dinner out with Colt. Laura had agreed to come over and sit with the kids. Laura had grinned when Carlie told her about Colt. The two women had met for lunch on Friday and Carlie had let Laura in on everything that had gone on that week. Laura had taken Carlie to Olive Garden for all you can eat soup, salad, and breadsticks. Laura's treat. "You lucky girl!" Laura had beamed. "He asked you to dinner and his friend gave you a new car all in one day?" Carlie had nodded. "Yeah, pretty much. But...." She had hesitated to finish her sentence. "But..." Laura had prompted. "How can I really enjoy myself or even consider falling for him? He's going to back to Colorado soon and I have no job." She had once again felt the tears filling her eyes.

"Carles, listen to me. Just enjoy the night. Don't think about your problems. Just focus on Colt. He sounds like a nice guy and who knows, maybe things will work out. He could be your Prince Charming!" Carlie had to laugh at that statement. "Yeah, but tell me something, Laura. Who does it work out for? Not me. Look what Joe did. I mean really, who does it work out for? Fairy tale princesses? Even at that, look at the messes the princes had to get them out of. Take Cinderella, for instance, her prince had to rescue her from slavery. Then there's Snow White, she was sent into a death sleep by an evil witch. Oh and let's not forget Belle, who hooked up with a beast!" Now Laura had laughed. Before long both women were laughing.

Carlie knew she had been silly, but in all seriousness she really wanted to know who true love worked out for. Now, as she plowed through her closet trying to figure out what to wear, she could feel knots forming in her stomache. Was she going to let Colt Storm get to know her a little more only to lose him? Well, she guessed she couldn't exactly lose him. She never really had him in the first place. Carlie had only met Colt just a few days ago. Sure, Colt Storm had done a lot for her; not to mention the emotions he had managed to arouse, but that didn't mean she could exactly claim him as hers. Everything had happened like a hurricane this week and Carlie felt like her head was spinning. Maybe she could at least slow down a little tonight. She decided she was going to have fun. Even if Colt was destined to go back to his home in Colorado, she was going to relax and have fun. After all, she was allowed to enjoy a nice dinner with a hot cowboy, wasn't she?

Carlie turned her thoughts back towards her closet. She continued to plow through her wardrobe, pulling out dresses and skirts and throwing them onto the bed as she did. Did she not have *anything* to wear that was appropariate and decent for a dinner date? Joe had always told her to dress simple. "Good church wives dress simple and conservative." he had told her. Little by little, Carlie was now starting to realize how controlling Joe had been. She was beginning to understand the puzzle just a little more. Yeah, her ex-husband wanted her to dress plain and simple while he went out chasing after a woman-child who dressed perogative and exciting. Oh! She wanted to slam something against the wall.

Carlie re-focused. *Concentrate on Colt and your date. Colt is a christian, so he doesn't need you to dress perogative. After all, he has seen you in jeans and a plain shirt.* Carlie reached deep into the back of her closet. She pulled out an elegant aqua-colored dress. She had worn it to Laura's wedding three years ago. The dress was form fitting and simple, but elegant. Carlie laid it out on her bed. She pulled her jeans and sweater off and slipped into the dress. It hung just above her knees. The dress' sleeves were long and tapered at the wrists. The neck line was v-shaped, modest and not too deep.

Carlie went over to her vanity and pulled out a set of pearls that her mother had given her. The matching three-piece set contained a necklace, bracelet, and earrings. Carlie sat down on the bench so she could look in the mirror. She placed the jewelry on and then took in her hair. Tonight she would wear her hair down. She had blown it dry with the blow dryer and it hung in waves down her back. She ran a brush through it and sprayed just a little hair spray to keep the waves in place. Next, she applied a light coating of foundation and finished with a rose lip gloss.

The woman in the mirror staring back at her did not look like a mom of two kids. This woman looked elegant and refined. Carlie did not know the last time she had dressed like this. Had it been three years ago when she and Joe attended Laura's wedding?

Is that why Joe had found someone else? No! Carlie Michaels was not going to blame herself. Joe was the one who had always told her that he liked the way she looked. He had wanted her to dress simple and plain. He had once told her that he didn't like his women wearing make-up. Ironic, considering whom he had taken off with.

Kat was a an agent for a modeling company. She never dressed in anything that was conservative or simple or plain. Kat always wore lots of make-up and bright red lipstick. Carlie wondered if maybe Joe had lost interest in her because she didn't dress sexier or wear a lot of make-up. No! Carlie was not going to take the blame for Joe running out on her and the kids. That had been *his* decision; *his* choice, not hers. Carlie stood and grabbed the matching aqua clutch purse. She did a turn in front of the full length mirror. Pleased with her appearance, she headed down the stairs.

"Wow! Mom! You look hot!" Roxy exclaimed as she looked up from a teen magazine she was reading "Whoa, Mommy, you look pretty!" Josh chimed in. Carlie smiled. "Thank you both." Then, changing the subject, said "Laura will be here in a few minutes. I left some money on the counter so you guys can order pizza tonight. Be good for her. OK?" Roxy and Josh both nodded. Just then the door bell rang. Carlie opened it to see Laura standing on the other side. Laura stepped into the living room as Carlie closed the door behind her. "Wow, Carles! You look gorgeous!" Laura exclaimed. "Your cowboy is going to fall over dead!" Carlie laughed. "Thank you, Laura. I doubt he will fall over dead, but thank you. And thank you for sitting with the kids. I left $20 bucks on the counter so you can order pizza." Laura nodded. "We will have fun."

Carlie pulled Laura into the kitchen, so the kids could not hear them. "It's all going too fast, Laura." Laura cocked her head to one side. "What do you mean?" Carlie pulled out a chair and sank down onto it. Laura sat too. "Just everything. I mean, look, the guy appears out of nowhere. He pays for the tow for my truck. He drives me home and helps unload my groceries. I mean, I let a stranger into my house without knowing anything about him except that he is from Colorado, has a ranch, and owns a furniture store!" Carlie took a deep breath before continuing. "Suddenly, I have a new car and my cable is paid for the next six months! This doesn't happen, at least not to people like me. Maybe this kind of thing happens in Hollywood on the big screen, but certainly not in small town Wilmington, Ohio!" Carlie stood and paced the kitchen. "I mean, come on, Laura! What does he want? What is Colt's angle? A man does not just do this kind of thing unless he expects something in return. I learned *that* from Joe."

Laura stood and took Carlie by both shoulders. "Carles, listen to me! It's not like the man is asking you to marry him! It's just dinner for goodness sake! As far as Joe....well forget that scum bag and just go and have a good time with Colt!" She let go. "Carles, maybe he just wanted to help. Did you ever think of that? Maybe he just saw the situation you were in and knew you needed a car and just wanted to help." Carlie nodded. "You are right, Laura. I guess I am just a little nervous and I am over reacting. After all, I haven't dated anyone since high school when Joe and I met." Laura smiled. "You will be fine." The two women hugged. Carlie was thankful for Laura's friendship. It was Laura who kept her grounded. The bell rang again. "Let me get it." Laura insisted. She opened the door.

"You must be Colt." Laura greeted him. "I'm Laura, Carlie's friend. Come on in, Carlie is just getting her coat." Colt removed his hat as he stepped over the the threshold and into the living room. Carlie appeared around the corner. Colt's heart stopped as he took her in. Carlie Michaels was breath-taking all dressed up. "Wow! You look amazing!" he exclaimed, pulling a bouquet of wild flowers from behind his back. Carlie smiled, blushing just a little as she took the flowers from him. "Thank you." She replied. "You look good, too." She noted, taking in Colt's black jeans, tucked-in dress shirt, and black boots. "Shall we?" Carlie nodded, handing the flowers to Laura. "You two have fun." Laura said as she closed the door behind them. Carlie smiled at her. "Thank you." Then, addressing Roxy and Josh, said, "You two behave for Laura." "We will, mom." They said simultaneously. Carlie gave them one last warning look before heading out the door with Colt. Laura noticed. She waved Carlie on. "We will all be fine." She said to Carlie, ushering her out the door.

Colt followed Carlie and opened the truck door for her.

After helping her climb in, he closed the door and got into the driver's side. "Where to?" He asked Carlie as he started the engine. Carlie was baffled. She hadn't thought about where they were going to eat. She thought for a minute. "Well, if you don't mind driving, we can go into Fields Ertle, it's just before you get to Cincinatti. There are a bunch of places there. *Olive Garden, Long Horn Steak House, TGIF*.....to name a few." Colt smiled. "Point the way. The steak house sounds very inviting." Now it was Carlie's turn to smile. "That would be a good choice." She directed Colt to the interstate. "Just stay on the interstate until you see the exit for Fields Ertle and then take a left at the light." She informed him. As they drove, Carlie started to relax. "So, Miss Carlie, are you nervous about leavin(leaving) the youngins?" Carlie grinned just a little. "Honestly?" Colt nodded. "Honestly." "Not quite as nervous as I was about going out with you tonight. Laura has been a friend for a while so the kids are in great hands. I was more nervous about being with you. I haven't dated since high school when I met...well you know." Colt nodded and took her hand in his. "I understand. It must be nerve racking. I don't want you to be nervous. Let's just have(enjoy?) a good dinner and have fun. OK? You know I won't try anything with you because I don't believe in that. We will see where everything goes." He turned and smiled at her as he squeezed her hand. Carlie smiled back at him, feeling so much more relaxed and relieved.

The restaurant lot was packed as Colt pulled in. He circled the lot several times before they finally found a space. "It will probably be at least a 45 minute wait." She supplied. Colt smiled at her. "Well, Miss Carlie, let's go find out." Carlie smiled back at him as he climbed out of the truck and came around to open the door for her. They entered the steak restaurant only to find out the wait would be an hour and a half versuses the forty-five minutes Carlie predicted it would be. She turned to Colt. "What do you want to do?" She asked quietly, as to not let the hostess hear. Colt put his arm around her. Carlie found herslef moving closer to him into the nook his arm formed, and it felt good. "Well, we can go do some shopping while we wait or we can find somewhere else." Colt suggested. Carlie thought momentarily. "Everywhere else is probably going to be the same." She said. Colt nodded. He removed his arm and led her to the hostess. "We will wait. The name is Storm, party of two. We are going down the road to do some shopping. We will be back in a little while." The hostess smiled as she wrote thier names in on her table seating placard.

Colt grabbed Carlie's hand and led her out of the restaurant. As they walked towards the truck, Colt asked, "Where to?" "There are a couple of places just down the road." She replied. Colt opened the door for her. Climbing into the driver's side, he put the truck in drive and pulled out of the lot.

They found a shopping plaza and decided to explore the shops. Carlie felt wonderful as the couple, hand-in-hand, made their way in and out of shops. She could get comfortable with this. *Don't do it, Carles.* She told herself. *Don't let yourself get too comfortable with Colt. After all, you've only known him for a few days and he is going to back to Colorado.* Carlie tried not to think about the fact that Colt would be leaving. She just wanted to enjoy tonight.

They found a little antique shop and decided to take a browse. As she admired several pieces of furniture, lamps, painitings, books, and even jewelry, Colt was watching Carlie carefully. He took notice of her interests and loved the way her eyes were sparkling. He just wished he knew for sure that having a relationship with Carlie Michaels was a definite possibility. He was falling for her only after a few short days of knowing her, and that was dangerous for him as well as for her. Love needed time to grow. Carlie and her children were still healing. Colt did not want to jump head first into another relationship only to be short-handed. The questioned remained, what to do about Carlie Michaels? The answer kept coming back. *Take your time and go slow. Pray before you jump in.*

Colt knew God was telling him to wait for the right timing. He wasn't sure if Carlie would be the one. Colt only knew he had to wait on God and that God would give an answer when the time was right. In the meantime, he would enjoy the night. Colt observed Carlie as she held up an anitque silver necklace with an oval locket. The middle of the locket was mother of pearl. It was beautiful. Colt walked over to the counter where Carlie had handed the necklace back to the cashier. "Would you like this in a box?"

The cashier was asking her. Carlie smiled and shook he head. "A little expensive for my budget." She said. "Thank you for showing it to me, though. It is exquisite."

Colt was impressed by Carlie's humble, yet classy demeanor. He could see the dissappointment in her eyes. He knew that she was used to dissappointment. He also imagined that she was used to giving up things that she wanted for the sake of her kids and what they needed and maybe sometimes wanted. He thought for a moment before stepping up to the counter. He had sworn after Jenna that he would not casually spend his money on whatever women thought they wanted or needed, but this was different. Carlie was not those other women. She had not even so much as entertained the thought of asking him to buy the necklace for her. She had simply admired the piece quietly and had humbly let the sales woman put it back. *That* had impressed Colt. He stepped up to the counter.

"We will take that." He said to the cashier. "But no box. I am going to let her wear it out of the store, if that's OK." The cashier looked a little surprised as she nodded. "Absolutely." She said as she rang up the neckalce. "That will be $321.00" Carlie gasped as Colt pulled out his credit card. The cashier processed the card as Colt fastened the necklace around Carlie' neck, removing her mother's pearls at the same time. He signed the reciept and tucked his card back into his wallet. He smiled at the cashier and thanked her.

Carlie was speechless as they left the store to go back to the restaurant. She wanted to say something, anything. She wanted to tell Colt thank you for the elegant gift, but nothing would come out. She just kept looking at him and smiling. Carlie took Colt's hand in hers and squeezed it. It was all she could do. He grinned at her, a huge cowboy grin. "You are welcome." He said, squeezing her hand. "Now, let's go enjoy a good steak dinner and each other's company." Carlie happily climbed into Colt's truck.

Colt's name was being called just as the couple entered the restaurant. "Just in time, Mr. Storm." The hostess smiled flirtatiously at Colt, ignoring Carlie, as she led them to their table. Colt had grasped Carlie's hand and squeezed it as if to reassure her that he was only interested in her and not the hostess. Colt waited for Carlie to be seated before seating himself. The hostess handed them menus, keeping her eyes solely on Colt. Colt gave her a polite smile. Carlie could not claim him as her boyfriend since he had not asked her and he was going back home.

"Can I take your drink orders?" The hostess asked. "I will have a sweet tea with a slice of lemon." Carlie ordered. "Uh-huh." The hostess replied. "And for you, handsome?" She addressed Colt. "I will have the same." Colt answered. "Perfect." The hostess practically purred. Colt cleared his throat. "Ma'am, may I ask what your name is?" The hostess grinned. "It's Kayla." She replied. "And I get off at 11:00." Colt glanced at Carlie who was obviously starting to feel uncomfortable as she pretended to glance over the menu. "Kayla, Can I make a request?" "Sure thing, handsome." Kayla replied. "Colt turned sligtly to face Kayla. "See this beautiful woman with me? My request is that you treat her with respect and that your service to her be at highest level of hospitality. My second request is that you stop flirting with me. I am clearly with a beautiful woman and I am clearly not interested in you. Oh, and one more thing, please bring Miss Carlie here a white rose." Carlie looked up at Colt. She felt her cheeks blushing. The hostess was flabergasted. "Yes sir. I will see that your lady here gets all the best service." She sauntered away.

Carlie leaned over the table. "Do they have white roses here?" She whispered. Colt grinned. "I don't know darlin, but I am sure they will find a way to get one." Carlie laughed. She was enjoying the way Colt could turn an uncomfortable situation into a humerous one. A few minutes later, a waitress came to the table with two sweet teas with lemon wedges and a beautiful white rose in a clear, glass vase. The waitress placed the drinks in front of them and the rose in the middle of the table. "Sir, you're dinner will be on the house. Our manager overheard Kayla and he would like for you to enjoy dinner on us tonight." Colt raised his hand. "Thank you, but I would like to pay for our dinner." The waitress smiled politely. "I'll tell you what we will do. If you insist on paying for dinner, we will give your date her dinner for free." Colt nodded. "Fair enough. Thank you." The waitress nodded. "Very well then. Are you ready to order?" Carlie looked up at Colt, then at the waitress. "Could we have a couple of minutes? Everything looks so delicious I can't decide." The waitress nodded again and left Colt and Carlie to make their choices.

Carlie leaned over the table. "Thank you." Colt eyes met her's. "For?" He inquired. "For everything. You have been such a help this week. I mean with my truck, the car, the money, now this exquisite necklace and dinner. Not to mention, the way you handled the hostess." Colt smile sheepishly. "You are very welcome, Miss Carlie. As for the hostess, I am not one to entertain flirtatious relationships that will only end up somewhere I don't want to find myself. Besides, I am with you tonight and I could tell she was making you uncomfortable."

It was Carlie's turn to smile. "Yes, she was making me a little uncomfortable." She admitted. "The nerve of some women, huh?" She said laughing. Colt laughed with her. He found it admirable that Carlie could turn an uncomfortable situation into a light-hearted joke. She clearly was able to laugh and have fun in the midst of what could have been a very uncomfortable dining experience.

Colt knew that he could not go down that road with Kayla, the hostess. The old Colt would have thought about it. The old Colt would have secretly gotten Kayla's number and would have had a rendezvous. But, that was the old Colt, before he became a Christian and changed his ways. The new and improved Colt did not have, nor did he desire to have, one night stands with flirtatious women with whom nothing would amount to. The new Colt wanted to find the one woman that he could spend the rest of his life with. The new Colt wanted to soley concentrate on Carlie Michaels tonight. The new Colt was praying and waiting on God's timing. He wanted to enjoy every minute of the rest of this evening with Carlie. He was enjoying seeing her outside of her "mom" role; outside of her realm. He enjoyed the fact that Carlie was relaxed and having fun. She was laughing and her eyes were shining. Colt had seen her tear up. He had seen her tense and worried. It was hard to believe that he had only met this amazing woman just a few short days ago.

The waitress reappeared a few minutes later and took thier orders. Carlie ordered a lettuce wedge with ranch dressing and a lobster tail with roasted asparagus. Colt ordered a ribye steak with a baked potatoe and green beans. They split an onion loaf, which Carlie had never had before but found amazing.

As they waited for their meals, they began to talk. "So, Miss Carlie, how is the car working for you?" Carlie smiled. "The car is great. I can not believe you and Jack did that for me." "Jack is the one who gave it to you."Colt supplied. "I take no credit." Carlied lowered her head for a moment. "What's wrong?" Colt addressed her. Carlie brought her head back up slowly and looked at him. She spoke slowly and thoughtfully "Colt, everything you have done for me and for my kids has been so great and truly appreciated." Carlie replied. "But..." Colt prompted her. Carlie took a deep breath.

"The thing is, you are going back home to Colorado pretty soon and I know it will be hard to develop and maintain a long distance relationship." She paused. "I know it *can* be possible, but hardly any long distance relationships actually work. Like I told you before, I have not dated anybody since Joe and I just don't want to fall for you only to lose you and get my heart broken again. It was painful enough the first time, you know? I have a lot riding on this or any relationship I enter into with someone. My kids are still healing and they come first. Roxy has been acting out and I know it is because of everything that has happened in the last year." She stopped there and took another deep breath. She looked at Colt who had his hands folded and was just listening to her. There was no judgement in his eyes. He was just listening to her talk.

Carlie had not known when the last time someone had actually listened to her was, other than Laura. Joe sure hadn't. Joe had always told her that he was the husband and whatever he said was law. Carlie continued." I like you Colt, a lot. I want to pay you back for everything you have done for me. I'm not used to being able to accept gifts like this. I hope you do stay in touch when you go back home, but I also know how hard that can be sometimes. Intentions can be good, but life happens and people forget." She shrugged as she stopped talking. She held her breath, waiting for Colt's response. She was sharing her heart. She wanted to just put it all out there on the table. No tricks. No deception. No hiding anything. Just pure honesty.

Colt reached across the table and took both of Carlie's hands in his. He was quiet for a couple of minutes. When he finally spoke, his voice was steady and soft. "Carlie, I know. I have thought a lot about you over the past few days too. I know it has only been just a few days since I met you, but I find myself intrigued by you. I see a woman who is struggling to heal from a hurtful divorce with two children. I see a woman of strength and weakness. I see a woman who tries to protect herself and her children from being hurt again. I see a struggling mother. I see a woman who is struggling not just emotionally, but financially as well. But I also see a woman who has a heart of gold; a woman who is intelligent and has yet to discover all of her talents." Colt paused. He looked directly into Carlie's eyes which were sparkling with tears. "Carlie, I am a praying man. I am praying for God's will to be done here. If we are meant to be, then God will make it happen. If we are not, then I hope we can keep in touch and just be friends. I am thankful that I was able to help you. I don't know all of what your relationship with Joe was like, but I don't expect anything from you in return and neither does Jack. I am finding myself falling for you too, but I also know that it has to be God who puts all of this together because if it is not of Him, it will not work." He squeezed her hands before letting go. He smiled at her. "The reason I asked you to dinner tonight is because I want to get to know you a little more. I also asked you because I know you needed a break and I thought it would be nice for you to just get out and enjoy an evening just being a woman."

Carlie smiled at him. Her heart was melting with his kind and sincere words. Colt too, was speaking from his heart. He too, had laid the cards out on the table. He had no secrets, no alterior motives. He just wanted to be her friend. Their meals came, and Colt bowed his head to say a prayer over their dinner. This time it was Carlie who took his hand in hers and bowed her head with him.

Carlie felt so much better as she practically devoured the lettuce wedge and lobster tail. She had not had a dinner out like this in a long time and it felt good. Colt took a bite of his steak, declaring how awesome it tasted. He gave Carlie a bite who in return gave him a bite of lobster. Both agreed that the food was absolutely delicious.

"This was definitely a good choice for a place to eat." Colt commented as the waitress took their empty plates away. "Would you like dessert?" The waitress asked. Carlie held her stomach for a second. "Yes we would, but give us a minute to decide." Colt answered her. Carlie looked at Colt with a surprised expression on her face. Why had he told the waitress they wanted dessert? She had not indicated that she wanted any dessert. In fact, she was not sure that she could eat another bite. She was stuffed from the lobster dinner.

Colt noticed the expression on Carlie's face. He held his hand up. "I'm not making decisions for you, darlin'. I just thought it would be nice to sit here a little while longer and just talk. Besides, if you can't eat it, you can take it home to the kids. After all, it is free for you, so why not?" Carlie laughed out loud. "You are a brat!" She teased. Colt laughed with her. "Oh darlin', if you could only have seen the look on your face." Carlie couldn't stop laughing. She must have looked absolutely horrified when he told the waitress they wanted dessert without asking her first.

Carlie and Colt both decided on cheesecake. The waitress returned with the biggest slices of cheesecake Carlie had ever seen. "Well," Carlie said, "I definitely am not going to be able to finish this!" Colt grinned. "I say we split one piece just for the heck of it." Carlie smiled. "Sure. Why not? You only live once." Colt placed one slice between them. Before long the piece was gone. Carlie held her stomache. "That was sooooo good." She noted. Colt nodded. "Yes it was, and now I am stuffed." Carlie agreed.

Colt summoned the waitress over, requesting a box for the other slice of cheesecake along with thier bill. The waitress promptly brought a box, but no bill. "Sir, the manager insists that you do not pay for your dinner. Enjoy the rest of your evening." She smiled as she walked away. Colt pulled out his wallet and placed a twenty-dollar bill on the table as tip. Carlie tried to hide the fact that she was impressed by such a generous tip. Then again, this whole night had been very impressive. Yet, Colt had been modest and had poured his heart out to her just as she had poured hers out to him. Maybe this was the beginning of a wonderful relationship. Maybe, just maybe, she and Colt could make a long distance relationship work. She didn't want to just write him off. She wanted to see where this would go, even if he did live half way across the country.

The couple ended the night with a movie. As they drove back to Carlie's home, Carlie felt at peace. Nothing could ruin this moment in time. Nothing in the whole universe could make her feel at any more peace than she felt right now. Colt had put her at ease. He had made Carlie feel special. She had put her cards on the table and Colt had, in return, accepted her right where she was. He understood her feelings and he understood her hesitation. It was as if God had brought him into her life, if for nothing else just to remind her that there are still a few good men in the world; well at least one good man. His name was Colt Storm.

Chapter 11

Carlie felt happy as she woke up the next morning. It was Sunday, 7 in the morning when Carlie awoke. She yawned and stretched as she rolled out of bed. Walking over to her bedroom window, she pulled back the drapes and stood, taking in the beauitful sun that was shining. Soon there would be snow. It was early October now and the weather was cooler and rainy. Today was a rare day where the sun was actually shining. Everything seemed perfect this morning. Last night with Colt had been the most amazing night she had had in a very long time. Colt had been such a gentleman.

Carlie still could not get over the necklace he had bought her on the spur of the moment. Just like that, Colt had laid out the money and just like that had placed the gorgeous silver antique necklace around her neck. The necklace, with it's mother-of-pearl setting, had quickly replaced the simple strand of pearls Carlie had been wearing. Carlie felt happy. She felt peaceful. She felt as if no matter what happened with her and Colt, God had smiled down on her and had given her the gift of feeling happy again. She had smiled and laughed with Colt. She had been able to be the old Carlie with him.

Carlie remembered a time where she had been funny, outgoing, and full of life. Then, junior year in high school hit and she met Joe Welsh. Her life had changed. She hadn't realized it then, but Carlie Michaels had become almost lifeless. Joe had made sure that she was not only submissive to him, but that she did not have a life of her own. Carlie had lost herself in trying to be the perfect "Christian" wife to Joe.

Now, after being with Colt Storm, Carlie felt as if her old self was revived. She did not have to hide who she was from Colt. He had accepted her for who she was and he understood her. It was if he could read deep into her soul and see everything that she wanted to be, but was hiding in the hurt and struggles. Carlie had not told Colt about losing her job. She did not want to burden him with anything more than she already had. Last night had just been about getting to know each other and having fun. Mission had been accomplished. Colt had even kissed her lightly on the cheek after dropping her off back home. He understood that for now she just wanted to be friends. Maybe that would change in the future. Neither Carlie nor Colt could be for certain what would to happen in the future, but one thing was for sure, and that was Carlie had fun with Colt Storm last night.

Carlie decided that she was going to wake up the kids and they were going to go back to church this morning. She knew that it would be difficult to walk through the doors of the church where she and Joe had once attended together. However, she also knew that she needed to get her family back into church. Carlie would brave the judgemental looks, looks of pity, and looks of concern for her and her children. At the very least if she felt unconfortable, she could leave.

She hadn't talked to the kids about going back to church yet, but had made a last minute decision. Carlie walked down the hall and opened the door to Roxy's room. "Rise and shine beautiful!" Roxy covered her head with the blanket. "Come on, Mom. It's Sunday!" Carlie smiled as she gently tugged the blanket off her daughter's head. "Yes. And we are going to church this morning. So get dressed." Roxy sat up half-way, her eyes bugging. "Church? Are you serious?" Carlie nodded. She could almost read the thoughts that were racing through Roxy's mind. "Yes. So get up and get dressed. Then come down for breakfast." Roxy groaned again, but obeyed and rolled out of bed. "Shower."

She mumbled as she stumbled down the hall towards the bathroom. Carlie smiled and shook her head. She entered Josh's room who was sitting up and rubbing his eyes. "Hi Mommy." He said as Carlie walked over to his bed. She tussled his hair, taking in his brown eyes. He looked just liked his father. Josh had inherited Joe's sandy-brown hair, brown eyes, and mischevious smile. "Good morning sport. Guess what?" "What?" Josh asked sleepily. "We are going to go to church this morning." Josh looked thoughtful for a moment. "Really?" He asked. "Really. So get dressed, OK?" Josh nodded. "OK." "Then come down for breakfast." Josh nodded again as he stretched and rolled out of from under his *Undertaker* blanket.

Carlie descended the stairs and into the kitchen to make breakfast. She pulled out the bacon she had set in the fridge the night before to thaw. She pulled out the electric griddle and set it on the counter top to heat. After mixing the pancake mix, she placed slabs of bacon on one side of the griddle and cirlces of pancake mix on the other side. She patiently waited for breakfast to cook as she brewed her morning coffee.

Roxy came down first, wearing jeans, a modest sweater, and boots. Josh bounded down the stairs a few moments later sporting jeans and a *John Cena* shirt. Carlie smiled at both of her children as she set the table with plates, forks, glasses, and napkins. She pulled out the maple syrup that had been heating in a pot of hot water. She finished placing the bacon and pancakes on a platter and sat it down on the table, serving the kids first, then herself. She poured syrup over Josh' pancakes for him and handed it to Roxy.

After pouring her coffe, Carlie sat down at the table. "Mom, do we really have to go to church?" Roxy inquired. She did not want to go back to church. What happened to her family was embarassing enough. Roxy dreaded the looks from the other kids in youth group and all the questions she would be forced to answer. It wasn't that Roxy didn't want to go back to church, but why did her mom insist on going back to their old church? Couldn't they just find a new church to go? Carlie could almost read her daughter's thoughts. She could only imagine what Roxy was thinking. More importantly, Carlie knew that it would be difficult to walk into a church where their whole family once attended and to fight those feelings of embarassment and shame. Carlie was having second thoughts as she studied her children.

Roxy was at a very impressionable age. She was caught between a child and a young woman. Roxy was already having a hard time of finding who she was. On top of the perplexing adventure of becoming a young woman, Roxy was obviously still dealing with a lot of hurt, pain, and confusion from the affair and divorce. Maybe the last thing she needed was to have her peers from her old youth group gathering around her and bombarding her with a bunch of questions that Roxy did not have the answers to. Carlie looked at both of her children carefully before speaking. "I know this is difficult for all of us and I have given going back to our old church some reconsideration." She paused there, waiting for their attention. She got it. Both of the kids' heads shot up. Both sets of eyes were fixed on her.

"Maybe we can skip church today and talk about going somewhere else. Maybe during this week we can all sit down and discuss other options and decide where we would like to visit." She took a deep breath before continuing. "We will probably have to visit a few churches to find one we are comfortable with going to. This is a small town, however, and it is not easy to avoid the fact that dad left. But, I think maybe we can find a church out of town or somwhere we can start fresh." "Sure Mom. And maybe we can just move out of Wilmington altogether." Roxy said unexpectedly.

Carlie could not tell from her daughter's tone of voice if Roxy was being sarcastic or not. Nonetheless Roxy's statement deserved a response. "Roxy, I am not saying we have to move out of town. I just thought maybe it would be too much to go back and have everyone bombarding us with a bunch of questions." Roxy nodded. "I get it, Mom. I just don't know if I am ready for all of that. I have a hard enough time at school."

There it was. The one sentence that explained the reasons for the behavior that Roxy had been presenting lately. Carlie reached over and touched her daughter's arm. "Honey, I know it is hard. And I am sorry. But we have to get on with our lives. It's not easy, but it has been a year and it is time this family gets moving back in the right direction." Roxy sighed as she got up to empty her plate into the trash and place it in the sink. "I know, Mom." Carlie watched her daughter retreat into the living room. A few seconds later, she heard the sound of the T.V.

Carlie was aware of how her daughter felt, the confusion, the fear, and the lingering hurt. The confusion and fear would fade away with time. The hurt would remain, only to be merely overshadowed with time. Carlie decided to give Roxy her space as she turned her attention towards Josh. "What about you, Sport? How do you feel about all of this?" Josh finished swallowing a piece of bacon and wiped his mouth on the sleeve of his shirt before answering. "I agree with Roxy." Was all he said.

Carlie sighed as she watched her son get up and put his plate in the sink before joining his sister in the living. Carlie cupped her face in both of her hands. *Happy now Joe?! Look at what YOU have done to your kids!* Carlie slowly got up. She would wash the dishes and then join her children in the living room. Maybe they would go to the mall today and do some light shopping. She still had a good amount of that check from Colt in her account. Her bills were caught up for the moment. Maybe what they needed was a good day out, like they used to.

Carlie slowly stood and made her way over tot he sink to wash up the dishes. As she filled the sink with with hot, soapy water, Carlie couldn't help but to wonder if she had made a mistake in not taking the kids to church this morning. Although, she understood that taking her family back to the church where they had attended when everything was right with her and Joe would be complicated, Carlie questioned her decision to not take them *anywhere* this morning. Life, as it was now, was definitely complex, but still she could not help but to feel that pang of guilt for not attempting to attend a church service this morning. She shoved the guilty feelings aside as she washed and dried the breakfast dishes and put them in their places in cabinets and drawers. She wiped down the stove, counters, and table before proceeding through the living and up the stairs to dress for their family outing. Carlie knew taking the kids out for a day would be good for all them. "Hey, you two." Carlie addressed her children as she stepped into the living room. "I am going to go up and get dressed. Then, I have a surprise for you." "What is it?" Roxy inquired in what seemed like a nonchlant I-don't -really-care tone of voice. Josh was a little more excited at the prospect of getting a surprise. "Well, I thought we could go to the mall and just have a day out doing some light shopping and just have some fun today. I have a little extra money stashed away and thought maybe we could spend a little of it." At the prospect of going to the mall, Roxy jumped up, practically running to her mom. She threw her arms around Carlie. "Thanks, Mom! I have been wanting to go out!" Carlie smiled at her daughter. "I think it will do us some good, sweetie." She said, gently stroking Roxy's cheek. "Let me grab my purse and then we will go." Roxy nodded and rejoined her brother, who was trying to pretend to watch the show on the television. Carlie caught Josh grinning, however, as she ascended the stairs.

The mall was about an hour's drive to get to. Carlie could feel the excitement building up in both of her children. Before leaving, she had quickly looked for near-by malls that would suit both her children's needs. She wanted Roxy to have fun shopping in all of the teen stores and she wanted Josh to be able to find places for him to hang out and have fun as well.

The mall was set back a little off of the highway. Carlie pulled in and found a parking spot just in front of the mall's main entrance. The trio climbed out as Carlie locked the SUV. "I've never been to the mall Mommy! This is so exciting!" Josh exclaimed as he gawked in amazement at the huge brick building that loomed before them. Carlie smiled, taking his hand. "We are going to have lots of fun here. But, it is important that you stay with me. OK? This is a very crowded place and you need to stay close." She instructed him.

Roxy was just a few feet ahead of her mother and brother. She waited at the mall's entrance doors for them to catch up. Her eyes were sparkling. They entered. Carlie was estacic to see the excited expressions on the faces of her children as they began to make their way through the mall and into different stores. She took them into each department store, where they explored every level and gawked at the expensive, vibrant, modern furniture and household items. They explored the sporting goods stores and bought Josh a couple pairs of new jeans and new wrestling shirts. Their next stops were a couple of the teen stores where Carlie let Roxy pick out a couple pairs of new jeans, a modest skirt, and a couple of shirts.

By one o' clock, they began to feel the hunger pains and wanted lunch. Carlie led her children up the escalator to the food court where she bought lunch for all of them. The great thing about the food court in the mall was that it catered to everyone's taste buds. Josh perfered chili dogs. Roxy wanted pizza. Carlie opted for Chinese. Later she would treat herself to an iced mocah-vanilla coffee.

After lunch, they continued to shop. Carlie purchased two new in-style dress pants and blouses for potential job interviews, a pair of jeans, and a casual sweater. After finishing shopping the clothing and department stores, the trio explored the gift shops, looking at Christmas decorations and gifts on display. Of course, they had to explore the toy stores for Josh and the music and movies stores for Roxy, and finally the jewelry and make-up stores for Carlie. By four pm, they were exausted and Carlie had reached her shopping budget. "OK. Gang, time to head home." Carlie announced. They headed out to the car and unloaded their packages into the back of the SUV. After everyone was buckled in their seats, Carlie pulled out of the parking lot. "One more stop before we head home." She said. "Where?" Roxy and Josh asked in unison. "Well, I thought it would be nice to stop at one of those little pastry shops and get a treat before heading home. "Yay!" Josh exclaimed. "Thanks, Mom. Today was really great." Roxy said, smiling. Carllie smiled back at her daughter. "We all needed this." She said as she pulled into a pastry shop which had ice cream and pastry decor on their windows.

The inside of the little pastry shop was set in the 1960's. Replicas of sixties style tables and chairs were scattered across the tile floor. Displays of old-style coke bottles stood in the self-serve refrigerator that sat to the right side of the counter. Even the waitress' uniforms resembled the ones that would have been worn in the nostaglic era of Elvis and poodle skirts. Carlie found a table with three metalic chairs. Roxy and Josh immediately picked up the one-sided menu and started to make their choices.

"This is so cool, Mom!" Roxy exclaimed. "Yeah, really cool." Josh chimed in. "It is, isn't it." Carlie agreed as she watched them gaze around at all the decorations. She took in the glows on their faces and the sparkles in their eyes. She had not seen her children this happy in a long time. All her troubles were forgotten for just this one day. She wished she could freeze today in time and never let it end.

A waitress came over to their table. "Are you folks ready to order?" She asked, interrupting Carlie's thoughts. "Yes. Go ahead kids." Carlie said. Josh ordered a chocolate milkshake with whipped cream and a cherry on top. Roxy ordered an old-fashioned root beer float with vanilla ice cream and whipped cream. Carlie ordered a mocha-vanilla iced coffee and a cheese danish. Their treats came quickly. As they ate, Roxy and Josh kept exclaiming over their new clothes and finds at the mall. They chattered among each other and to Carlie about how this was the greatest day ever.

Carlie was so pleased that she had been able to make her

children smile today. They finished their deserts. Carlie paid and left a small tip on the table. Once inside the car, Carlie made her way back to the highway and home. "Mom, this was the best day ever! Thank You!" Roxy said. "Yeah, Mommy. I had tons of fun." Josh agreed. Carlie smiled. "You are both welcome."

The rest of the trip home was silent as Josh fell asleep and Roxy stared out the window watching the landscapes pass by. *Yes.* Carlie thought. *This was the best day ever, at least since Joe left.* As Carlie merged onto the interstate, her thoughts returned to a time where going to the mall or out to eat, even going to the amusement park, had been an every weekend thing. Once again, Carlie was left with memories of being told what they were going to do and where they were going and what was appropriate for her to wear.

Carlie began to realize that her marriage to Joe had always been about pleasing him and bending her life around what he wanted. Her thoughts turned to Colt. Colt seemed different than what she was used to. For one, Colt talked a lot about God, prayer, and church. Those topics were never discussed with Joe outside of church. Carlie was beginning to think the whole church thing for her family, had been nothing but a facade.

The Welshes had appeared to be the perfect family; good down-to-earth people. Joe had worked a respectable job while maintaining the good-guy-of-the-community facade. Carlie had pretended to be the perfect wife and mother, staying home and taking care of the house and kids like a good little church wife should do. Carlie shook her head and breathed deeply. Maybe the divorce had been for the best. Sure, the affair had hurt her and the kids. Joe leaving them had been very difficult and painful, but now as Carlie reflected back on their life before the affair, she couldn't help but to wonder how much turmoil she had been brewing inside of herself before their seemingly perfect life had fallen apart.

Chapter 12

Colt Storm paced the floor of his hotel room. He could not get Carlie Michaels off of his mind. Last night had been nearly perfect, with the exception of the waitress flirting with him, of course. He could not get Carlie out of his head. Maybe it was the way her eyes sparkled when she laughed. Maybe it was the fact that she had looked out of this world in that dress she had worn or the way her hair flowed down her back. He had been charmed by her humility and the way she had not even hinted at the fact he should buy the antique silver necklace for her. Colt had bought it any way. He figured that Carlie Michaels deserved something just for her. He imagined she sacrificed so much for her kids. She seemed like the kind of person who would just go without in order to make sure her kids had everything they needed. Colt was impressed by the way she didn't make a big deal about the flirting waitress. Sure, she was probably not comfortable with the idea of another woman flirting with him. After all, Colt had been her date. He could not tell if Carlie was falling for him as he was for her. He knew she had to have be having doubts. After all, he was going to have be leaving to go back home to Colorado. His horses would need tended to, although he was positive the ranch hands were doing thier jobs. Colt, however, was starting to get home sick. He needed to ride his mustang. He needed to get his hands on wood and create a new master piece. He dreaded having to leave Carlie. He dreaded not knowing if they would stay in contact. He hated the feeling of just not knowing.

Colt sat down on the foot of the bed. It was 5pm. Church this morning had been good. He missed his home church, but he had enjoyed the service this morning at the church he visited. He wondered if Carlie had taken her kids to church this morning. He guessed she hadn't. It would probably take her some time to go back to church. He couldn't blame her. Colt wondered what Carlie had done with her day. He wondered if he could convince her to join him for one last meal before he had to go back home. Colt extremely enjoyed being with Carlie. But, once again, he knew this matter would have to be placed in the Father's hands. Colt realized that God still had a lot of work to do on Carlie's heart. He wasn't sure about the kids. He had only talked to Josh briefly and had not really met Roxy, except for the one second he had seen her when Roxy opened the door. He could tell Roxy had a lot to work out in her own heart. He had seen the look she had given her mother when the two had walked out the door to go to dinner. He hadn't said anything to Carlie about it. That was something that really need to be be worked out between mother and daughter. Although, Colt could understand how Roxy must be feeling. In the world of a teenage girl, Mom should not be going out with other men. Colt figured that Roxy had hope that her father would magically return and everything would be great and perfect. Colt hoped that Roxy would realize that her father was not going to just magically return. He hoped that both of the kids realized what a wonderful and loving mother they had. Carlie was magical in her own way; the way she dealt with the kids, holding a job down, and having to deal with all that hurt. Colt could not even begin to imagine some of the tricks that Carlie had to pull out of her sleeves sometimes. How many times did she hold back the tears for the sake of her children? How many times did she give up something she needed or wanted so that her kids could have what they needed? Colt shook his head and stood. Yes, he decided, Carlie Michaels was the most wonderful woman he had ever met. Yet, he knew that God would have to bring it all to pass if the two were meant to be.

Colt sat on the edge of the bed for quite a while debating how much longer he could stay here in Ohio. Part of him just wanted to pick up the phone and tell Carlie to have the kids and herself packed and to whisk them off to Colorado with him. The more logical part of him knew that asking Carlie to uproot her life was just foolishness. He had not known her for very long and while she was probably the most amazing woman he had ever met, Colt knew that it would take time for her to fall in love again. These kind of things could not be rushed. Love took time. Trust had to be rebuilt. The children had to understand that their mom was allowed to be happy with someone else.

It all was so frustrating to Colt. The way he felt about this woman was real. Yet, he knew that he could not just jump the gun and haul off and marry Carlie Michaels. It was way too soon to be having thoughts like that. Colt could only imagine how Carlie must be feeling. All of this must be confusing and frustrating to her as well. He wanted to throw something. He wanted to just take Carlie with him.

Last night he had wanted to take her into his arms and just hold her. He had wanted to kiss her. He wanted to make it all OK. for her. He wanted to somehow explain to her kids that it was ok for their mother to be happy again. He wanted it all. However, he knew he could not have it all, not just yet. He would be patient. He would pray and let God work on the Michaels family and do the healing that still needed to be done. Colt himself, needed to pray. He needed God to settle the restless feeling that was occupying the depths of his heart. Colt did just that. He bowed his head and he prayed. He prayed that God would settle his own heart and bring peace to him. He prayed that the Lord would heal Carlie and her children and bring them the peace they needed. He prayed that Carlie would feel God's love for her and that she would no longer be afraid to go back to church; that she would submit herself to the Lord and let him lead her. Finally, he prayed that God's will would be done as far as the relationship between himself and Carlie.

Colt lifted his head and wiped the tears from his eyes. Whoever said that real men don't cry? Well, Colt Storm did cry whenever he felt heavily in God's presence or whenever something was weighing heavily on his heart. He neither regreted crying nor was he ashamed to cry. He stood slowly. Colt decided that he would leave first thing Tuesday morning and head back to Colorado. He had his plane ticket which was an open ticket. He picked up the phone and dialed the number for the airport in Columbus where he had flown in. After confirming the early morning flight, Colt called Jack to inform his buddy that he would be going back to Colorado and to ask if Jack could follow him to the rental car place. He needed to return the car and then have Jack take him to the airport. Fortunately, Jack was available to do so.

"What about your lady friend?" Jack asked Colt. Colt sighed. "I hate to leave her, Jack, but I can't just haul her and those kids to Colorado. These things take time and definitely need tweaking." Jack chuckled. "Colt, ole boy, ya got yerself in quite a bind." Cole couldn't have agreed more. "Well Jack, ole buddy, if it's meant to be, then the good Lord will bring it to pass. I hate not knowing if I will ever talk to Carlie Michaels, let alone see her again, but it's in his hands." Jack agreed and the two hung up the phone with Jack promising to be at the hotel at 5am to get Colt to the airport. Colt sighed. Now, he faced another dilemma. Should he ask Carlie to have dinner with him tomorrow night before he left or should he just call her and tell her that he had to go back to Colorado?

Colt picked up the phone, sighed, and replaced the reciever. If he had dinner with Carlie one more time, it would break her heart and his. He couldn't hold her like he would want to. He couldn't kiss her goodbye like he would want to. Those gestures would bring about too many emotions; emotions that he did not need to stir up in either of them. Yet, if he simply called her and said goodbye over the phone, it would haunt him the rest of his life that he didn't take her to dinner. Either way would leave Carlie confused and full of emotions that Colt wasn't sure she was ready to deal with. Oh why couldn't he have just helped her and left it at that? Because he was attracted to her. He had been attracted to her from the minute he had seen her yelling and hitting her truck. "Ole Blue" she had called the broken down pick-up. He laughed out loud now as he remembered the horrid look on her face when she realized she had been caught. Colt had seen something in Carlie when she had told him about the divorce. He had felt her pain. He had seen something in her children when he first met Josh and later Roxy. Colt felt helpless. He didn't want to hurt Carlie. He didn't want to leave her. But, he definitely could not and did not want to stay in Ohio. His heart and his life were in Colorado. He loved his home, the ranch, his furniture company. "OKOk Colt. Settle down.' He said to himself. "It's not the end of the world. You have her number. You can call her. You can keep in touch." Colt finally talked himself into asking Carlie to have dinner with him before leaving for home. He knew if he didn't, he would regret it. He knew Carlie would hate him for it. He picked up the phone and dialed her number.

Carlie rushed in the door, dropping her packages from the mall on the couch, grabbing for the phone as she did. "Hello?" "Carlie, it's Colt, I was, uhhh...I was uhh.. well I was wondering if you would like to have dinner with me again tomorrow night?" He paused. "That is, if you are not working." Carlie swallowed hard, She had not told him she had lost her job, so of course having dinner with Colt did not require making any adjustments in her schedule. "Ummm, sure tomorrow evening would be great." She finally answered. Colt sighed a sigh of relief. He did not tell her over the phone that he was going to be leaving to go back to Colorado. He would save that for dinner.

Carlie was estatic at the prospect of seeing Colt Storm again. Although, something inside her was warning her to not get carried away. Carlie could not help but to get excited over having dinner with Colt. She realized he would be going back to Colorado soon. She was smart enough to understand that she should not be falling for someone who was destined to leave her to go back to his hometown. Yet, the feelings that had been stirred deep down inside her over the last week trumped the doubts of not being able to have some kind of relationship with Colt Storm. She couldn't explain it.

Carlie knew it was foolish to be thinking this way. For pete's sake, she was acting like a high school girl all over again. She had made the mistake of letting her girlish crushes lead to heartache once. She could not afford to make that same mistake again. True, there seemed to be substance to Colt. But, what did she really know about the man? So he was from Colorado, went to church and prayed. Well, so had Joe for that matter, and look what he had done.

Colt owned a ranch and a furniture store. That was all just geography. He was generous with his money, but Carlie Michaels was not a gold digger. Carlie had to really get to know a man before she jumped into a relationship with him. She thought she had known Joe, but nothing she had known about her ex-husband was real. Their whole marriage had been based on their high school crushes on each other. She had played the good little wife and he had played the devoted husband and church member to a T.

Their lives and marriage had been fake from the start. So no wonder Joe went off to be with someone else. No wonder it had all come crashing down. Carlie was not going to jump into a relationship with any man based soley on the fact she thought he was cute. No sir. Never again. If she was going to give her heart to someone, she was going to have to know the person inside out.

She wanted to get to know Colt like that, but knew it was impossible to do that long distance.Carlie sat at the kitchen table, twirling her cup of tea as these thoughts went through her mind. She had agreed to have dinner with Colt tomorrow night, but something inside her told her that this would be the last dinner with him for a very long time, if not forever. She was so mad at herself for engaging in lunch and dinner dates with someone she knew there was no possible way she could engage in a relationship with. Why hadn't she just thanked him for his help and left it at that?

She tried, Carlie reminded herself. Colt Storm was the one who just had to go and give her a new car and a $5,000 check. *He* was the one who had not left well enough alone. Carlie sighed. She would have this last dinner with Colt Storm. She knew he was going to be leaving for Colorado soon. His work was done here. Whatever he had been doing here Ohio in the first place she didn't know. Carlie hadn't asked him either, which was curious because she was quite interested in what he was doing in Ohio, other than helping her. It didn't matter, she concluded. He had helped her more than she could have asked and she was extremely grateful for Colt's generosity. Someday she would pay him back. After all, Carlie Michaels never took anything for free. There was always repayment to be made. Nothing in life was just handed to anyone. Nothing was ever really free. One day, somehow, she would pay Colt Storm back for everything he had done for her.

"Mom." Roxy's voice jolted Carlie out of her deep thoughts. "Sorry honey, I was lost in thought." Roxy smiled. "Yeah, I noticed." It was Carlie's turn to smile. She studied her daughter momentarily, taking in Roxy's long, blond hair and deep blue eyes. "Is that the new skirt and sweater you got at the mall?" Carlie asked, noticing how beautiful her daughter looked. "Yeah. What do you think?" Carlie stood as Roxy twirled. "You look gorgeous, honey. I love it." Roxy beamed. "I'm gonna go change into my jams. I just wanted to show you." Carlie lovingly placed her hand on Roxy's cheek. "You are so beautiful and that outfit just looks amazing on you." Roxy grinned as she turned to go upstairs to put on her "jams".

Carlie smiled at the way Roxy had her own terms for things

like clothing. She wasn't sure when Roxy had become so grown up. Even though the girl was only 13, she seemed more like 18. Carlie had to reel Roxy in at times and remind her that she is still just a girl and not a full grown woman. Josh bounded into the kitchen next, showing off his new *John Cena* pajamas. "I love them, Mommy! They are awesome!" Carlie laughed as she tussled his hair.

Roxy entered the kitchen looking all cozy and ready for bed. Carlie glanced at the kitchen clock. It read 8pm. "OK you two. Movie and snack time, then off to bed you go." The two practically ran each other over as they sprang into the living room. Carlie checked her chart to see who's turn it was to pick out a movie. Charts were becoming Carlie's friend. They kept the kids from arguing over who's turn it was to do what. Carlie had movie charts and chore charts. They had become lifesavers. Carlie figured every mom should have charts. It was Roxy's turn to pick the movie. Fortunately for Josh, Roxy still liked some of the animated cartoon movies and adventure movies. Carlie placed a bag of popcorn into the microwave.

As she waited for it to finish popping, she checked to see what the movie of the night was. *Spy Kids* was the choice of the night, which Carlie thought was a great compromise. Roxy had not been selfish in choosing the movie. She had picked something that she and Josh both would like.

Carlie dumped the piping hot popcorn into a large bowl and carried it into the living. She dug a two liter of Pepsi out of the fridge and poured the cold beverage into three glasses. After she carried the glasses into the living room and distributed them, she settled down on the couch to join her kids in the adventure of *Spy Kids*.

The movie ended. Josh yawned and stretched. Roxy also stretched. "OK you two, up to bed you go." Carlie smiled as the two of them bounded arm in arm up the steps. Roxy paused on the steps. "Thanks again for today, Mom. It was awesome." Carlie smiled at her daughter as she gathered up the glasses and popcorn bowl and carried them into the kitchen. She dumped the popcorn seeds into the trash before placing the dishes in the sink. She ran a shallow sinkful of hot, soapy water and washed the bowl and the glasses.

Once the dishes were dried and put away, she headed up the stairs to tuck her kids in and kiss them good night.Carlie stopped in Josh's room first. He was already under his blanket and his eyes were half shut. She tucked the blanket in a little more snug around him and kissed his forhead. "Good night Josh, I love you." "Good night Mommy, love you too." Carlie smiled as she exited his room, leaving the door slightly ajar so the hall light could shine into his room. Next, she made her way up the hall to Roxy's room. She could hear music playing softly.

She opened the door to find Roxy sitting cross -legged in the middle of her bed reading a book. "Hey Rox, don't stay up too late,OK" "I won't Mom." Roxy hugged her daughter and kissed her on the cheek. "Good night, Roxy, I love you." Roxy looked up. "Night, Mom. Love you too." Carlie exited Roxy's room and left her daughter's door slightly open as well so that she could hear if Roxy tried to sneak out or tried to stay up later than she was supposed to. Carlie made her way down the hall, past the bathroom, and to her bedroom at the end. She got into her silk pajamas, grabbed a book off the shelf, and snuggled under her grandmother's quilt to read a while before finally closing her eyes. She couldn't concentrate on the *Nora Roberts* book, however, as he mind was on Colt and their dinner plans for tomorrow evening.

Chapter 13

Monday evening came and went way too fast for either Carlie or Colt's liking. Colt informed Carlie that he would be leaving first thing the next morning. Carlie had given him a brave smile, holding back the tears that she refused to let fall. As Colt packed his small suitcase, he couldn't help but to feel a lump form in his throat. He had only known Carlie Michaels for a week, but somehow that one week felt like he had known her for years. He hated to have to leave her. He hated not knowing if he would ever see her or talk to her again. Yet he knew that his life in Colorado was waiting for him. He had business to catch up on. and he had horses to tend to. He had furniture pieces to create, orders to catch up on, and inventory to do at the the store. He had ranch hands to pay as well as the few employees at *Colt's Unique Furniture* store. Colt zipped shut the suitcase and took one last look around the room to ensure he had not forgotten anything. Satisfied that he had everything he'd brought with him plus a few items he had picked up, he stood by the window momentarily and stared out at the road. Colt sighed. He silently prayed that Carlie would stay in touch with him. Colt took a deep breath and grabbed his suitcase. The knock at the door told him that Jack had arrived. Colt opened the door to greet his long time friend. "Ready?" Jack asked him. Colt nodded. "As ready as I'll ever be." Jack noticed the raspiness in Colt's voice. He knew his buddy was torn between having to go back home and staying here with Carlie. "She will be fine, Colt. If it's meant to be, then God will bring it all together for both of you." Colt nodded again. "I know, Jack. I don't know why I am having all these feelings for her. I've only known the woman for a week, yet I feel like I have known her forever." He stopped there. Jack placed a hand on Colt's shoulder. "You will be fine too, ole buddy. Call her once in a while. Let her know you are thinking of her. Leave this in God's hands. He will make a way." Colt forced a smile. Jack was right. Colt had a life to get back to. Carlie Michaels would remain in his heart, but for now, he had to let her go. "You are right, Jack. Let's go." The elevator door opened and the two men stepped inside. As strong as Colt was trying to be, he wasn't sure that his heart would understand why he was leaving Carlie Michaels behind.

***

Carlie paced the floor of the kitchen. She had woken up at 4am and could not get back to sleep. Now, dressed in her silk pajamas, a cotton bath robe, and slippers, she paced. Colt told her he was leaving for Colorado this morning. He had explained to her that he had to go back to his life. Colt had told her that he had could take some time later on to come back to visit Jack and his family. Colt had also told Carlie that while his feelings were real for her, he could not rush a relationship with her. Carlie understood that Colt's life was not here in Ohio. She understood that even though it had only been a week, he had real feelings for her. Carlie fought back the tears. She had started to fall for Colt Storm. Everything within her wanted to pack up and go with him. But, Colt was right. They would be foolish to just rush into a relationship. They needed time to get to know each other. How in the world were they supposed to get know each other when they lived hundreds of miles apart? Carlie was frustrated. She was dealing with feelings she wasn't ready to deal with. She wanted to scream. She wanted to throw something. She wanted to call Colt and beg him to take her and the kids with him. She wanted to hate him for starting whatever this was with her. She wanted to fall in love with him for all he had done for her and for letting her be herself. She wanted to hate him for leaving and not taking her with him. She wanted to love him for being who he was. She hated and loved him all at the same time. Carlie finally collapsed into a chair. She buried her head in her arms and cried. She realized she couldn't have it all. She had to let Colt go home, back to his life in Colorado. It wasn't like she had a choice. He hadn't asked her to go with him. He hadn't asked her to be his wife. Good grief! She was acting foolish. She needed to get it together. Carlie lifted her head and folded her arms in front of her on the table. For the first time in a long time, Carlie Michaels prayed. She looked upwards. "God, it's me. I know I haven't talked to you in a long time. I know I have ignored you and church and everything that I should be doing spiritually. I have a confession. I hated Joe for what he did to me and to our children. I hated him. I don't understand why you let it happen or maybe you didn't. I know you gave us free will and Joe chose to do what he did. God, it's been a year. I need to move on. I need to get on with my life. So do my kids. I know you brought Colt Storm into my life for a reason. So, God, if we are meant to be, then make it work. Make it work between me and him. Make it work with my kids. Just please don't let me get hurt again. Amen." Carlie lowered her head back down. She felt peace. Maybe this wasn't the end. Maybe it was just the beginning. Maybe she had spent too much time blaming Joe and looking back. Maybe it was time to look forward; time to make some changes. It was time to move on. Carlie wasn't sure what moving forward entailed. She wasn't sure where to begin, but she knew she couldn't stay in the past. After all, Colt promised to keep in touch with her.Carlie would wait for God to put all the pieces together. After all, moving on was her only option. And just maybe, that would include Colt Storm. Just maybe.....

***

He parked across the street. He noticed her kitchen light was on. It was 5am. She never got up this early. He wondered how the kids were doing. He noticed that the old blue pick up truck had been replaced by a new SUV. He wondered where she had gotten the money for a new car. New man maybe? It had been a year. He hadn't been by the house since he left. Joe Welsh sighed as leaned his head back against the his car seat. A Toby Keith song played in his mind as he sat and studied the house. *Who's That Man Runnin My Life?* Joe didn't know if Carlie was seeing someone or not. He really didn't care. He had made his decision a year ago to leave his family for Kat. Now he and Kat were going to get married and travel the world. He could do that with her. He wouldn't be tied down with kids and church with Kat. They could do whatever they wanted to do. He would be able to live the life he had imagined with Carlie, with Kat. Joe didn't know why he drove by the house so early. He was trying to get up the nerve to let her know that he was signing off his rights to the kids. He loved them, sure, but he didn't want the responisbility of being a father any longer. He agreed to pay child support. At least he would do that much for them, but he did not want to see the kids or Carlie. He did not want to deal with every other weekend visits. That would tie him down too much. No. Joe wanted to live free of any responsibilities that came with being a father. The kids would understand in time. Carlie would explain it to them. Maybe when Roxanne and Josh were older, he would come back. Maybe not. For now however, he would live a life of adventure with Kat. Joe sighed. He started the engine and slowly drove away. Maybe later he would knock on her door and hand her the papers he had signed to give up his rights. Maybe he would just mail it to her. As he drove down the quiet street, Joe wondered what Carlie's reaction would be once she got the news. He knew he would have to deliver the papers soon one way or the other as he and Kat were leaving for Paris next week to get married. He also had a contract he was going to sign in London, England on remodeling an old historic building in the center of England's majestic city. Joe pulled into a drive-way and turned around. He parked in front of Carlie's house. Carlie's house. Not the Welsh's house. Joe and Carlie Welsh no longer existed. Now it was Carlie Michael's house. She had gone back to her maiden name. Joe sighed deeply. Oh well. It no longer mattered. Soon he would be married to Kat. He opened his car door and crept up the steps to the porch. He carefully slipped the envelope with the signed papers into her mail box. He stood momentarily as the memory of carrying Carlie over the threshold crossed his mind. He shook his head and pushed that memory away. He crept back down the steps and left. He would never look back. He wished the best for Carlie. He hoped that Roxanne and Josh would grow up to be fine citizens. Joe Welsh drove away and never looked back.

***

Carlie brewed a pot of coffee. She decided after dropping the kids off at school, she would buy a couple of newspapers and see what jobs were available. She did not have much training and was not sure what type of job she would be qualified to work. The idea of going back to school still played in the back of her mind. She always loved reading. She liked to write and create. She loved to cook as well. Maybe she could go to an arts college and take literature and culinary classes. Maybe she could become a great writer or famous chef. A smile played at the corner of her lips. At her age? Was she delirious? There was no way she could start a whole new career at her age. She bit her lower lip as if in deep thought. Then again, maybe she should. Maybe she should follow her dreams. Maybe now was the time to find out. After all, she did not have much else to work with and she needed to do something with her life other than hop from one retail store to the next. Carlie wanted to use her brain and pursue her dreams. She loathed the idea of being stuck in a mundane job, such as running a cash register, for the rest of her life. She wanted to create. She wanted to travel. And she wanted someone who would support those dreams. Joe sure hadn't. Oh, sure when they had first gotten married, Joe had wanted to travel the world with Carlie. But then she became pregnant with Roxy and everything changed. Joe had become more controlling and Carlie became subserviant and almost lifeless. Carlie shook her head. No! She was not going to continue to blame herself! It was time to move on. It was time to put the past where it belonged; in the past. It was time to follow her dreams and it was definitely time to make a fresh start for her and her children.

The struggle needed to come to an end. She needed to find peace. She needed to go back to church. Carlie just needed to move forward.

Chapter 14

Colt sighed a sigh of relief as he pulled into the the little town snuggled (nestled) between the Mountains where he called home. There was not much to this one-horse town, but it suited him just fine. There was just enough to keep him happy. A General Store, a diner, a few craft and home decor shops scattered here and there, and a hunting shop where one could find everything he needed to fish or hunt. Colt pulled into the diner. He was starving since he hadn't stopped too often during the long trip from Ohio back to Colorado. Colt had stopped briefly along the highway just long enough to get gas, a cup of coffee, and grab a sandwich which he was sure was not made fresh and had been wrapped in cellophane. It hadn't tasted very good either and he had thrown half of it out the window. Now, as he strode into the little diner, his stomach reminded him of just how hungry he was as the aroma of fried potatoes lingered in the air. Tracy, the diner's beloved owner, was busy on the grill, frying up whatever the meat of the day was. In this case it appeared that burgers and chopped steaks were the meats of choice. Colt took a seat at the counter. Tracy noticed him out of the corner of her eye. "Hey look who's back!" Colt grinned. "Good to be home." He said. "What's good in here today?" He looked over the menu. "Burgers and chopped steak seem to be the popular choice today with fried taters and fresh green beans." Colt thought momentarily. "In that case I will have a chopped steak with mushrooms and onions, a side of fried taters with onions and peppers, and a spoonful of those fresh beans. Oh, and a cup of coffee with a glass of ice water. " Tracy smiled as she took the menu from him. "You got it." Colt glanced around the diner as he waited for his food. The usual dinner crowd was there. Merchants who had just closed up their businesess for the day were bustling in and filling up the round tables. The sherrif and his deputy were seated at a corner table with their typical cups of coffee and cheeseburgers with everything on them. A few out-of-towners were busy chattering about how beautiful the moutains were. Colt smiled. It was good to be home.

His food came and he ate it greedily as if he was never

going to eat again. He sipped his coffe and left a generous tip on the counter. He lifted his hat and placed it back on his head as he exited the diner and climbed into his truck. He had missed his Chevy dual-cab work truck. Although the one he had rented in Ohio, the one he had picked Carlie Michaels up in, was nice, he'd missed his truck. He sighed another deep sigh as drove down the long gravel road to his ranch house. As he drove by the pastures, he took in the horses grazing and running about the pastures. He took in the trees and how beautiful the leaves were beginning to look as the colors changed from green to oranges and reds. He took in the mountains. Yes. It was good to be home, yet his heart hungered to see and talk to Carlie. Now what was he going to do about her? About them? About whatever this thing was that had started between them? Could he keep the relationship going? He wondered how Carlie was doing. He wondered if she felt the same loneliness that was suddenly consuming himand the restlessness that once again was beginning to settle in his heart. Colt parked the truck in front of his large log cabin home. His faithful black lab, Sly, greeted him, his tail thumping at the sight of his beloved owner returning. Colt bent down and petted the dog. "Miss me, boy?" As if to answer, Sly licked Colt's face. Colt unlocked the door, noticing that there was food and fresh water in Sly's bowl. The ranch hands had remembered to feed and water the pet. Colt stepped into the sunken living room and placed his suticase down by the sofa. He was home. He sunk down onto the couch and slipped off his boots. He needed to rest after the long drive. He would check in on the ranch hands and the horses in a couple of hours, after a good long nap.

Colt bolted upright at the sound of Sly barking. He rubbed his eyes, noticed the time on the clock and figured he had slept at least three hours, much longer than he intended to. It was dusk. Putting on his boots, Colt stood and stretched out his back. He made his way to the front door to see Rich, one of the ranch hands standing on the porch. Rich's hands were rugged and dirty. Colt knew his man had been working hard. Rich was holding his hat in between his hands."I'm sorry to bother you, sir, but we have a horse down and we need your help." Colt grabbed his hat and went out the door." Which one?" He inquired of his ranch hand. "Red mare." Rich replied. "She went out to have her colt but we can't get her back up." He paused there. "The colt's fine, but his mama ain't lookin so good."

Colt sighed. The red mare was one of his best horses. He did not want to lose her. "Well I'll saddle up Lightening and ride out with ya and see what we can do." Rich nodded as he headed to the barn, Colt by his side. Colt and Rich rode out to the meadow where they found the red mare lying still. Colt jumped off his horse and grabbed the saddle bag where he kept rope and medical supplies. He was no vet, but he knew enough to be able to keep his horses alive and well when they did get sick.

Colt checked the mare and gently placed a rope around her neck. He pulled out a pump and filled it half way with water that he had brought along in a canteen and caster oil. He attached the end of a short hose to the end of the pump, placing the other end in the horses mouth. He checked her teeth before pumping. "Looks like she ate some bad hay." Colt said to Rich. "Hold this end of the hose in her mouth while I pump. We have to get her to move and get her up." Rich did what Colt instructed.

Colt pumped the fluid into the horse. She lifted her head once and then laid back down. "Come on girl. You need to get up and moving. Your baby here needs you." Colt said to Red as he watched her colt nose around his mother's neck. Colt pumped and pumped and pumped until finally Red lifted her head. He instructed Rich to remove the hose.

"We have to make her stand up." Colt said. Rich pushed while Colt took the rope around the horse's neck and pulled. Finally, Red kicked her hind legs and was on her feet. Rich jumped out of the way in order to keep from being crushed. "Good girl!" Colt stroked Red's mane. He handed the harness to Rich. "Get her walking around while I check on the colt. She had a rough delivery, but she ate some rotten hay. That's what made her sick and go down." Rich nodded as he urged the mare to walked forward.

Colt caught the baby horse and checked him out thorougly. "You seem to be healthy, young fella. Your mama did good." Colt laughed as the baby wobbled trying to run to his mother to nurse. Rich brought Red back over. They watched the colt nurse before leading mama and baby back to the barn. Once the horses were in their stalls, Colt said, "Keep them in for a few days. I want to make sure Red's OKok before I let her back out into the pasture." Rich nodded. Colt left the barn and strode back toward the house to clean up.

As he mounted his horse, Lightening, and headed back to the barn, he took in the sun beginning to set over the mountains. The orange sky mixed with just a little blue and white clouds were beautiful against the white tips of the mountains. Colt couldn't help but to think how Carlie would love to see this view. Carlie. Colt could not help but to think about her and wondered if he should call her after he had his supper. Her face flashed across his mind. Sparkling eyes. Chestnut- colored hair. A smile that could light up the darkest night. Colt sighed. He already missed her. As he climbed off his horse and put Lightening back in his stall, Colt pondered as to whether or not it would be too soon to call Carlie. After all, it had been just this morning he left Ohio and arrived back here. Maybe he should wait a couple of more days. He had been gone about a month and needed to settle back in and check things around the ranch and his furniture store. Yes. Colt decided. It would be best to give it a couple of days before calling Carlie Michaels. Tonight he would enjoy a good ole fashioned steak and potatoes meal. Tomorrow he would check the ranch and check on Red and the new colt. Thursday he would go to the furniture store and check to see what orders that needed to be filled and work on catching up on business. Maybe Friday he would call and check on Carlie and the kids.

She was standing in the meadow, wearing jeans, cowboy boots, a flannel shirt, and a tan cowgirl hat. She had a rope in her hand, training one of the young colts. He stood at a distance watching her. Her chestnut hair glowed in the early rays of the sunrise. He heard her laugh as she instructed the colt to gallop. She brought the young horse to a stop. Walking over to the animal, she brushed her leather gloved hand along the side of the horse's neck. She was whispering something to the horse that Colt could not hear. The young animal let out a gentle neigh and she led him towards the fence leading out of the meadow. She smiled at him. She tied the rope to the fence and strode over to him. She slid her arms around his waist and kissed him on his lips. Her silver wedding ring gleamed against the sun light.

Colt sat up and gasped. He must have dozed off again. He checked the clock above the T.V. It read 9:00. Colt had dreamed of Carlie. Here. Married to him. He wasn't sure what that meant; what the dream meant. He slowly stood and stretched. He gave Sly a pat on the head. His dog was looking at him like he had seen a ghost. "What Sly? Haven't you ever had a dream before?" Colt smiled. Of course he didn't figure that dogs had dreams and if they did, they more than likely dreamed of chasing squirrels or rabbits or some other small game. "I am gonna go hit the shower, Sly. Then check my emails and hit the hay. Been a long day ole boy." Sly wagged his tail in approval and laid down on his rug in front of the fire place. Colt smiled and headed to the bathroom for a well needed shower. His mind was on Carlie Michaels and the dream he had just had about her. He wasn't much for trying to interpret dreams, but this one had gotten to his core. It had seemed so real. Once again, as he stepped out and dressed, Colt said a silent prayer over Carlie and her kids, adding in that if God wanted him to be with Carlie Michaels, then there would be a path made for them to be together.

Chapter 15

Carlie woke up Wednesday morning feeling exausted. She had not slept well last night. Tuesday had been emotional for her with Colt going back to Colorado and she couldn't understand why. They had made absolutely zero committments to each other. Carlie had laid out all the cards on the table for him and he had done the same. They had both come to the understanding that they would just be friends. Then why was she so restless? Why was there this panicky feeling in the depths of her being that she might never see him again? Why was she feeling so sad? Carlie could not understand for the life of her why she felt this way. In some ways it was the same feeling she felt when Joe had declared his lust for another woman; yes *lust, not love.* At least that was the way Carlie had seen it. Yet in another way, this feeling was different. She *wanted* to see Colt Storm again. She wanted to be able to have dinner with him. However, she wasn't sure how anything could work out between her and Colt with the distance in between them. She certainly was in no shape to just uproot her kids and move to Colorado. Carlie set the coffe pot to brew before waking up her kids for school. She had thought about looking for jobs today, but she needed a day off from looking. Besides, for whatever reason, she just wasn't in the mood to go out and do any job hunting today. She shook her head and tried to clear the grogginess she felt consuming her as she climbed up the stairs first to Roxy's room to wake her up and then to Josh's to check on him. She yielded to a yawn as she knocked on her daughter's door. There was no answer. She knocked again."Rox, it's time to get up for school." Still nothing. "Roxy?" Carlie opened the door. She took in the still movement of the lump beneath Roxy's balnket. "You really must have been chilly last night, kiddo. You never sleep completely under your blanket like that." Just as she said it, Carlie felt a cold breeze come through the room. She turned and noticed that the bedroom window was wide open. Carlie felt panic in her heart. She walked over to the bed and pulled back the blanket only to reveal that the unmoving lump was nothing but Roxy's pillows. She ran to Josh's room. He was standing in the hallway. "Mommy?" Carlie forced a smile. "Hi baby." She hugged him. "Hey have you seen your sister?" Josh shook his head. "Nope." Carlie nodded. She checked the bathroom, with Josh in tow. No Roxy. She raced back down stairs and checked the living room, kitchen and the spare room. No Roxy. Carlie gently took Josh by the shoulders. "Did Roxy mention anything to you about spending the night at a friend's house?" Josh once again shook his head. "Nope." Carlie nodded. She was in sheer panic mode now. *Think, Carles, think! The open window. Had Roxy run away from home or just snuck out to meet one of her friends?* She turned back to Josh. "Honey, I need you to go get dressed. OKOk?" Josh nodded and obeyed. Carlie followed him back up the stairs. She calmly went to her room and shut the door. She pulled out her jeans and a flannel shirt. After getting dressed, she pulled on her favorite fall boots. She threw her hair up into a pony tail and then went back down to the hall to Roxy's room. She started searching her daughter's closet and drawers. She opened Roxy's notebooks and flipped over her mattress, searching for any signs of where Roxy may have snuck out to. Only the small teal duffle bag that Carlie had given Roxy for her birthday was gone. Carlie found a notebook where Roxy had scribbled down some phone numbers. Carlie flew out of her daughter's room and down the stairs. She grabbed the phone from off her desk and dialed the number for the police station. After giving them the report of what she had discovered and that her daughter was missing, she called for Josh to come down. After getting him settled at the table with a bowl of cereal and some juice, Carlie poured herself a cup of coffee. She debated on whether or not she should start calling the numbers she found. She picked up the phone and dialed the school who politely informed her that Roxy had not shown up for school. The door bell rang. "Stay right there, Josh." Carlie instructed her son as she raced to answer the door.

Two officers from the Wilmington Police Department stood on the welcome mat in front of the front door. "Officers, please come in." Carlie greeted them. " Miss Michaels, I am Officer Dunloe and this is Officer Kenton. We understand your daughter was missing from her room this morning. " Carlie nodded, fighting the panic that was rising up in her. "Yes. I went to get to her up for school and her window was wide open. She wasn't in her bed or anywhere in the house. A small duffle bag I had given her for her birthday was gone, but nothing else. I asked my son if his sister had said anything to him about going to a friend's house or anything. She hadn't. I don't know where she could be. I searched her room and found a notebook with some phone numbers in it. Nothing in her room was disturbed or out of place. I have been kind of hard on her lately because she had been skipping school and had come home drunk one day after skipping school and going to the mall. "Carlie realized she was rambling. She was trying to feed the officers important information, but knew she sounded desparate. What mother wouldn't be in her situation right now?

Josh appeared in the living room. "Mommy, did they find Roxy?" He asked, pointing to the officers. "That is why they are here." Carlie told him. "Go get your book bag and your jacket. Your bus will be here soon." Josh turned toward the stairs, but Officer Dunloe stopped him. "Josh, what is your sister's name?" He asked. "Roxanne, but Mommy and I call her Roxy." Officer Dunloe nodded. "Did Roxy say anything to you last night about going out or going to a friend's house or anything?" Josh shook his head. "No. Mommy asked me that this morning, but Roxy didn't tell me anything. Is she going to be okOK? Are you going to find her?"Josh inquired. Officer Dunloe gave Josh his best smile. "That's why we are here. You can go on and get your stuff. I assume you are going to school." Josh nodded. "Yep. Mommy says I have to go every day 'cause education is important." Officer Dunloe smile. "Your Mom is right." With that, Josh raced up the stairs, grabbed his book bag and jacket and came back down just in time for his bus to pull up. Carlie gave him a hug and kissed his cheek before sending Josh out the door.

Carlie watched the bus drive away before turning her attention back to the officers. "I called the school and they said that Roxy had not shown up this morning." Carlie informed the officers. She bit back the tears that threatened to fall. "Miss Michaels, do you have the notebook with the numbers?" Carlie nodded. "It's in the kitchen. I'll get it." She turned to go to the kitchen where she retrieved the notebook off the counter. She held it a moment, sliding her right hand over the drawings of horses on the cover. Roxy was talented when it came to art. A tear slid down

Carlie's cheek. She grabbed a paper towel and quickly wiped her eyes. After regaining her composure, Carlie took the notebook into the living room and handed it to Officer Dunloe. He thumbed through it before handing it to his partner. "We would like to stay here and make the calls. We also would like to be here in case your daughter shows back up." Carlie nodded. "I can make you some coffee." "Thank You. That would be appreciated." It was Officer Kenton who spoke this time. Carlie returned to the kitchen. She took her time making the coffee, methodically rinsing out the pot and refilling the coffee maker with fresh water and coffee grinds.

Carlie took the hot mugs of coffee into the officers who were both on their phones. Carlie was sure they were making calls to the numbers in Roxy's notebook. Carlie paced the floor. She could not imagine what in the world would make Roxy run. Sure, Carlie had told her daughter that Roxy could not just do whatever she wanted when she wanted and that she could not wear certain types of clothing. But seriously, since when did that make daughters run away from home? Carlie sighed. Mercifully, Josh could stay at school and keep his mind off his missing sister for a few hours. Although, Carlie knew her son better than that. She knew Josh would worry anyway. Carlie knew it would be hard for Josh to concentrate on class. She knew he would worry and she also considered the fact that he would expect his sister to be home when he got off the bus this afternoon. Carlie could not make Roxy just reappear and she did not know just how she would be able to explain this to Josh. She wanted to cry and scream at the same time. She walked over to her desk to see if she could hear anything the officers were saying. Then she saw it. The opened envelope was there on the desk with a letter on top of it. It was in Joe's handwriting. Carlie's heart sank as she picked it up. She read the contents over and over as she sank down onto the couch:

Carlie, I am signing over my rights to the kids. I am moving on with my life. I will send you child support in the amount of $600 each month. However, I no longer want to or need to be a part of this family. You and the kids need to move on without me. I am leaving tomorrow with Kat to go to Paris where we will be getting married. I am sure you and the kids will be just fine without me.

Enclosed are the court documents giving you sole custody and all rights to the children. Please understand.

Sincerely, Joe

Carlie couldn't breathe. She couldn't think. She just sat there, frozen, letter in her hand. She was completely oblivious to the officers talking to her. "Miss Michaels, are you okok?" Carlie looked up at Officer Dunloe. "The letter." She managed to get out. "Roxy must have seen the letter. She ran to find him." Officer Dunloe gave her a minute before he spoke. "Who, Miss Michaels?" Carlie looked up at him, tears in her eyes. "Her father, Joe Welsh." She handed him the letter. Officer Dunloe read the document and nodded. Carlie let the tears fall as she wrote down Joe's address. Roxy had run off to confront her father. Joe had written them off as if they were just pieces of merchandise he no longer wanted. Carlie could understand if he didn't want anything to do with her. She felt the same about him. But his own kids! How could he just write off his own children! Anger began to replace the hurt. Now she was furious. Oh! She could just kill him! Carlie stood, hands clenched at her side. She had to pull herself together. She had to focus on Roxy and getting her back home safely.

The doorbell rang. Carlie started towards the door, but Officer Dunloe stopped her. With one hand on the holster on his hip, he slowly opened the door as Officer Kent moved into a cover-his- partner position. Carlie gasped as the door fully opened. Joe. Roxy. Joe was standing with Roxy. Roxy slowly made her way in the house. Joe barely looked at Carlie. Carlie was doing all she could to not run at him and knock him down and punch him over and over. Instead, she engulfed her daughter in her arms. Joe lowered his eyes as he spoke. "I explained everything to her. I have to go now. Goodbye." Carlie let go of Roxy for a moment as she approached the door. She walked up to Joe, slapping him hard, not caring that there were two officers in her house. She didn't care that they were watching her. She was full of fury. "How *dare* you!" Carlie screamed. "How dare you just write our children off like they are pieces of merchandise you simply don't want anymore! You are not a man'"" Carlie screamed as the tears slide down her face. Joe looked at Carly as he touched his face with the palm of his hand. He turned and walked back to his car, leaving mother and daughter to once again watch him walk away. Carlie turned and looked at Roxy."I am so sorry, honey. I did not see the letter and I am so sorry your father is doing this, *again.*" Roxy looked up at her mother." I'm sorry, Mom. I saw that letter Dad...I mean *Joe* wrote and I freaked out. I just wanted answers. I'm really sorry."

Carlie took in all the anguish on her daugher's face. She wrapped her arms around Roxy and held her tight. Officer Dunloe and Officer Kent made thier way over to the couch. Carlie let go of Roxy as the officers approached. "Young lady, do you understand the dangers of what you did today?" Officer Dunloe questioned Roxy. Roxy nodded. "Yes Sir." Carlie rubbed her daughter's arm. "Next time you get upset with either one of your parents you need to talk to your mother. I am sorry your father did this to you and your little brother, but running away is not the answer. If your mother has to call us out here again, the consequences will be a little harsher." Roxy nodded. "I understand." She said weakly. She really wanted to curl up and cry. Roxy wanted to hit something. She was glad that her mom smacked *Joe.* She refused to call him her dad any longer. He was not a father to her now.

Carlie stood and walked the officers to the door. "Thank you officers." Carlie thanked them and closed the door behind the officers. She turned back towards Roxy who looked weary and about ready to cry. Carlie's heart was breaking for her daughter and she did not feel like now was the time to deal with the running away issue. Now was the time to deal with the fact that Joe had written off his kids as if they were not important or just pieces of trash to be discarded. The officers had said nothing about her smacking the scumbag.

Carlie wanted to scream, but she had to stay calm for Roxy's sake. She was thankful that Josh had not been here to see his father....er....*sperm donor...* walk away. Joe was no father. Carlie could not believe what was happening...*AGAIN.* Joe had managed to hurt them again. The last year spent trying to repair the hurt and confusion and pain had just been flushed down the drain. In just a few seconds he had managed to bring back all the agony and confusion. Carlie felt the tears slipping down her cheeks. Her mind went to Colt. She wanted to call him. She wanted him here to hold her and tell her it was all going to be ok. But he wasn't here. He was in Colorado, where he belonged. Carlie was on her own to deal with all this once more and she hated Joe for it. She hated Colt for not being here when she needed someone. She was angry at God for it. She wiped the tears away and turned back towards Roxy who was now softly crying. Carlie went over to her. She sat down next to Roxy and gently wiped a strand of hair away from her face. "Roxy, I am so sorry your dad did this to us again. Why don't I make you some hot chocolate and you can just hang out on the couch and watch T.V. for the rest of the afternoon." Roxy nodded as she pulled the quilt covering the back of the couch around her. Carlie made her way into the kitchen, returning shortly with the promised hot chocolate. Roxy took the mug and gave her mom a faint smile. Carlie returned the smile and headed back to the kitchen where Roxy couldn't see her mother cry.

Carlie browsed the freezer to set something out for supper. Screw it. She would order a couple of pizzas tonight. Screw Joe. Screw Colt. Screw Mr. Marley. Screw life itself. Why was this all happening to her? Just when she felt like she was going to be happy again. And why was she blaming Colt? He had nothing to do with this. So what if he had waltzed into her life, cared about her, and then left her to go back to Colorado. It wasn't his fault. It wasn't like she had known him all that long anyway. Sure she cared about him, but what would it lead to? Heartache? Carlie was not quite sure what would happen between her and Colt Storm, but it really wasn't fair to blame him for any of this. It certainly was not his fault that she had married a controlling scumbag. She struggled with wanting to never talk to Colt again. What would their relationship lead to any way?

Every once in a blue moon he would come back to Ohio to visit her? If she was lucky she might get a phone call once or twice a month. So really, what was the point of trying to maintain any kind of anything with Colt Storm? It would lead to heartache and right now she couldn't take any more heartbreak, hurt, or confusion in her life. Joe had manged to bring back all that into their lives once more. Was it going to take Carlie and the kids another year to heal from this? Carlie wanted desparately to throw a plate or something against a wall. She wanted to scream. She wanted to hunt Joe down and do something so terrible to him so that he would never be able to enjoy his life. He was the one who had it easy. It was like he had made a check list. Have an affair: check. Divorce wife: check. Cause confusion and hurt: check. Destroy his kids' lives: check. Write his kids off and just walk away: check. So what if he sent her child support every month?! No amount of money could ever heal the damage he caused today. Not ever.

Carlie had once thought that Joe was her ace in the hole in life. She would have it made with him. They were going to travel the world and live a life of adventure. But that had been their high school dreams. They had grown up and gotten married. Joe had still talked about traveling the world. Then Carlie became pregnant with Roxanne.

Joe had changed. She hadn't been able to see it until now, but looking back she had known there had been something different about her husband. The sparkle in his eyes had faded. He smiled less and he had seemed restless. Carlie knew it then, but had chosen to ignore it. She had chosen to pretend that they still had an exciting marriage. A baby wasn't going to change thier lives all that much. Yet it had. Joe had started becoming controlling. Church was neccessary to maintain thier facade as a happy couple.

Carlie had welcomed Roxy with all the planning and glow and happiness of a true new mother. Joe had accepted it from a distance. Then a few years later, Josh had been born. Joe became more and more distant. Why hadn't she seen it then? Or maybe she had and had just chosen to ignore it. At church, they were the perfect couple. At home, they were worlds apart.

Carlie put her hands over her face. She needed to stop looking back. But how could she not? Today had brought back all those painful memories. How was she going to heal again? How was she going to heal Roxy again? Roxy had never completely gotten over her dad leaving in the first place. How was she going to react now? Carlie let the tears fall. She couldn't help it. She never let her kids see her cry. Normally she would lock herself in her room after the kids were in bed and cried. But now she could not help it. The hurt and confusion Joe had just caused was too much for anyone to bear.

Carlie grabbed a paper towel and wiped the tears from her face. She gently blew her nose, then leaning over the sink she splashed cool water on her face in attempt to erase any signs that she had been crying. After all, Josh was due home from school any minute and he did not need to see his mother falling apart. Carlie pulled herself together, dutily setting out a plate of cookies and a glass of milk for her son's after school snack.

Chapter 16

Colt let the phone ring a few times before he heard her answering machine come on. "Hey you have reached Carlie. Sorry that I missed your call. You know what to do." He didn't leave a message. He would try to call her later. She must be busy with the kids. Colt glanced at his watch. Yep. It was about that time when her kids would be coming home from school. He would call her later this evening. Colt was missing Carlie, but he would have to accept the fact that she was not under any obligation to pick up her phone or talk to him. She had made it clear to him that they could only be friends, but Colt wanted more. In the short time he knew Carlie Michaels, he knew that he wanted more than just friendship with her. He had been praying and he could not shake the feeling that was consuming him.

He really believed that God had brought this amazing woman into his life. Colt just did not not know how to pursue this relationship with Carlie.Today he especially felt a sudden urge to talk to her. He felt something telling him that she needed to talk to him too. Colt sat down on the couch and folded his hands on his knees. He prayed out loud. *God, I know you know what Carlie and her kids need right now. I believe you have brought her to me for a reason. I can't shake this feeling that we are meant to be together. Yet, tonight I come before you, not as a man who wants this woman, but to pray for her. Whatever she is dealing with right now, I ask that you put your arms around her and those kids. I pray that you give her strength to confront the enemy that has been attacking this family. I pray that she will feel your presence and know that you are there for her and for her kids. Give her wisdom. Lord. Let her know you care about her and that you love her. I care about her too, God. Bring us back together. In your name, Lord, I pray. Amen.*

Colt raised his head. He wiped the moisture from around his eyes. He could not help but feel emotional when it came to praying for Carlie and her kids. He knew the hard times she had been through and was still going through. He did not know what had happened today or what she was facing, but he felt it urgent enough to take a moment to pray for her and to try and call her again. Colt had a strong sense that Carlie needed him right now, but more than him, she needed God the Father. For even if Colt could comfort her right now, he knew that only God could bring the healing that needed to be done. Only God could give Carlie a new future.

Colt wanted that future to include him. He wanted more than anything to give Carlie and her kids a good life. He wanted to help her to forget all the bad memories and to replace them with good ones. Colt had seen what Carlie was like when she was relaxed and happy. *That* Carlie Michaels, he knew, was the real Carlie.

Barkis is Willin. Colt smiled at the thought. *Barkis is Willin* is a phrase that he tended to use a lot, but not in the way it was meant to be and certainly not in the way he meant it for Carlie Michaels. The phrase originated from a character in *David Copperfield*, a play by Charles Dickens in the year 1850. It meant that one was willing to propose to the woman of his dreams. However, the phrase soon came to apply to any type of willingness. Colt only knew the phrase because he had been forced to study Dickens in an English class in college. Colt grinned to himself. Carlie Michaels wasn't the only one who knew a little about old time playwrights and poets. Although, Colt was willing to bet she knew a lot more about old time poets, authors and playwrights than he did. At any rate, given the right time, place, and opportunity, Colt was willing to propose to Carlie. He would marry her in a heartbeat. *Barkis is Willin.* However, he knew that Carlie still had some healing to do and although he did not know what had happened today, Colt could sense that something was wrong. Thus the reason he felt the urges to both call and to pray for Carlie.

Colt stood and made his way to the kitchen. He was hungry. Not yet being dinner time, he rummaged through the cabinets for something to munch on. There wasn't much he could find. He had made a point to go to the store and stock up on some food, but Colt Storm hated grocery shopping with a passion. He hated any kind of shopping really, except for the kind he could buy himself a new tool or equipment for the horses and the ranch. He frowned when all he could find was half a bag of stale nacho chips, no salsa, an empty box of snack cakes that one of the farm hands must have neglected to throw away, and a half-eaten stale angel food cake. Colt muttered under his breath as he checked the time. Maybe he would check on the horses and the farm hands and then go into town for an early dinner. He would make it a point to stop at the General Store on the way back home. By then, maybe things at the Michaels residence would be calmed down enough for him to call Carlie. *Barkis is Willin* he thought again as he grabbed his leather jacket, tugged on his worn cowboy boots, and headed out to the stables.

Satisfied that the horses were in good hands and that Red Mare was doing better after her complications of birthing her colt, Colt went to the wash barn to clean up. After washing his hands and face, he climbed up into his truck and headed into town. Just as he was ready to pull out of the drive, his phone rang. Without looking at the number, he answered. "This is Colt Storm, talk to me." A brief silence hung in the air like a heavy fog. Then he heard her voice. *Carlie Michaels.* He sighed and pulled the truck off into the grass. "Carlie, Hi. I was wondering if you got my message." He could hear her sigh a deep sigh. "I did." Her voice was shaky. He instantly knew something was not right. It seemed like an eternity before Colt could respond to the soft, frightened voice on the other end of the phone. Maybe frightened was not the right word, more like hurt or scared or confused. Maybe she was experiencing all of the above.

"Carlie, what's wrong?" He asked, getting straight to the point. He already knew there was something wrong. There was no sense in beating around the bush about it. Carlie cleared her throat. When she spoke, her voice was a little husky. Colt could tell she had been crying. *Dang it!* He hated the thought of tears falling down that soft, beautiful face of hers. He leaned his head back against the head rest of the truck seat, holding his phone to his ear. "Carlie talk to me." She sighed deeply. "It's Joe." She said. "I don't know where to begin." She paused. "I woke up this morning to find Roxy gone. She wasn't anywhere in the house. I ended up calling the police. I sent Josh to school with promises I would find his sister."

Carlie was talking faster then she intended to talk. She was trying to get the story out before breaking into hysterical crying again. All she could think of was what would lie ahead of her as far as healing her kids again. She took a deep breath to try and slow down. Colt sat, silently listening.

He let her take her time. "Anyway, I don't know what to do." Carlie continued, her voice still shaky, but a little calmer now. Colt was glad for the slight calmness. Carlie knew that talking to Colt Storm would calm her a little. That was why she decided to return his phone call. Sure she had her friend, Laura, who had been there for Carlie through thick and thin. Yet, Carlie somehow knew that Colt was the one she needed to talk to. He was the one who could calm her. She didn't understand what drew her to him, but she knew there was something about him that she needed and wanted in him. She was well aware that there wasn't a darn thing Colt could do about the situation, but hearing his voice calmed her and gave her a sense of peace and comfort. The fact that Colt could calm Carlie down and be her voice of reason did not make sense to her in the least little bit. How could a man she barely knew keep her calm? What propelled her to call him and dump all of her junk on him in the first place? Colt Storm was under no obligation to sit on his phone and listen to her whine about her ex-husband and how he managed to torment her and the kids *again*. Likewise, Carlie knew, she was under no obligation to be calling him. *What is he supposed to do about it anyway?* She thought to herself. *Why would Colt even care? Why would he want to listen to me or help me? After all I told him that this probably wouldn't work because of the distance. Why am I bothering him?*

There was nothing but dead silence as Carlie let these thoughts filter through her mind. Colt waited patiently for her to speak again as he knew that Carlie must be thinking on what exactly she should tell him and what she should keep to herself. Colt was fully aware of the fact that it took Carlie a lot of courage to have called him. After all, they had agreed to just be long distance friends, for now. Colt still was holding on to the hope that this would turn into more. He could not ignore the fact that he had prayed only an hour ago for Carlie and now she was calling him. Colt prayed a silent quick prayer for wisdom for Carlie. He knew she had a lot to say and was struggling to tell him in spite of the fact that he seemed to be comforting to her somewhat. About two minutes passed before Carlie finally spoke again. "Colt? Are you still there?" Her voice still sounded weak. Colt hated to hear weakness in her voice. "Yeah, Carlie, I'm here." He answered. "I'm sorry." Came her apology from the other end of the phone. Colt did not know for the life of him why Carlie apologized. She had done nothing wrong. Maybe she felt like he didn't want to be bothered. He didn't know. "No need to apologize." Colt tried to reassure Carlie.

Another sigh. "It's just that I shouldn't be dumping all my crap on you." She paused momentarily. "It's just that I don't really have anyone to talk to. I mean you were so generous and nice to me when you were here and I felt a connection with you. I just...." Her voice trailed off and Colt heard a sob escape her throat. He hated that she was hurting like this. He hated it with everything inside of him. He wanted to be there to hold her, to comfort her, to tell her that everything was going to be ok. Colt wanted to tell Carlie face to face that no matter how awful her life seemed right now that God had a plan for her and the kids and that she would be better off without Joe interfering in her life at all. He wanted to move heaven and earth for Carlie Michaels and her two children. But how? How could he tell this woman that everything was going to be fine when all she's seen is disappointment? What could Colt say to Carlie to assure her that he was here for her and her kids?

He longed to go back to Ohio and pack up Carlie and the kids and move them here with him in Colorado. But he knew that would take a lot more planning than just showing up and hauling them off. Colt pondered these thoughts before continuing the conversation. He wanted with every fiber in his being to tell her that he would be there in a couple of days to pick her and her kids up and move them to Colorado. But he could not do that. Not just yet anyway. He had to be 100% sure and Carlie had to be willing, healed enough and in her complete right mind to agree to move.

Barkis is willin. He reminded himself again. He was willing for sure, but was Carlie Michaels willing and ready? That was the question of the moment. "Colt," Carlie's voice came back over the phone. "I'm here, Carles." Carles. He was the first person that ever called her that besides Laura. Colt didn't really know why he called her that. It just came out naturally and felt right at the moment.

"Joe wrote off his kids. He left a letter in the mailbox saying that he never wanted anything to do with them again. HOW COULD HE?! Roxy went to find him and Joe brought her back and walked away. *Again.* I don't know how to heal them again." She paused. He could hear her crying softly. Colt ran his hand through his hair. He didn't understand why that jerk did this to Carlie and her kids again. He knew he shouldn't call Joe names, but this made Colt angry. Now he really wanted nothing more than to go back to Ohio and pack up Carlie and her kids and get them away from all that heartache. Carlie was back on the phone.

"Colt, I know this sounds completely off the wall, but..." She hesitated. "But what?" Colt prompted. Carlie took a deep breath. "I think the kids and I need to get out of Ohio, at least this town. We need a fresh start somewhere, anywhere. We need to go somewhere where no one really knows our name or our situation and just start brand new. New schools, new friends, a new home. We need to go somewhere where we don't have to think about Joe every time we turn the corner or hear his name every place we go. We just need to start over."

Colt could not believe what he was hearing. Should he offer up his suggestion of her moving here? He was stunned at the statement that Carlie had just made. Statement or suggestion? He wondered. What exactly was she suggesting? Was she giving him a hint about possibly moving out to Colorado close to him? Was he reading into her statement too much? Colt did not know what to say. He did not know how he should respond to what Carlie had just said. He knew he needed to say something, but what? He couldn't think. For once in his life, Colt Storm was speechless. He had to try and say something to her. She was waiting for him to respond, to give her some kind of answer.

"Colt?" He heard her say. "Yeah, Carlie, I'm here." "Well, what should I do?" Colt was struggling. Every fiber in his being wanted to tell her that he would be there within a few days to get her. A nervous lump formed in his throat. "I don't know, Carlie. I can't tell you what to do." He paused. " I can tell you that I have a place out here if you want to move out here and be close to me." Dang it! He should have left the "be close to me" out! He held his breath for a brief second as he waited for her to respond.

"I would really love to, Colt. I want to get to know you." She took a deep breath before continuing. Colt could hear the "but" coming before she even said it. "The thing is, I have to sell the house. I have to prepare the kids. I just need a couple of weeks to try and think this through and get things settled to where we can move. Do you understand?" Colt breathed deeply. She hadn't exactly said yes to his proposal yet, but close enough. She definitely had not said no. There was hope yet. *Barkis is willin* he thought for the hudredth time that day. Geesh! He needed a new phrase to quote. He smiled. To Carlie he said,"I understand, Carles. I can be patient. I know you need time to figure things out and to get your kids ready and to do what you need to do. I am here for you. Call me any time and any time you want to come visit, let me know. I will get you and the kids out here." He left it at that. He wanted to say more. He wanted to tell her that he would be there in a couple of days. He wanted to tell her how he was feeling for her. "Thank you Colt." Carlie said. Her voice seemed calmer now, not as shakey. Colt was glad he could offer her some comfort. "I promise I will call you soon. And Colt?" "Yeah?" Carlie sighed. "Thank you for all you have done and are doing for me. You don't know how glad I am to have met you. Who knew that an old blue truck would lead to this. To us. Who knows. Maybe this will lead to something after all. Well, good night, Colt Storm." She almost said "I love you." But that was way too forward and way, way too soon to express any of those kind of feelings. "Good night, Carles. I'm here for you any time you need me. Good night." With that,both parties hung up their phones. Colt sighed deeply. He was starting to fall even harder for Carlie Michaels.

Chapter 17

Carlie smiled as she hung up the phone. She still did not understand what drove her to call Colt and whine to him about Joe. But, she was glad that she had. He calmed her down. She still felt angry, but she didn't feel alone. She knew that Colt would be there any time she needed to talk. She climbed up the stairs and checked on the kids one more time before heading to her room. She changed into her favorite flannel pajamas and picked up the *Nora Roberts* book she had started to read the other night. With her mind being more relaxed and her heart somewhat settled a little, Carlie was able to get into the first book of the three book series she so desparately had been wanting to read. Carlie got through the first two chapters before she fell asleep. Colt Storm was on her mind as she drifted off. Her last thought before peaceful darkness consumed her was what it might be like to be in Colorado with him.

The next morning, Carlie felt energized. She started to feel some anxiety and stress lift. She was still unsure what her future would hold. She knew she had to talk to the kids and that there was a lot of healing to be done. Another thought hit her like a bullet flying through the air and hitting her right smack in between her eyes. Maybe it would be best for her and the kids to move out of this town. Maybe what they really needed was to move to where noone knew them or Joe or their fantasy story gone wrong.

Carlie was very aware of the fact that in a new town there would be questions about where they were from and what her story was. On the other hand, Carlie was sure that it would be better than the sideways glances and looks of pity and accusations she had gotten accustomed to here. Then again, moving was a very big deal. Carlie paced the floor of her room as a million and one thoughts and questions ran through her mind. She shook her head to clear her mind. She would think through this whole idea of moving once the kids were off to school. She went down the hall to Roxy's room and slowly opened the door after knocking. Roxy was already awake and dressed.

"Hey Rox, you sure are on the ball this morning." Carlie observed. Roxy smiled. "Yeah. I did a lot of thinking last night,

Mom. I really want to try harder. I don't want to keep screwing up. Dad...I mean *Joe...*" Roxy paused. She shrugged her shoulders as she comtinued. "I just don't get why this is all happening. I mean, *Joe* giving up on us like this. It hurts all over again. Is anything ever going to be ok or normal again?" Carlie wiped a tear from her daughter's face. Her own tears felt heavy as she struggled to find an answer for Roxy. Unfortunately, there was no easy answer or way to deal with the hurt. There was not going to be an easy way to remove the black cloud that was looming over them.

Carlie sighed as she sat on the bed next to Roxy. "I can't tell you that it is going to be easy to get over what your father has done to you..to Josh..to us. Roxy shot her mother a look of disdain. "*That* man is *NOT* my father." She reiterated. Carlie placed her hand on Roxy's back. "Honey, I know you feel that way now, but you may one day reconcile with him. I am not saying that what he did is right in any way. In fact it is a sin against a sin. It is wrong in so many waysand I know you feel like you will never be able to forgive him. I can't imagine forgiving him either, but somehow we must in order to go with our lives." Carlie took a deep breath and let that sink in. "Roxy, honey, we can't hold bitterness towards your father. That will only hurt us in the long run and then he wins. Forgiving him does not mean accepting what he has done and is doing. Nor does it mean we have to let him back in our lives. It just means that we need to move on from here and do our best to build our lives without him. We can be happy again. Just wait and see. Ok?" Roxy nodded, wiping the tears from off her cheek. Carlie hugged her daughter and rose from the bed. "Mom?" Carlie looked down at Roxy. "Yes?" Roxy flipped her hair over her shoulder. "Do you think you will ever see that guy Colt again? I mean I'm sorry I tried to run him off. He seemed nice enough. I was just mad. You know?" Carlie smiled as she lovingly placed her hand under Roxy's chin. "Yeah, I know. And maybe. I do talk to him on the phone. We'll see what happens. Ok?" Roxy nodded. She smiled at her mother. "Ok." Carlie nodded. "Ok now get ready for school. You don't want to be late." Roxy nodded.

Carlie exited the room, closing the door behind her. She paused outside the door for a moment to let thier conversation sink in. She took a deep breath and headed down the hall to Josh's room.

She knocked on the door and opened it. Josh was already up, dressed for school and watching T.V. She smiled at the sight of her little sandy-haired boy sitting crosse-legged on the bed. "You are up bright and early." Carlie said, smiling. Josh nodded. "I was just thinking about Daddy." Carlie took in another deep breath. *Here we go...*she thought as she waited patiently for Josh to continue. He turned to her. "Mommy it's just not fair! Why doesn't Daddy love us? Did we do something wrong?" Carlie's own eyes filled with tears once again as she looked at her son. Anguish was written all over her son's young face. *God! He shouldn't have to ask these kind of questions!*

She sat on the edge of Josh's bed and put her arm around his shoulder. "Oh, sweetie. It's not that Daddy doesn't love you. It's just that he is busy doing other things right now." She let that sink in. "You and Roxy did nothing wrong. I don't have all the answers for you, baby. I wish I could explain why Daddy is doing what he is, but I can't." She paused, taking in her son's expression. "But know that I love you and I am always here for you. Someday when you are older, maybe you will be able to ask Daddy those questions. But for now, you, me, and Roxy just need to focus on us. It will be ok, I promise." Josh looked at Carlie with those deep brown eyes. He wiped the tears away and smiled. "Ok, Mommy. I love you bunches." Carlie smiled as she wrapped her arms around him. "Love you bunches more!" She held her son in her arms for just a few seconds longer than she intended. When she finally let go, Josh gave her a kiss on the cheek and turned back to his show. "Now," Carlie informed him. "I am going downstairs to get breakfast ready." Josh smiled and nodded. Carlie exited Josh's room and descended the stairs.

As she entered the kitchen and pulled out cereal bowls and spoons, Carlie thought about the brief conversations she just had with the kids. She hoped her answers were enough to help them understand a little. Carlie didn't have all the answers that her children needed. Heck, she didn't have the answers she needed. The tough thing was that she had to find a way to heal all of them. How was she going to do that? She needed to heal so she could heal her kids *again.*

With the kids off to school, Carlie knew she would have

time to think things through a little more. She poured herself a strong cup of coffee and took it upstairs with her so that she could get dressed for the day.

After pulling on a pair of jeans, a light sweater and a pair of loafers, she sat on the edge of her bed. Carlie replayed the conversations with her kids through her mind one more time. She had hoped she gave them enough to satisfy thier questions for the time being. She was fully aware of the fact, however, that no matter what she told them, they were never going to be completely satisfied. Her children, Carlie knew, would carry these scars in thier hearts for the rest of thier lives. Even if there was ever the possibility of Joe reconciling with his kids, Carlie knew that Roxy and Josh would neither easily forget nor would they forgive him for what he had done to them not just once, but twice.

Carlie sighed deeply as she sipped the last bit of her coffee. She could not stand being in this house anymore. She needed a day out. She decided to call Laura and see if she was available to go on a shopping and lunch date. Carlie had not talked to Laura since she had gotten fired from the store. The last time she had talked to or even had seen Laura was the night Carlie had gone on the date with Colt. Carlie missed her friend and decided it had been way too long since the two of them had talked or hung out together.

Carlie picked up her purse and dug out her cell phone. She found Laura's number and dialed. "Hello?" Came the sleepy voice from the other end. "Hey, Laura. It's Carlie. Oh, I'm so sorry. Did I wake you?" Carlie heard Laura yawn. "Oh No, I was wide awake and taking a jog." Came the sarcastic reply. Carlie laughed. She had always loved Laura's sense of humor. That was one of the things that had made them such good friends. The two of them had always been able to make wisecracks about other co-workers, their bosses, and those annoying customers who always asked about coupons and sales.

"I'm sorry" Carlie apologized. "I just got the kids off to school and I was thinking about getting out of the house. Are you free today?" There was a pause. "Yeah. I'm actually off today." Laura answered. "What did you have in mind?" Carlie smiled. "A day of shopping and having lunch. Sound good?" She could hear rustling on the other end of the phone. No doubt Laura was removing blankets and getting out of bed. "Sounds great! Did you get another job?" Carlie sighed. "Not yet." "Oh. You sure you can afford to go shopping? I know how much you have been struggling." No sooner had she said the words, Laura regreted them. "I'm so sorry. I didn't mean..." Carlie smiled. "It's OKok. I have left over money from Colt Storm's charity fund. "She reported to her friend. Now it was Laura's turn to laugh. "Great! What time?" Carlie checked the clock on her bedroom wall. "Meet you in an hour? Maybe we can head to Field's Ertle and do some shopping there. There's that mall and all those little shops and maybe lunch at the *Olive Garden?"* "Sounds great!" Laura said. "I'll be at your house in an hour." The women hung up. Carlie smiled. She was looking forward to hanging out with Laura. A girl's day out was exactly what she needed.

She decided to change out of her loafers and put on a pair of her favorite boots instead. She decided her black low-heeled boots would be more stylish to go out in than the pair of worn out loafers she wore around the house. Not that Carlie Michaels was an expert on fashion, but she did like to look and feel like a woman every now and then. She went to her vanity. Sitting in front of the mirror, she let down her hair and brushed it out, letting it fall naturally down her back. She applied a light coating of foudation, blush, eye shadow, and mascara. She finished off her look with a rose lip gloss. Satisfied that she was ready to face the world of fashionable women, Carlie took her coffee mug downstairs and refilled it. It was just one of those mornings where an extra cup of coffee was most needed. Besides, hadn't she just seen on the news that coffee was now good for you? Carlie smiled as she exited the kitchen and went into the living room where she seated herself on the sofa and flipped on the T.V. Carlie settled in to watch *Live with Kelly and Michael.* She didn't usually get a chance to watch the show, but Carlie thouroughly enjoyed the two talk hosts whenever she did get to sit down and watch it.

True to her word, Laura arrived exactly one hour later. Carlie opened the door and greeted her friend with a hug. "Hey, how you been?" Laura smiled as she closed the door behind her. "I'm good. Long time no see." Carlie nodded. "I know. I'm sorry. Just so much stuff going on." Carlie apologized as she made her way to the kitchen to place her coffee mug in the sink. Laura followed Carlie. She leaned against the kitchen counter and folded her arms across her chest. "So what's going on? I heard that Roxy got into some trouble and that the cops were here." Carlie rolled her eyes. "I hate this town!" She exclaimed. "Nothing is private anymore." Laura burst out laughing. She held a hand up. "I'm sorry, Carles. It's just, what did you expect? Everyone here knows everyone and their business."

Once again Carlie nodded. She knew Laura was right. The problem though was that everyone only *thought* they really knew what went on in thier neighbors' lives in this town. Carlie waved Laura off. "Don't apologize. Roxy wasn't in any serious trouble.It had to do with Joe." Now it was Laura's turn to roll her eyes. " Joe? What did he do now? I mean it's been a year since you and the kids have even seen him so I don't understand." Carlie shrugged. "Well, Joe had left a letter in the mailbox. Roxy got to it before I did. She ran away to find him. Of course, I had no idea where she had gone. I woke up the other morning to find her missing. I called the cops. While they were here trying to track down her friends, Joe and Roxy showed up. I finally saw the letter on my desk." Laura could not believe this. She probed deeper. "What did he want?"

Carlie crossed the kitchen to grab her purse and jacket that were hanging on the back of one of the chairs. "He signed all his rights over with promises of paying child support. Said that he didn't want anything to do with the kids. I guess Roxy wanted an explanation." She paused. "I guess I can't blame her. I wanted one too. I just wish she had come to me and talked to me before running off." Laura could not believe what she was hearing. "You've got to be kidding! How can that jerk do this to you and those kids again? Wasn't the first round painful enough?"

Carlie could not agree more. She slipped on her jacket. "I know. I couldn't even talk to him. I slapped him. I slapped him hard with the officers standing right there watching the whole scene." Laura shook her head. "I'm sorry Carles. You don't deserve this." Carlie smiled. "No I don't and neither do the kids." She paused. "Life goes on. With that said, you ready to go? I'm dying for some shopping therapy!" Laura laughed. The two women headed out to Carlie's car for a girl's day out; or as Carlie had called it, *shopping therapy.*

Chapter 18

The two women climbed into Carlie's SUV. Once their seatbelts were in place and Carlie had turned out of the driveway, Laura turned to her friend. She finally asked the question she'd been holding in and dying to know the answer to. Flipping her hair over her shoulder, she asked, " So, have you talked to Colt since he went back to wherever it was that he came from?" Carlie grinned. "Colorado." She corrected Laura. Laura shrugged her shoulders. "So?" Carlie turned left at the light, heading for the interstate. "I have spoken to him over the phone a couple of times. I called him the other night after everything had happened with Roxy." Carlie stopped there. Laura knew there was more than what her friend was telling her. She waited. Carlie turned onto the interstate."I don't kow, Laura. I have been thinking that maybe the kids and I need a fresh start." Laura looked as if she was in shock. "You mean like moving?" She didn't add the out-of-state phrase. She was pretty sure that was what Carlie meant. Carlie nodded.

"Well, yeah. I mean I am tired of this town and the looks I get every time I go down the street or around the corner. Roxy's been having trouble at school with kids teasing her about the divorce and her dad. Josh, I don't know, but I can tell he is hurting too. He has been asking some hard questions and I try to answer the best I can." She paused. Laura was silent for a moment as Carlie skillfully maneuvered in and out of heavy traffic. "Well, where would you go? I mean I understand wanting to start over and all, but leave Ohio completely?" Carlie shrugged. "I know. But I have lived here all my life and I think it would be really good for us." She paused there. "And as far as where to go," She continued. "Colt offered to let us move out there. He thinks it might be good to get the kids around horses." Both women laughed. "Horses huh?" Laura snickered. "Yeah, he says horses have a way of healing a person's soul." Carlie replied. Laura doubled over laughing. "What?!" Carlie excalimed. "Have you ever been around the animals? He does have a point. Horses tend to calm you and they do have a way of making you forget all your problems. For example, when I used to ride on my parents' farm, whatever was bothering me at school or whatever, riding and being with the horses made me feel like there wasn't a worry in the world."

Laura stopped laughing and cleared her throat. "Ok, ok. But honestly, Carles, I think this has more to it than just big, beautiful animals. I think you really like this guy and he really likes you and whether or not you are ready to admit it, I think you are in love." Carlie pulled off the interstate, made a left at the light and pulled into the *Pier One* parking lot. She found a parking space and shut off the engine. Taking off her seatbelt, Carlie turned to face Laura. "I hardly even know the man." She argued. Then taking a deep breath, she continued. "Maybe you are right. I mean ever since I met him in the parking lot at Kroger, there's just been this connection with him. I can't explain how after only knowing the man for a couple of weeks, I can't stop thinking about him and longing to be with him. It's like there is this magnet pulling me to him." Carlie admited. Laura gave her a knowing smile. Carlie continued as the two women climbed out of the vehicle.

"And believe me, Laura, the last thing I wantedor want to do, is to fall in love with Colt Storm." Laura nodded. "I get it. Joe hurt you and I know that the last thing you want to do is to jump into a relationship, especially with someone that you barely know." Carlie threw her hands in the air. "Exactly! Yet I just can't get him out of my head. I even called him the other night after the issue with Joe and Roxy. It's weird, Laura, but he calms me and after talking to him, I just felt so much better." Laura grinned. "Like the horses." She teased. Carlie laughed. "Yeah, like the horses."

The two women entered the store. "Well, to be honest, Carles, I saw it when he came over that night to take you to dinner. I saw the way he looked at you and believe me it was a lot more than just lust. He had this look of respect and interest, and yeah maybe a little lust. But, I don't think he just wanted to sleep with you. I think there was something more there. You didn't notice because you were too busy being nervous and lecturing the kids. But there was definitely something there and maybe you should take the chance." Carlie stopped and picked up an exquisite candle holder. It was silver and turquoise with a gold strip wrapped around it. She picked up a blue candle and smelled it. It smelled like the ocean and Carlie decided she had to have the piece. She turned to Laura as she carefully picked up the holder and the candle. "Maybe you are right. I don't really know if this thing with him, whatever it is, is going to go somewhere. But isn't moving to Colorado a little ecentric? I mean if it doesn't work out or if I am reading his signals wrong, I am stuck in the same situation I am here." Laura placed a hand on Carlie's shoulder. "Carles, take the chance. I am telling you if Colt Storm didn't want to have anything with you, he would not have suggested that you move out there. Listen to me, he is crazy about you! And he likes your kids." Laura said as she picked up a red and gold decorative pillow. "$40 bucks! Geesh!" Laura exclaimed changing the subject. She reexamined the object in her hand. She noticed the sale sign that said "Two pillows for $40." She picked up the matching pillow. "That's more like it. These will look amazing on my new tan couch I just bought." Carlie agreed. "They are beautiful. Definitely worth that price for both of them and they would look perfect with that sofa you just purchased!"

The women circled the store to see what other finds they could convince themselves they wanted or needed. Carlie picked up a lantern that looked as if it was from the early eighteen-hundreds. The piece was not that ancient, of course, it was just a replica of an old lantern that would have been used in the homes of the pioneers. The lantern was another candle holder. Carlie decided to keep the silver and turquoise candle holder. She carefully placed the lantern back on the shelf. Always stick with your first instincts. Not doing so often results in a regret of choice. Carlie had learned that lesson from her mother.

She picked up a antique looking bronze flower vase off the clearance shelf. She put it back as an interesting art picture caught her eye. The art piece looked to be hand-painted. The background was done in blue-gray which was made to look like leather. A pile of old books was painted in a criss-cross stack form in the middle of the painting surrounded by abstract streaks of colors, such as red, dark blue, and green. The price tag read $25. Carlie decided she just had to have it. Being a book lover, the piece would suit her just fine. She could hang it abover her desk in her bedroom. Laura had picked up the lantern that Carlie had chosen not to purchase.

"This is cool." She remarked. Carlie nodded. "Yeah I thought so too, but I decided to keep this candle holder." Then turning Laura's attention to the art piece, she said,"What do you think about this? I thought it would look good hanging above my desk in my bedroom." Knowing that Carlie was a book lover, Laura thought the piece was perfect. "I think you should get it, Carles." She paused. "Of course, if you move to Colt Storm's neck of the country, you may have to ask him permission to hang it in...umm.. the bedroom" Carlie lightly tapped Laura's arm. "You are too much!" She exclaimed, laughing.

The women headed to the register. The cashier rang Carlie's candle holder and candle up. "Is this all for you?" She asked politely. Carlie noticed the name tag on the girl's shirt. *Tangie* "I would like to take that art piece hanging on the wall in the corner there. The painting of the books." Tangie nodded. "That piece has been here for a while. Seems like no one appreciates books anymore, or art for that matter." She said as she walked around the counter and skillfully removed the piece from the wall. She brought the painting back to the counter and carefully wrapped it. "You are in luck. This is a clearance item and is half off the original price. Carlie felt like whooping. But of course, she didn't. She held her excitement to herself. "Thank you, Tangie! I love it even more now!" Tangie smiled as she took Carlie's credit card and ran it. Carlie signed the reciept and moved over so that Laura could make her purchases. Once Laura's transaction was completed, the two women exited the store and carefully loaded their purchases into Carlie's SUV.

Once inside the vehicle, Carlie took note of the time. The clock on the panel read 11:00. "Wow. I didn't realaize we spent an hour in there." She exclaimed. "Laura smiled. "So much to look at and too little time." She said. Carlie nodded. "Early lunch at *The Olive Garden?"* Laura nodded. "Absolutely! We have to take advantage of their all you can eat soup, salad, and breadsticks!" It was Carlie's turn to laugh. "I was thinking more of a favorite pasta dish like chicken alfredo or shrimp scampi with that all you can eat yummy salad.: Laura grunted. "My figure will suffer!" She teased.

The women laughed as Carlie pulled out the *Pier One's* parking lot. Turning left at the light, she made a bee line for *Olive Garden.* Once parked, the women went inside. The waitress seated them right away, handing them menus along with the drink specials of the day. As tempted as Carlie was to order a margarita, she turned it down and ordered an iced tea with lemon instead. Laura ordered a glass of Merlot with ice water on the side. The waitress went off to fill their drink orders as Carlie and Laura studied the menu. Laura nodded toward a nearby table where a college boy was cleaning it off. "He is cute." She noted. Carlie grinned. "A little young for you, and what would your husband think of you hitting on college boys!" Laura grinned back. "Hey just because I can't eat the food doesn't mean I can't look at the menu." She defended herself in a deviant and sort of comical way. Carlie laughed. "You have a point, my friend." She replied.

The college boy must have overheard them for he casually approached thier table. "Ladies." He greeted them in a friendly voice. "The name is Eric. I am 25. I recently graduated from Dayton University and this is my last week here at this infamous and amazing restaurant before I begin my adventure as a defense attorney." The two friends could only stare. Both women could have died right then and there of total embarrassment. Eric continued. "However, I do thank you for the compliment on my looks and I hope you enjoy your lunch. And may I add that you two are the most beautiful women that have entered this fine establishment today." That did it. Carlie and Laura could not contain thier laughter anymore. They both burst out in uncontrollable laughter. Eric was grinning from ear to ear. "Well, Eric, I hope you enjoy your new job and congratulations." Eric smiled at the two women and thanked them. He turned on his heels and finished cleaning off the table.

By the time the waitress had returned with thier drinks, Carlie and Laura had composed themselves. "Thank you." They said in unison. The waitress smiled. "I'm Charlotte. Are you ready to order?" The women nodded. Carlie ordered the shrimp scampi while Laura ordered crab bisque, salad, and breadsticks. The salad and bread sticks were brought out first followed shortly by the shrimp scampi and crab bisque. The two women talked some more about Colt, then changed the subject to Laura's job. Carlie learned that Laura was on the verge of getting another job as a freelance writer for the local newspaper. Laura had gone to college and had studied journalism. "That is so great, Laura! I'm so happy for you!" Laura grinned. "*Mr. Scrooge* isn't thrilled about me leaving. He said that I was the best cashier he had working in the store. He even offered me a promotion and a raise if I stay." She shook her head as she finished off the bisque and a bread stick. "I can't believe you guys are still calling him that." Carlie laughed. "Seriously though, you will do a lot better using your journalism degree." Laura nodded. "I'll be happier, too," She paused as she took the last sip of her wine. "So what about you? Do you think you will move to Colorado and try to make this work with Colt?" Carlie? sighed. "I don't know. It would be great and we do need a change of atmosphere and Colt is such a great guy. Joe certainly doesn't want anything to do with his kids. Maybe it would be good for us. I have to talk to the kids about it and see what they think. Plus I want to look into what kind of jobs are around there." She paused as she took a drink of tea. " Don't get me wrong, Colt has money and all and I probably wouldn't have to work. But, I want to work and I want to find something I enjoy doing. I am thinking about taking some cooking or creative writing classes and becoming a chef or a writer, or maybe I can do both." Laura nodded. "I can totally see you doing either or both of those. I think you should go for it, Carles. Talk to Colt. See what colleges are out there and see what jobs are available in his town. But, I think you should just do it."

The women paid their bill and headed out to the shopping mall where they explored the book and craft stores. Hauling their purchases to the vehicle, they were ready to hit the road and head home. Carlie turned back to the interstate. Once back in Wilmington, the women decided they had enough time to stop at the dairy store to finish off their day with milkshakes. Carlie ordered a chocolate caramel shake while Laura went with the peanut butter shake. Once finished with their treats, they headed back to Carlie's house. Carlie pulled into the drive and parked. She unlocked the back and helped Laura load her purchases into her car. Carlie hugged her friend. "Hey, thanks for today, Laura." Laura smiled as she climbed into the driver's seat. "Anytime, girl. Call me later or tomorrow after you talk to the kids and Colt. But, I think you should give this whole thing a chance."

Carlie waved as she watched Laura pull away. She carried her purchases into the house and up to her bedroom. As she slowly unpacked and admired all the items she bought. Her items included the painting of the books, the exquisite candle holder and candle, the two books she purchased at the bookstore, and the writing materials and fabric she purchased at the craft store. Carlie couldn't help but to begin to think that Laura was right. Maybe it was time she took a chance. Maybe this moment in her life was the moment to do what she wanted to do with her life and to take the chance of falling in love again. Maybe now was the time to start healing and to start over. Maybe it was time to end this struggle that she had been going through for what seemed like an eternity.

Carlie checked the time. It was nearly three p.m. Any moment now Roxy would be heading through the door announcing her arrival from school. Carlie tucked away the bags and wrappings of her shopping trip and made her way down the stairs to fix Roxy an after school snack. As the pepperoni hot pocket heated in the microwave, Carlie sat out a glass, filling it with ice and Pepsi. Just as the microwave beeped, Roxy breezed into the kitchen. "Hey Mom." Carlie smiled as she placed Roxy's favorite snack on a plate and placed it on the table.

"Hey, Roxy. How was school?" Roxy sighed as she plopped down into a chair and reached for the glass. "I hate this town! I thought that all this crap with Joe was over." Carlie ignored the fact that Roxy did not refer to Joe as *Dad*. "What happened honey?" She inquired, taking the chair accross from Roxy. Roxy folded her arms accrossed her chest. "I'm tired of the teasing and the jokes Mom. All I ever hear anymore is how Joe took off with a younger woman and maybe I'll gain a *sister*!" Roxy wiped a tear away. "Can't we just move out of this God-awful town, Mom? Isn't there someplace we can go where we aren't reminded of what happened every time we turn the corner?"

Carlie handed her daughter a tissue. She didn't say anything for a moment. Finally, she looked at Roxy. This was as good a time as any to talk to Roxy about moving to Colorado. "Roxy, I've been doing a lot of thinking. I talked to Laura today about this too." Roxy looked at her mom. "What is it, Mom?" Carlie took a deep breath. "Well, I have been talking to Colt and he offered to let us move out to Colorado with him. He suggested that maybe we all just need a change and to get away and start over. I talked it over with Laura today and she agrees."

There was silence for a long period while Roxy nibbled on the hot pocket and proccessed what her Mother was telling her. Finally, after what seemed like an eternity, she spoke. "Mom, I know you like Colt and I think he likes you. You know me. I don't like change, but I think I could handle moving out of this town, this state, and going somewhere where I can make new friends." She paused. "Colt has horses too doesn't he?" Carlie nodded. Roxy's eyes lit up. "I have always wanted a horse you know." Carlie didn't know. "

Honey, you never said anything about wanting a horse. I know you like to read about them and you draw horses, but you never mentioned your interest went to wanting to own one." Roxy nodded. "Well I do. I think it would be cool, Mom. I think we should move. Josh and I can make new friends and we can be somewhere where people will stop teasing us and giving you looks as if you were the one who did something wrong."

Carlie was stunned. She had not realized how observant Roxy had been over the whole situation with Joe and with small town talk. Carlie nodded. "It will take a little while to do. I'll have to put the house up for sale and see how fast it will sell. Then there is all the packing and cleaning that will have to be done." Roxy nodded as she finished off her snack. "We can do it, Mom." Carlie stood. "Well, I guess it's settled. I'll call Colt tonight and see what he can do in helping us move to Colorado." Roxy smiled as she stood and placed her plate and glass in the sink. "Mom, for the first time since this all happened, I feel relieved and happy." Carlie smiled as she watched Roxy head into the living room. Now to tell Josh.

Carlie wasn't sure if he would feel the same way as his sister. He hadn't complained about any teasing from his peers at school, but nonetheless, Carlie felt as if Josh would embrace the change as well as Roxy did.

An hour after she had her talk with Roxy about moving to Colorado, Carlie was prepared to talk with Josh. She set out a plate of cookies and a glass of milk. Just as she filled her mug with coffee, Josh came in through the back door. "Mommy!" He ran into Carlie's arms. Carlie hugged her son tightly. "Hey, how was school?" Josh hung his back pack on a hook along the wall and sat down to devour his snack. "Good. Except for one thing." Carlie waited as he took a big gulp of milk and wiped his mouth on his sleeve as boys do. "I hate getting teased. Kids at school are saying that I am going to get an older sister and that my dad is nothing but a low-life cheater." Carlie was enraged. She didn't show it however as she sat next to her son at the table. "I'm sorry, honey." Josh swallowed. "It's not your fault, Mommy. I know it's not your fault. I don't like this town anymore." Josh said as he stood and placed his plate and glass in the sink. Carlie sighed. This was definitely a sign that she was making the right decision about moving. Josh had been fairly quiet about everything until now. She hadn't realized that he had been getting the same treatment at school that Roxy had been getting. Josh had always been a little more quiet and reserved about things. But then again, he was only eight and Carlie knew that children sometimes just needed to proccess things on their own and in their own way. Carlie patted the chair. "Sit back down for a minute, sweetie." Josh obeyed. "I already told Roxy, but I want to tell you too and see what you think and how you would feel about something. I know you and your sister have had it rough this last year. I didn't know you were being teased too. I'm sorry, baby." Josh shrugged. "It's OKok Mom." He said. Carlie nodded, even though she knew it wasn't all ok, but she let it go.

"You remember Colt, right?" Josh nodded. "Yeah, I like him." Carlie smiled. "Well, he has offered to let us move to Colorado to be with him. And I thought that maybe it would be good for us to move there and get out of Wilmington and out of Ohio altogether where we all can start fresh and be somewhere where we aren't being teased or talked about. Colt has a horse ranch and you can learn to ride horses and stuff." She paused to let that sink in, "What do you think?" Josh didn't say anything for a little while. Finally, he spoke. "Mommy, I would like that. What does Roxy think?" Once again, Carlie smiled at her son. "Roxy likes the idea. It would take a little time though. I have to put up the house for sale and we have a lot of packing to do." Josh nodded. "Ok, Mommy. I'm excited though. Will we be there for Christmas or here?"

Carlie sighed. Christmas was two months away. She wasn't sure if the house would sell that fast. "I'm not sure, Josh. It depends on how fast the house sells and how fast we can get moved. But, I promise you this. I promise that either way, you and your sister will have a great Christmas. Ok?" Josh nodded as he stood. "Ok." He gave Carlie a hug and headed to the living room to watch T.V with Roxy.

Carlie sat at the table for a few minutes, twirling her mug. She had a lot of details to work out and she needed to call Colt tonight to make sure the offer was still available. Carlie knew that this was the right move to make. Both of her kids had not even hesitated about moving. Carlie took that as a sign that this was what she needed to do for her family. She could not know for sure, though, that happily forever after would be found with Colt Storm. However, she did know that by moving, she and her kids could finally heal and start a new life. And maybe, just maybe, the struggle would finally end.

Chapter 19

That night, after the kids were fed and tucked into bed, Carlie went to her room and dressed for bed. She picked up her phone and dialed Colt's number. After several rings, she got his voicemail. *Howdy. This is Colt. You know what to do. Leave a message and I'll get back to you. Have a great day.* Carlie didn't leave a message. She quickly hung up. After flipping on the T.V., she couldn't focus on the show she was watching. She looked at her phone which seemed to be begging her to pick it up and call Colt again.

Carlie bit her lower lip as she stared at the device which seemed to be haunting her. She glanced at the clock. It was nine p.m. She contemplated trying to reach Colt again. She needed to let him know that she had made the decision to move to Colorado, providing the offer was still on the table. Carlie didn't see any reason why Colt's offer wouldn't still stand. She couldn't take it anymore. She reached for the phone and dialed Colt's number for a second time.

She got his voicmail again, but this time, Carlie left him a message, "Colt, this is Carlie. Listen, I have been doing some thinking. I talked to to my best friend, Laura and the kids. Please call me back as soon as you arc available so we can talk. Thanks. Talk to you soon." Carlie wanted to add *I love you,* but she refrained. She did not understand why she wanted so badly to say the three forbidden words to a man she had only known for a very short time nor did she understand what drew her to him, but there was just something there. She could not explain it. Carlie only knew that somehow God must be working in her life and trying to do something amazing for her and her children. After all, he knew all the hurt and struggles they had been through over the past year and were still going through. Carlie conceded that maybe this was God's way of healing her family and showing up for her in a way she could have never dreamed or could have even began to ever imagine. After all, look at all that he had done through Colt Storm over the last two or three weeks.

It seemed that God had brought Colt to her in the most unexpected way and at the exact moment she needed someone.

Colt had just happened to be in the parking lot where Carlie's truck broke down. He just happened to know a towing company who also just happened to have a spare vehicle to give to Carlie. Colt just happened to be able to pay for her cable and to give her enough money to pay for the title, plates, and insurance on the new vehicle and enough to keep her going for a little while. He just happened to be there when she needed to talk to him and needed him the most.

Carlie felt the tears run down her cheeks. She bowed her head. *God, if this is what you want for me and my children, then you make this possible and let the house sell quickly and give us what we need to be able to move. You do this God, if it be your will. Amen.* Just as she lifted her head, her phone rang. She quickly wiped her eyes and cleared her throat. "Hello?" She answered. "Hey, Carles, it's Colt." Carlie smiled. Her heart fluttered.

"Hey. How are you?" She could hear Colt grinning through the phone. "I'm good. I got your message. I'm sorry I missed your call. I had an emergency out in the barn. One of my men got his leg broken by a new horse we just brought in. I had to get him off to the hospital." Carlie gasped. "Oh. I am so sorry. I hope he is going to be ok." Colt smiled. "He will be. Doc is putting a cast on him now. He will be down for a few weeks, but I reckon I'll get along while he recovers." Carlie smiled. Colt Storm had to be one of the most caring people she had ever met. "So anyway, what's up? Your message seemed a little urgent."

Carlie took a breath. "Not really, but I have been talking to my friend Laura and I talked to the kids. Is your offer still good about us possibly moving out there to be with you? I mean, we need a change and the kids agree that they are ready to leave this town and to start a new life somewhere where their dad can't hurt them anymore. We just need to put the past behind us and move on with our lives. The kids want this too. We all need a change." She paused, taking another deep breath before continuing. "And Colt, I don't like long distance relationships. If there is something between us, then I need to be there with you." She waited. Carlie hoped she wasn't being too forward and that Colt felt the same way. Her heart was pounding hard in her chest as she waited for him to respond.

Colt couldn't help but to feel happy inside that Carlie Michaels was actually considering moving closer to him. He had felt from the beginning that he had crossed her path for a reason. God was working in a way that Colt could never had imagined. He had given up his wild ways of drinking and shacking up with women and had given his heart fully to the Lord. He had been waiting for God to send someone wonderful into his life. Colt had been hoping that Carlie was starting to feel the same way. He knew that Carlie had not been going to church, but Colt could also see that the woman had a heart of gold. He knew that she had been hurt and had sworn off everyone and everything. He knew that she had blamed God for the affair and divorce and all the hurt and pain. Yet, Colt had sensed that Carlie's heart was not as hardened as she wanted others to believe it was. Deep down, he knew, her heart still longed for the presence of God.

Colt wanted to be the one to show her real love. Ever since that day he helped her with her truck and heard Carlie's story, Colt Storm had wanted to be the one to bring this beautiful woman back to life. He had wanted to be the one to show her how a *real* man treats a woman. Colt wanted Carlie and he had prayed and left it in God's hands. Now it seemed as though God was opening the doors and answering those prayers and Colt was thrilled. Although, even if God had not let Carlie be the one, Colt knew he had served a purpose in the woman's life and he would have been grateful to have been a small part of the miracle Carlie Michales had needed at the moment. But, it seemed as if God was opening the doors for something bigger and better than Colt could imagine. God was bringing Carlie to him.

"Carlie," Colt said. "I want you and the kids to move here. I really believe that God brought us together for a reason and I believe we are supposed to be together. I have been praying over you and for your family since the day I met you. Now I know it doesn't make any sense that two people could fall in love over such a short period of time, but I believe that God is making a way for us to be together and I believe he brought us together. Yes. The offer is still valid and I will do whatever you need me to do to help you move." Colt stopped there. He didn't tell Carlie he loved her. He would save that for the right moment when they were face to face.

Colt Storm was not one to jump the gun, but he was ready to buy a ring and ask Carlie Michaels to marry him. He would wait to pop the question, though. *Barkis is willin.* He reminded himself again. He knew that Carlie would need time to sell the house and pack and get moved out here. He would look for an apartment for her and the kids. Something temporary until he felt it was the right time to pop the question and they could make wedding plans. Colt could hear Carlie crying on the other end of the phone. "Oh, Colt. I am so relieved. I miss you and I need to be there with you and the kids are excited too." Colt smiled. "I miss you too, Carles. Just let me know what you need me to help you with and I will make arrangements to be there." Carlie agreed.

After talking for a few more minutes, Carlie bid Colt goodnight with promises that they would talk soon. Colt told Carlie that he would send her a check so that she could hire a realtor to sell the house. Carlie thanked him and bid him goodnight. As she hung up the phone, she leaned back against the headboard. She wiped the tears from her eyes and said a silent prayer. She thanked God for sending Colt into her life. Carlie could not believe how the events of her life had been changing over the last few weeks.

Carlie picked up the phone to call Laura. She knew it was late and that her friend would probably be in bed sleeping. Laura usually had to be at the store by seven a.m to run register for the early birds who were picking up their lunches for the day before going to work. She hated to wake Laura up, but Carlie could not wait to tell her best friend the news. Carlie Michaels was moving to Colorado!

Carlie dialed Laura's number. "Hello?" A sleepy voice answered on the other end. "Whoever this is calling better be dead or seriously injured!" Carlie could not help but to smile at Laura's humor. "Laura, it's Carlie. Sorry to be calling so late, but I just got off the phone with Colt Storm and I have some news." Laura sat up. She was awake now. "I'm awake. So what did you tell him?" She inquired, yawning and taking a sip of the water that was sitting on her night stand. "I told him that the kids and I would move to Colorado to be closer to him. I told Colt that if we were going to have a relationship that I don't do long distance ones and that I needed to be there with him." Laura smiled. "And.....?" She prompted. Carlie breathed deeply. "And he said he would do what he could to help us move. He is going to send me some money to hire a realtor and he would come up with a trailer to help us move. He is also going to be looking for a place for us." Laura was silent for a moment. "Not moving in with him?" She asked, as if shacking up with Colt Storm had been in the agreement of Colt helping Carlie move. "No, Laura. We both agreed that we should not move in together. We want to wait and make sure this is going to work and if it does get more serious, we want to wait until we get married."

Laura was beside herself with glee. "Married! Oh, Carles!" She exclaimed. "Hold your horses, Laura. I said *IF.* And that is a big IF. We both agree that we met for a reason, but it is going to be a big adjustment for Josh and Roxy and we also want to make sure they are ok with Colt and I being together. We really want to take time to get to know each other and he really wants to get to know the kids. The kids are going to have to adjust to a new town and a new school and a new relationship. We just want to take this slow and see where everything goes." Laura could understand that. She knew that the move would be a big change and adjustment for Josh and Roxanne. Carlie was right. Moving in with Colt Storm would not be wise at this juncture in her friend's life, but Laura also had a feeling that it would not be long before Colt Storm would be putting a ring on Carlie's finger. She kept that last part to herself, however.

"Carles, I am so happy for you! This is what you need for yourself and those kids. I'll help you too. I know a great realtor I can put you in touch with." Carlie thanked Laura. "Oh, Carles, just one more thing before we hang up. Promise me if you do get married, I get to be you maid of honor." Carlie grinned. "I promise." The two women bid each other good night with promises of having dinner and discussing the moving plans. For the first time in a long time, Carlie felt happy. She felt excited and a little anxious about the move. Yet, she knew that this was the right thing to do and deep down, Carlie knew that she had met a man who would stand by her side and love her and her children no matter what. She finally fell asleep with continued thanks to God above for sending

Colt Storm into her life.

After Colt had hung up with Carlie and waited in the waiting area of the local hostpital for his handy man to be released, he could not help but to offer up a silent prayer. He once again thanked God for bringing Carlie Michaels into his life and for allowing her to move closer to him. Colt took into consideration, however, the impact that the move and changes would have on Carlie's children. Carlie had informed him that both Roxy and Josh were excited about moving, but still, Colt couldn't help but wonder how the kids would fair once they actually moved here. He was aware of the fact that Roxanne and Josh would be starting a new school, would have to make new friends, get used to an even smaller town, and get used to their mother being in a new relationship. Colt hoped that he had made a good impression on both of Carlie's children during his brief encounter with them while in Ohio.

Roxanne did not seem to want him around, but Colt had taken her reaction to him wih a grain of salt, realizing that Roxy had seen him as just another man who would probably hurt her mother. He also knew that Roxy was having problems accepting the fact that her father was gone for good. Colt knew that deep down both of the kids had hoped that Joe would return or at least be a part of their lives. Colt could not even begin to imagine the pain and hurt and confusion Roxanne had endured from this last stunt Joe Welsh had pulled. No child deserved to be hurt as Carlie's children had been. No woman deserved to be hurt and to have to struggle the way Carlie has had to. Colt could only hope and pray that he would be able to step up and be the man that Carlie and her kids needed.

He would be, he decided. He would give them everything they needed and more than matertial needs and wants, he would give them the love and attention they all deserved. With God's help, Colt Storm would be the husband that Carlie Michaels needed and the father figure that her children needed. He hoped that he could end the struggle and the hurt that Carlie and her children had endured. Colt could not wait to begin his life and adventure with Carlie Michaels and her children.

Carlie had never felt more releived, excited, and happier

than she was feeling at this moment. As she climbed underneath her Grandmother's quilt, she reflected back over the events of the last few weeks since Colt Storm had entered her life. Looking from the outside in, one would think that Carlie had lost her mind for even considering uprooting her children and moving to Colorado to be with a man she barely knew. But Carlie knew that the move was the right thing. There was no explanation for it. There was just the knowing that her life was about to change for good, but for much better.

Carlie thought about the house and if it would sell quickly. She wondered if she should wait until after the holidays to sell and move. She wanted to have one more Thanksgiving and Christmas here before the move to Colt Storm. Then as if lightening had struck her, she sat straight up. She would have to tell her parents and her brothers that she was planning on selling the house and moving to Colorado. Her Mother! Carlie knew that her mother would not take the news easily. Although, Regina Michaels would want the best for her daughter, Carlie knew that her mother would do everything to persuade Carlie to stay put. Even with this thought, Carlie had peace that everything would work out. She decided to have one more holiday season here and then start the move in January. It would be the perfect fresh start to a brand new year. Thanksgiving was only a month away now and Carlie wanted to have a big dinner here at the house with her parents and brothers and their families.

Christmas, she decided, would be the big farewell party. She would go ahead and start looking for a realtor. Carlie figured it would take at least two to four months for the house to sell. Colt had informed her, though, that she could conduct all the real eastate business from Colorado. She could transfer her accounts to a bank there in Colorado and have the funds from the sell directly deposited into her bank account. Carlie wanted to be here when the house sold, however. She wanted to close the deal in person. After all, inspite of Colt's offer to help her with the move and the expenses of moving, Carlie did not want him to. She wanted to use the money from selling the house to pay for the moving expenses herself.

Carlie did not want to use Colt for his money. She was

starting to love him and she wanted to be the type of woman that wasn't going to be accused of being a gold digger. She wanted Colt to feel and to know that she really loved him and she wanted to be the woman for him that he deserved. Carlie giggled out loud. She could not believe she was already thinking about a marrying the man and planning a wedding! With these thoughts, Carlie drifted into a deep, peaceful sleep. Life was turning around for her and her children. God was working. The struggle was coming to an end.

Colt Storm left the hospital with Mark, his handy man, who had finally been released with a cast on his leg, crutches, and instructions from the hospital doctor to follow up with the bone doctor in three weeks to check the healing process. The doc had warned Colt that Mark would not be able to stand or work with the horses until his leg was completely healed. Colt, however, knew how stubborn Mark could be, and therefore decided that his handy man could wobble around to feed the horses if he chose to do so. On the other hand, Colt did not want the man to reinjure himself.

As he helped Mark into the truck, Colt said, "Now, you heard the Doc. I want you to take it easy on that leg. You have to heal properly now or you won't be any good to me or that wife and those kids of yours. You got it?" Mark nodded, grinning. Colt shook a finger at him. "Now, I mean it. Jane would kill me and you both if she knew I was letting you hobble around trying to work." Mark laughed. "Yeah she would. She is a good woman, but she would kill both of us. I promise, I'll follow the doc's orders and take it easy." Colt closed the door and climbed into the driver seat.

As Colt turned the key, causing the truck to roar to life, Mark turned to his boss. "Speakin of good women, what is happening with you and that lady you met in Ohio? What's her name again? Carol? Carrie?" Colt grinned. "Carlie. Her name is Carlie Michaels. And since you asked, she is moving to Colorado within the next couple of months. We are going to try and make something of this relationship or whatever this is that we have going on." Colt paused as he turned out of the hospital parking lot."I know it sounds crazy, but I really took to her when I was there and I think I am in love with her. She and her two kids have been through hell." Mark nodded. "Yeah, you told me."

Colt glanced over to his handy man. Mark was not only one

of Colt's best ranch hands, but had also become one of his best friends. "Well," Mark continued. "It's not what other folks think. It's what the two of you feel is the right thing to do. Now, I'm sure when she and her kids get out here, folks will ask a lot of questions, but as long as you think you will be happy, then go for it. You deserve a good woman, especially after that Jenna chick." Colt laughed. "I appreciate that, ole buddy. Now, let's get you home. I'm sure Jane is anxious to see you." Mark nodded. "Yep. She will be all worried." Colt turned down the gravel lane that led to Mark's stone house. After helping him out of the truck and instructing Jane to take good care of her husband, Colt returned to the truck and headed back to the ranch, once again with Carlie Michaels on his mind.

Chapter 20

The next morning, Carlie woke up with a start. She stretched and swung her feet over the side of the bed, feeling for her slippers as she did. She felt so much more energized this morning than she had in a very long time. Everything inside of her seemed to be dancing with glee. Carlie smiled as she thought about her conversations with Laura and then with Colt last night. Everything was falling into place.

As Carlie began to think about all the plans and phone calls she needed to be making, she felt every inch of a queen. In other words, she was finally starting to feel whole again; like a real person instead of the robot she had been feeling like. Carlie put on her robe, tying it as she headed down the stairs to brew her morning coffee. To her surprise, Roxy was already in the kitchen, fully dressed and eating waffles accompanied a by a glass of orange juice.

"Hey Mom." Roxy greeted Carlie. "Hi honey. You are up early." Carlie said as she poured water into the coffee maker and measured out the coffee grinds. "I couldn't sleep. I am so excited about moving and stuff. I can't wait to get out of this town!" Carlie smiled. "Well, it will take a couple of months at the very least for the house to sell and for us to pack and get moved." She paused as she reached into the cabinet and pulled out her favorite coffee mug. "I think we will have Thanksgiving and Christmas here one final time. Christmas will be our big farewell party." Roxy grinned. "Yay!"

Carlie laughed as she poured coffee into the mug, adding cream and sugar. "It will definitely be fun and exciting." Carlie told her daughter. "Josh is excited too. He snuck into my rom last night and we sat up and talked about moving and how great it is going to be to have new friends and a new school. Josh is especially excited about the horses and having a new 'dad.' I'm glad you and Colt met, Mom."

Carlie gasped. She wasn't surprised at the fact that her children were excited about startng over. She was, however, shocked at the fact that her son was already seeing Colt as a father figure. "Well, honey, you know you don't have to call Colt 'dad' if you don't want to. He really wants to get to know you guys and just be there for you." Roxy put her dishes in the sink and gave her mom a kiss on the cheek. "We know, Mom. But, I think he will be good for us and you too." With that, Roxy turned to grab her bag and head out the door to the bus, leaving her mother in a state of pure shock and happiness.

Just as Carlie had poured herself a second cup of coffee, Josh came bounding into the kitchen, throwing his book bag on the back of a chair. He rushed into Carlie's arms, giving her the biggest bear hug he could muster up. "I love you, Mommy." Carlie hugged him back. "I love you too, kiddo." Josh grabbed a bowl and poured himself some cereal. After adding the milk, he looked at Carlie and said,"You know, Mommy, I am glad that Colt is going to be our new dad. He seems nice and cool and he is a *real life cowboy!*" Carlie laughed. She loved her son's sense of humor. "Well, like I told Roxy, you guys don't have to call him Dad. He and I aren't married yet." Josh wiped a drop of milk off his mouth with his sleeve. "Don't worry, Mommy, you will be." Carlie smiled at her son. *Perhaps we will be.* She thought to herself. To Josh she said, "These things take a little time, honey. But, I suppose it is something that can happen. I do like Colt a lot." Josh put his bowl and spoon in the sink. Grabbing his backpack, he headed to the door. He paused as he turned back towards Carlie. "Mommy, I know you like Colt and I know I like Colt. Roxy likes Colt. So we are going to be a real family again. Love you. Bye!" With that, Carlie watched her son get on the bus.

She was stunned by the conversation that had just taken place with her eight year old son. He was too wise for his age. If her kids could foresee a marriage with Colt, then maybe she could too. After finishing her coffee, Carlie went back up to her bedroom to get dressed for the day. It was going to be another cold fall day in Ohio. As she pulled on her skinny jeans and her turquoise sweater, Carlie couldn't help but to wonder what autumn in Colorado was like. She wondered how Colt celebrated the holidays and she could not wait to experience it all with him.

Carlie ran a brush through her hair and applied a light coat of makeup and lip gloss. Slipping into her favorite fall boots, she made her way back down the stairs. She settled in at her desk to make the phone call she had been dreading to make since last night. She dialed the number. "Hello?" Came the older female voice from the other end of the phone. "Hey, Mom, it's Carlie." Mrs. Michaels sounded genuinely surprised to hear from her only daughter. "Carles! How are you!" Carlie smiled. "Mom, Listen. There is something important I need to tell you." Carlie began. "Is this about that young man who helped you with your truck a few weeks ago? Collin something or other?" Carlie placed her hand on her forehead. "His name is Colt, Mom, Colt Storm. And how did you hear about that anyway?" She waited as she could hear her mother rustling around in the kitchen. "Oh, Jay called me. He said he ran into Jack who owns the tow truck company in town and Jack told him all about how that Colt guy helped you with your truck and how Jack gave you another vehicle and how this Colt guy is head over heals for you."

Carlie was impressed at how much her mother knew even though her parents no longer lived in Ohio. Jay was the oldest of Carlie's two brothers. He was also the town male gossip. Carlie couldn't help but to laugh. Men always think that women are the gossipers. Yet, the males seem to do just as much gossiping as women. If Carlie had wanted her mother to know about Colt Storm, she would have called her like she was doing now.

"What's so funny, dear?" Regina Michaels interrupted her daughter's thoughts. Carlie had not realized that she had laughed out loud. "Oh nothing, Mom. I was just thinking how much men gossip." She paused. "Anyway, I am calling you because I have made a very difficult, but important decision. One that I believe will be beneficial to the kids and I." There was a second of silence. "Oh? And what would that be?" Carlie took a deep breath. "I have decided to move to Colorado with Roxy and Josh. That is where Colt is from and to be honest we need to get out of this small, gossiping town and go somewhere where we can just start over. I will be putting the house up for sale, but I am going to have one last holiday season here before I do. Do you think you and Dad could come up for the holidays?"

There was no immediate response for a few moments. Carlie knew that her mother was pondering on what Carlie had just unloaded on her. "Well Carles, are you sure? I mean, selling the house that you grew up in and that we gave you is one thing. But, uprooting your whole life for a man you have only known for a few short weeks, that's a whole different story. How do the kids feel about this? Have they met Colt?"

Carlie knew that her mother would be concerned. Carlie didn't have time to go into all the details of how she felt about Colt. "Mom, I can't explain to you how natural it feels to be with Colt Storm. When we talk, it is like we have known each other forever. As far as the kids are concerned, they are all for it. I just think this is the right move. Besides, it isn't like I am just jumping into another relationship or marriage. Joe does not want anything to do with the kids. We are not moving in with Colt. We are just moving there so we can really get to know him, but mostly to get a fresh start somewhere where the kids aren't getting teased and I'm not getting pity looks every time I turn the corner. It has been a year since Joe left. The divorce is final and it's time for us to move on." Carlie explained. She felt like she had to defend herself. Regina Michaels could be very condescending at times and Carlie knew this would be one of those times. This was a defining moment in her life and she knew her mother would not take it well. Carlie expected the perverbial motherly lecture of the how's and why's and are you sure you know what you are doing. However, Carlie also wanted her mother to trust her enough to know that she was making the right decision. After all, Carlie was thirty-eight, not fifteen.

As Carlie explained the details of selling the house and moving to her mother, she couldn't help but to just feel more excited about it all. She had to again defend her relationship with Colt Storm. Regina Michaels just did not understand how her daughter could just up and move herself and the kids to Colorado to be with a man she had just met a few weeks ago. Carlie finally stopped trying to explain what she had felt with Colt and what he felt and wanted with her. Carlie knew that her mother would never understand, but she also knew without a shadow of a doubt that she was doing the right thing. Carlie finally bid her mother goodbye and replaced the phone in its cradle.

Emotionally exausted from their mother-daughter conversation, Carlie decided to get out of the house for a little while. She would hit the local library for a good book to read. She had finished the *Nora Roberts* book she had been reading and was in search of new material to read. Maybe a good *James Patterson* or *Mary Higgins Clark* thriller would be the cure. Or maybe she would find some new author to read. Who knows? The library was full of books waiting to be read. After the library, she would treat herself to lunch at the local deli. A turkey reuben at *Jen's Deli* with a side of *Jen's* famous potato salad and a coke would be just the thing.

Carlie smiled as she lifted her keys from the wood key holder that hung on her wall beside the front door and headed out. She knew there would be certain things she would miss in this town, such as the deli, but she was also looking forward to new and better adventures in Colorado with Colt Storm. Carlie unlocked the doors to the SUV just as an unfamiliar car pulled up in front of the house. Carlie turned to face the uninvited stranger. A woman got out of the car. She was fairly tall and lim with shoulder-length auburn hair. She was dressed in a navy skirt, white shirt, and suit jacket.

"Hi." She greeted Carlie. "My name is Meghan Crone. I am the owner and realtor of *Crone Realtors* located in Lebanon." Carlie nodded and shook Meghan's hand. "Hi. I'm Carlie Michaels. What can I do for you?" Meghan stepped into the driveway, holding a portfolio in her hands. "I recieved a call this morning from a Jack Bryant. He owns a tow company here in town. He said he got a call from a Colt Storm in Colorado and asked him if he knew of a good real estate agent and Jack contacted me. He said you were looking to sell the house." Carlie nodded. She was still a little fuzzy on what was happenning. "Um...yes. I am wanting to sell the house and move to Colorado with my two kids. It's a three bedroom." Meghan smiled. "Do you have a few moments? I would love to take a look inside and we can sit and discuss figures."

Carlie shut the door to her vehicle and ushered Meghan inside. Thankfully, Carlie had cleaned the house up last night before going to bed. She led Meghan upstairs first, showing the agent the three bedrooms and the bathroom."I see all the bedrooms have great nice-sized walk-in closets. That will up the selling price for sure. And the master bathroom has a hot tub with a nice-sized separate shower. Also good." After Megahn had taken her notes down on the upstairs, the two women descended down the steps.

Carlie led the realtor into the living room and the downstairs bathroom and finally the kitchen. "I see the kitchen has a nice little mudroom off to the back of it." Carlie nodded. "Shall we sit down and talk selling price?" Carlie pulled out a chair at the table for Meghan. "Would you like some coffee or something to drink?" Carlie offered. "Jut a glass of ice water would be fine. Thank you." Meghan accepted. Carlie fished out a glass and filled it with ice. After filling the glass with water, she joined Meghan at the table.

"I'm sorry. I am just a little hazy on how this happened so quickly. I mean I just spoke to Colt las night." Meghan grinned at her and Carlie decided that she liked the woman. "I know. The man did not waste any time. He seemed anxious to get you to Colorado from what Jack told me." Carlie couldn't help but to smile. "Ok. Down to business." Meghan said. "Now, the house is in excellent condition. Of course, we will have to have it appraised and see what it is worth and we will work from there. But from what I have seen, I would estiamte the selling price to be right around $80,000. Maybe more. But you will definitely get a good price for it, even after closing costs." Carlie nodded as the two women stood. She shook Meghan's hand. "Ok. Well, thank you." She managed, unsure of what to really say being that this was just sprung on her without any warning.

She led Meghan to the door and opened it. Megahan handed Carlie a business card. "Listen, I will call the appraiser this afternoon and will call you. We will set up a time where he can come out and appraise the house and we will go from there." Carlie again thanked Meghan and gave the woman her cell number. After Meghan left, Carlie climbed into the SUV and headed to the library and lunch alone, still pondering what had just happened. She would have to call Colt tonight and remind him that she needed a warning before real estate agents just showed on her front porch out of nowhere. Of course she would tell him in a teasing, friendly sort of way. Carlie pulled out of the drive and turned to head to the library.

Well Carles, at least you have a good real estate agent. Now all you have to do is start planning for the holidays and the farewell party at Christmas and start packing. Carlie dreaded all the packing that would have to be done. She knew she could count on Laura to help her. Colt said he would come up and help load everything. Carlie hoped the house would sell for a decent price. She would put her profit from the sale into the bank. She needed to research schools and jobs near where Colt lived. As these thoughts circled through her mind, Carlie knew there was a lot to be done. Yet, she knew she would not regret this decision. This move would change her life for the best. It would allow her kids to be free from the gossip and teasing as well. Carlie smiled as she found a spot in front of the library's steps.

Carlie entered through the glass doors. As she browsed the shelves of books, deciding which book would take her on the next reading adventure. She had forgotten how much she loved coming to the library. She loved the smell of old books. She loved to browse the shelves lined with endless possibilities. Carlie decided to check to see if the library had a book on Colorado as well. Since she was moving there, she figured she might as well find out all she could about the state, specifically the part of Colorado where Colt lived and where she would be moving her family to. Carlie approached the reference desk. The librarian gave her a list of books on Colorado and pointed Carlie to the geographical section. Carlie took her time browsing through the list. She picked two books that seemed to be most pertinent to what she was looking for. After choosing the books on Colorado, Carlie made her way back to the fiction and mystery aisles. She decided on a *James Patterson* novel. She looked at the title; *"The Murder House"*. Just when she thought she had read every *Patterson* novel ever written, Carlie was amazed to find one that she hadn't read. She walked over to the shelves where new books were placed. She picked up a new novel by *Tami Hoag*. Satisfied with her selections, Carlie walked over to the movie section. She figured she would pick out a couple of movies for the kids to watch; one for Josh, one for Roxy, one for herself and one or two they could all watch together. After making her selections, Carlie checked out the books and movies at the desk and exited the library.

Chapter 21

Carlie pulled out of the library parking lot and turned down Main Street. As she cruised down the street, deciding which restaurant she wanted to catch an early lunch in, Carlie thought again about how fast everything was suddenly happening. She could only believe that this was God's will otherwise why would everything be falling into place the way it was? True that Carlie had not actually attended a church service since the affair and divorce. The fact was that she had blamed God and had a very difficult time forgiving Joe. Mostly Carlie knew that she had to forgive herself for any part she had played in the whole divorce.

She realized the affair had not been her fault. But, she also acknowledged that she had not been very pleasant during the divorce proceedings. In fact, her attorney had warned her several times to keep her lips sealed. Carlie had been so hurt and devastated that she had wanted to lash out and call Joe every ungodly name she could think of. But for the sake of her children, Carlie had refrained. Instead, she had gone home and screamed every name she wanted to call Joe to her walls. Oh, she had called him a few to his face. She was not going to just stand by and let him not be punished somehow. But now, a year later, Carlie had been able to forgive Joe and herself. She no longer blamed God for her marriage falling apart. She was pretty certain that Colt Storm had played a big part in the healing and forgiving process.

Carlie wondered if she would have been able to heal and forgive had Colt never crossed her path. She started fervently believing that God had sent Colt to her, not just for her time of need, but maybe forever. Maybe God was showing her love again. Carlie thought about church, the children she used to teach in Sunday school and the worship band Joe had led. The perfect family in church; literal hell outside of church. Her and Joe's marriage had been a fake. They had wanted everyone to believe that they were the quintessential American family. She and Joe had put on the show to it's fullest. They had been high school lovers turned into the perfect ccouple. They had been church goers and leaders in the church. To top off the façade, two children, one boy and one girl. They had become the ultimate American dream, the perfect family. All that had been stripped away.

Now, Carlie was not really grateful that it all had happened the way it had, but she could forgive, heal and move on. She could think about church again...maybe. The thing was Carlie wanted to attend church. She just could not bear the looks and sideways glances and the whisperings of gossiping women. Church was supposed to be a safe place, yet whenever Carlie had stepped through the doors, she had been looked upon like one of those lepers that the Bible talks about, being cast away in exile outside the city gates. Carlie could not stand it any longer and that is why she never went back to church. Maybe in Colorado, she could go to church with Colt. At least there, there would be no one casting her pitiful or accusing glances. In Colorado, there wouldn't be mean kids teasing Roxy and Josh. No one would know Carlie Michaels and her two children. It woud truly be a fresh start; a chance to truly start over and to be free from all the struggles she had faced here in small town, Ohio.

Carlie smiled to herself as she turned back through town and headed towards downtown to *Jen's Deli*. A turkey ruben and *Jen's* infamous potato salad would be just the cure for Carlie's hunger. She would take a book inside with her to read while she ate. Rule number one for eating alone was to never be unarmed. Always have a book on hand to read or a paper and pen to make it appear as if you are writing a letter or in Carlie's case, the start of the next great novel. *Now wouldn't that be something.* Carlie thought to herself as she parked the car in a parking space. *I could be the next great novelist.* Carlie grinned to herself as she grabbed the *Tami Hoag* mystery novel and headed into the deli. As she waited in line to order her food, Carlie wondered what kind of book she would write if given the chance to do so. Maybe the next great murder mystery or the next greatest love story, or an autobiography. She could title the autobiography *The Story Of Me.* Carlie entertained the thought for a moment. *Wouldn't that be something, Carles. You, the next best selling novelist!* Carlie shook her head as she stepped up to the counter and ordered her sandwich with a side of potato salad and a coke.

***

Colt entered the ranch house exhausted from the day and from the long wait at the hospital. He grabbed a cold pop from the refrigerator and settled down on the sofa to take off his boots. As he opened the can, a smile tugged at the corner of his mouth. He remembered the days of grabbing a cold beer out of the fridge and Jenna pouring herself a glass of red wine. Colt remembered the arguments he and Jenna had had over her spending his money on frivolous items such as *Guci* handbags she didn't need or another $600 dress that would she would only wear once or twice and then hang in the back of the closet and never wear again. Colt shook his head. Oh how much he had changed since those days. Breaking up with Jenna and kicking her out of his house was the best thing he could have ever done.

Shortly after the hostile break-up with Jenna, he had found the Lord and his life had really begun to change. Now there was Carlie Michaels. Colt leaned back against the couch as he took a sip of the ice cold Pepsi. Images of Carlie danced in his head. The very first time he had seen her, he was in love. Well, not in love per se, but definitely attracted. He laughed at out loud at the memory of seeing her kicking her truck and yelling at it. She had been at what he thought was her worst and still he had been instantly attracted to the woman. He had had no idea how complicated of a woman Carlie Michaels really was and how complicated her life was until he started to actually talk to her. Even after everything he knew that had happened to her and to her children; her husband's affair and all that, Colt still wanted to be with her. Oh, Colt was fully aware of how difficult it would be to gain Carlie's interest, let alone her trust. Yet, somehow he had. He credited that accomplishment to God. There was just no other explanation as to why and how Carlie Michaels seemed to have trusted him from the start.

Colt had stopped trying to figure out the whys and the hows. He had just trusted God to work. Colt often wondered if he could have been as strong as Carlie Michaels had been if the shoe was on the other foot. At least with Jenna, the choice to break up with her had been his. Carlie did not ask for her husband to have an affair and to write off his children. Yet somehow, behind the pain and the countless tears Colt knew Carlie had to have cried, she stood strong and had rallied for her children. And, Colt knew, that had been no easy task. The woman was strong. Yet, Colt had been able to see a happy, relaxed, and fun Carlie Michaels. He imagined the fun and happy Carlie was the true woman.

Now, as he contemplated Carlie and her kids moving here to Colorado with him, Colt had a lot of work and planning to do. He had called Jack and set in motion for a well-known and good real estate agent to contact Carlie. Colt needed to go back to Ohio and help Carlie as much as he could. He had to finish out the week in the furniture store. He needed to pay some attention to the store and see how business was doing. He would go in first thing in the morning and get the sales results for the month as well as see what new items were being made and what the best sellers were. Colt had insisted from the start of the business that every piece of furniture would be hand crafted. He himself had made many of the pieces, his favorite being the antique style rocking chairs. Colt would visit the store first thing in the morning. He would spend the week handling the store's business. Then on the weekend he would book a flight to Ohio to see Carlie Michaels and to discuss moving plans and arrangements with the woman he loved.

Colt woke up at the crack of dawn. After checking on the ranch hands and checking on Mark, Colt took a shower and dressed for his business day. He put on a pair of Levis, a blue button down flannel shirt and his good brown boots. He ran a comb through his hair and trimmed his five-o-clock shadow. Satisfied with his appearance, Colt headed out. He decided to stop at the diner for breakfast before going to the furniture store. Once inside the diner, he ordered the farmer's breakfast which included scrambled eggs, bacon, pancakes, and hash browns. He orderd coffee with a glass of orange juice. Colt grabbed a copy of the newspaper to read while he ate breakfast. Colt Storm had a rule: Whenever eating alone always have something to read. As he ate, Colt wondered what Carlie was eating this morning. He wondered what she would be doing today. It was getting closer to Thanksgiving and he imagined that Carlie was decorating her house and getting ready for the holidays. Colt smiled to himself as he caught himself thinking about Carlie Michaels. Just as he had swallowed the last gulp of orange juice, he heard a familiar voice coming from beside his table. "Well, well, well, if it isn't Colt Storm.: Colt looked up to see Jenna standing beside his table. "Are you going to ask a lady to join you?" She said, smiling. Jenna was dressed to the tilt. Her long hair cascaded down her back. She was wearing black leggings with a long black and silver cowl neck sweater and black high-healed boots. Colt smiled politely. "I was just leaving, but it is nice to see you, Jenna." He stood up, but Jenna blocked him. She stood between Colt and the exit. "Oh I miss you, cowboy. We used to have good times." Colt did not reply. "Come on cowboy," Jenna purred, running a finger down the buttons of his shirt. "Take me out to dinner tonight and let's have some fun." Colt politely went around her. "Sorry Jenna, I am seeing someone and I am no longer interrersted. Have a good day." With that Colt made his exit, leaving Jenna standing in the diner alone. Outside, Colt shook his head. *Unbelievable!* He thought to himself. *That girl has some nerve!* Colt climbed into his truck and headed to his store. He turned his thoughts back to Carlie.

She was the one he wanted. Jenna had been history for a long time now and there was no way Colt would ever go back to her. Colt was falling in love with Carlie Michaels. He decided that once Carlie and her kids were settled in, he would ask her to marry him. Colt smiled as he pulled into the store's parking lot. Yes. He decided. Carlie Michaels would soon be Mrs. Colt Storm. Colt hoped and prayed that Carlie would agree to be his wife. After all, she was the one he had been searching to find. She was the one that he longed and needed to be with. Colt knew that there was no one else for him. Carlie Michaels was the one.

As Colt drove to the store, he hoped that after dismissing her at the diner that Jenna would leave him alone now. He had not expected to see her back in town. He thought that Jenna had moved to California or somewhere but there she had been, back in Colorado. Colt shook his head. As long as the ocean was wide, Colt would never go back back to Jenna. She had tried to seduce him by running her fingers down his shirt, but he had not responded in any way. The old Colt would have jumped at the chance to have a little "fun" with her, but the new Colt would not give it a second thought. Colt Storm was not the same man and he had his sights and heart and soul set on one woman only; Carlie Michaels. There was nothing and there was no one who was going to change his mind. Try as Jenna may, and Colt hoped that she wouldn't try anymore, Colt was committed to Carlie. He wanted nothing more to get Carlie here to Colorado and ask her to marry him. If he had things his way, Carlie would be down here tomorrow. However, Colt knew that Carlie had to pack and get everything ready for the house to sell. Colt prayed that the house would sell quickly as he was anxious to start the rest of his life with Carlie Michaels.

Chapter 22

Thanksgiving was approaching quickly. Carlie busied herself with menu preparations along with entertaining potential buyers for the house. It was Friday and the kids would be out of school the very next Wednesday for Thanksgiving break. Carlie kissed Roxy and Josh goodbye and sent them off to school. She had one appointment this morning at 10:00 to show a new couple the house. Meghan was going to meet her at 9:30 to go over the details of the couple's offer. The house had been appraised at $90,000. Carlie would be happy to get at least $80,00 out of it.

She watched the school bus pull away and turned to start a pot of coffee. She was also setting some appetizers out. She set the temp on the oven and pulled the mini quiches out of the freezer. They looked delicious even frozen as she set them on a cookie sheet to bake. She also had bought some muffins just in case her guests did not like egg, bacon, sundried tomato and cheese quiches. She took out a serving plate and arranged the blueberry and banana nut muffins and sat the plate in the middle of the table. She glanced up at the clock. It was 9:20. Ten minutes until Meghan arrived. With the coffee going and the quiches baking, Carlie had a few minutes to spare to get her mind on the meeting. Meghan had stated that the couple had shown a real interest in the house.

Carlie set the table with small plates and coffee mugs. She took the creamer out of the refrigerator and set it, along with the sugar on the table. Exactly at 9:30 the door bell rang and Carlie greeted Meghan. "Hi. Come on in." Meghan stepped over the threshold and Carlie closed the door behind her. "It smells delicious in here." Meghan commented as the two women made their way into the kitchen where Carlie had just pulled the quiches out of the oven and had arranged them on a separate platter. Carlie poured Meghan a cup of coffee and then herself before joining the real estate agent at the table.

Meghan pulled out the papers from her briefcase. She sat the pile of documents on the table. The documents included the selling contract along with several photos of the house, both inside and outside. Carlie was anxious to see what the couple was offering for the home where she had spent all of her life. Now as the reality of actually selling the only home she had ever known hit her, Carlie felt a little pang of sadness. Even though she wanted nothing more than to be with Colt, Carlie still couldn't help but to feel somewhat saddened by the prospect of never seeing this place again.

The door bell rang and Carlie excused herself as she went to greet the prospective buyers. "Hi. Come on in." She greeted them as she opened the door. "Hi. You must be Carlie. I'm Mike Hanes and this is my new bride Jane." Carlie smiled at the lovely beaming couple. Jane was beautiful and radiant standing approximately 5'6" with shoulder-length auburn hair, green eyes and a figure any woman would die to have. Mike was handsome and beaming at no less than 6' with curly brown hair and brown eyes. Carlie estimated the couple to be barely in their twenties. Both still had that child like way about them. Carlie remembered being young and in love and newly married. She hoped that the couple would last. She led Mike and Jane into the kitchen. After seating them at the table, she poured them coffee and told them to help themselves to the appetizers. Jane reached for a quiche and Mike chose two quiches and a blueberry muffin. Carlie seated herself at the head of the table.

"Ok." Meghan said once everyone was settled. "As you know, Carlie wants to make sure that she is selling to the right buyers. This house was where she and her two brothers grew up. She has lived here all her life. So you can see it is more than just a piece of nice property. It is a home and she wants nothing more than for it to continue to be a home." Meghan addressed Mike and Jane. Mike nodded. "We understand that perfectly. And we have decided to make an offer. I think you will find it more than generous. We may be young, but we both have graduated college. I have a business degree in finance and Jane has just passed the bar to become a defense attorney." Carlie smiled. "Congratulations to both of you. Those are quite some accomplishments, Any children in the future?" Jane blushed just a little. "Oh yes. We both want children some day. At least three."

Carlie couldn't help but notice how Mike affectionately squeezed his bride's hand. Meghan pulled out the contracts. "We are ready to hear your offer." She addressed Mike. Mike took out a pen and wrote the offer on a piece of paper and slid it to Meghan who seemed to be a little shocked at the price he had written down. She slid the paper to Carlie who was equally shocked. Both Meghan and Carlie were at a loss of words for a moment. "Could you excuse us just for a moment?" Meghan said to Mike and Jane. "I woud like to discuss the offer with Carlie. Feel free to take another look around the house."

Once the couple exited the kitchen and Meghan was sure they were out of hearing range, she addressed Carlie. "This is quite a bit more than what the house was even appraised at. They want the furniture too." Carlie took another look at the price Mike had scribbled on the paper. "$150,000! Can they afford that? I don't want to accept the offer only to find out that they can't afford it and have to go through trying to resell the house." Meghan nodded. "I agree. I think before you agree to this offer we should talk to them some more. I will request as much financial information as possible." Carlie took a deep breath. "I suppose I could sell them some of the furniture, but not all of it. I want to keep the kids bedroom sets as well as mine. I also want to keep my good dishes as they were my grandmother's. The rest I would be willing to part with." Meghan nodded. "Let's bring them back in and talk to them some more." Carlie nodded as she refilled her and Meghan's coffee cups.

An hour and a half later, Carlie agreed to the offer. After careful researching into the new couple's finances and their backgrounds, both Meghan and Carlie agreed that the Cranes were not only legitimate, but could handle the responsibility. The transaction was not as grueling as Carlie expected it to be. The couple was pleasant and had willingly given Meghan all the information needed to complete the deal. After the contracts were signed and Meghan had walked out with the couple, Carlie cleaned up the dishes and put away the left over food. She took a deep breath and wondered if she should call Colt or wait until tonight. He was probably busy working at the ranch or his furniture business. She decided it would be best to wait until this evening to call him as he would more likely be available to talk to her. She would need his full attention on this one.

As she exited the kitchen, Carlie debated on how to spend the rest of her day. Her brain was on overload with all the decisions that now had to be made. The house had sold quicker than either she or Meghan had expected it to. Carlie had to decide whether or not to stay for Christmas or move to Colorado after Thanksgiving and spend Christmas and New Year's in their new home and with Colt. The decision to move, Carlie guessed, would all depend on how fast she could pack. She had sold all the furniture along with the house with the exception of the bedroom sets and her grandmother's china, including the tea set.

Carlie decided that a Thanksgiving shopping trip was what she needed to clear her head. She still had a few hours before the kids would start coming home from school. Roxy would be able to stay home a few minutes alone should Carlie run a little late. Carlie was amazed at the way Roxy's attitude had changed since she had told her they were moving. Carlie would break the news to the kids tonight about the house selling. She hoped they would be as excited as she was. She would also discuss their holiday plans with the kids and go by what Roxy and Josh decided to do.

The Hanes' had said they wouldn't be able to move in until after Christmas so if need be Carlie could have one last Christmas at the house. Part of her, though, wanted to spend Christmas with Colt. Carlie shook her head as she grabbed her purse and keys and headed out. She decided to go to Wal-Mart to do all-in-one shopping. She could browse for table cloths and other decorations. She may even splurge for new outfits for her and the kids. She locked the door and climbed into the SUV. Just as she was ready to close the door, she heard footsteps approaching.

"Hey darlin, where are you in a rush to?" Carlie turned just in time to see Colt striding up the driveway. She climbed out the car and blinked a few times to make sure she wasn't seeing things. "Colt! What are you doing here in Ohio?! At my house!" She ran into his arms. "Well now I am glad to see you too." Colt said as he enveloped Carlie in his arms. Carlie let him hold her for a few moments. It felt so amazing to be in his arms. She finally forced herself to let go as she looked into his eyes. "You didn't answer my question." She said smiling up at him. He smiled back at her. "You didn't give me a chance to answer." Carlie grinned. "Fair enough. So what are you doing here?"

Colt walked her back to the car. "Well, I took care of

business at the store and decided to take a spur of the moment flight to help you with the house and stuff and to see where you are at with everything." Carlie smiled. "I was going to call you tonight and give you the news." She paused. "I was headed to the store, but would you like to go get some lunch instead? We can talk about everything." Colt grinned at her. "I'd like that very much." The couple climbed into Carlie's vehicle and headed to the Mexican restaurant in town.

Carlie let Colt drive. She settled into the passenger seat. She could not believe he was here. He had actually taken a last minute flight to see her! She could not be more happy than she was at this moment. She could not wait to tell him that the house had sold and how much she got for it. Colt drove with one hand on the wheel and the other he clasped around Carlie's hand. He was beaming at her. She looked amazing today in those jeans and white sweater and boots. She had worn her hair fully down, which he absolutely loved. She had a very light amount of make up on; another one his favorite things about her. Carlie Michaels was just a beautiful woman inside and out. Colt could not wait to have her as his forever. He knew that she was bursting to tell him some news. He had a feeling it was about the house. He wondered if Carlie and her kids would be moving to Colorado quicker than either of them expected. He had some news of his own to tell Carlie. He had already found a great place for her and her kids as well as a school for her to attend if she still decided she wanted to take classes. He had also found a part-time job for her, providing she liked to cook. Colt, of course, was not going to force anything on Carlie Michaels. He just wanted to present her with what he had been able to find based on what she had told him she wanted to do and be. She, of course, could decide for herself if she wanted the job or go to school or even wanted the house he had found. Colt was excited to have Carlie and the kids to move closer to him. He was prepared to even let Carlie come to his store and pick out some of his furniture. Colt could imagine Carlie sitting on his porch in one the rocking chairs he had made. He imagined her sipping coffee and reading her Bible or a favorite novel.

Colt pulled into the parking lot and parked. He slid out of the driver's seat and walked around to open the door for Carlie. She smiled at Colt as she took his hand. He held her hand all the way into the restaurant. Carlie kept glancing at him, smiling, still not believing that Colt flew here just to help her out with the house and moving preparations. Mostly she was thrilled that he wanted to see her; wanted to be with her. And she did not mind delaying her holiday shopping plans one bit. She could go tomorrow and if Colt wanted to, he could tag along.

Once inside, the couple was seated at a booth in the corner. The restaurant was fully decorated in traditional Mexican motif. There were pinatas hanging from the ceiling in various forms of animals and dragons. The walls were painted sunset orange and yellow. The tables were dark cherry wood and the seats were chushioned with seat pillows that matched the walls. The lights were dim and it gave the place a more calm romantic feeling. Carlie and Colt both ordered Pepsis to drink.They requested the waiter to give them a few minutes to look over the menu.

"So, Carlie Michaels does drink more than sweet tea." Colt teased. Carlie laughed. "Oh I love my Pepsi." Carlie answered him. Colt smiled as he looked over the menu. He decided on the combination lunch which included one enchilada, one taco, and one chilli releno. He opted for the spanish rice but no refried beans. Carlie decided on steak fajitas with spanish rice on the side. As they waited for their order, Carlie decided to break the news to Colt. "I still can not believe you flew here just to see me." She began. "I was going to call you tonight to tell you that I sold the house this morning to a young newly married couple."

Colt could not believe what Carlie was telling him. "What! Are you serious?" Carlie nodded. "And to make the news even sweeter, let me tell you what it sold for. Well, first let me tell you what it was appraised for." She paused. "The house was appraised at $90,000. But, the Hanes, that is the name of the couple, offered $150,000! They bought the house plus all the furniture I decided I didn't want to keep." Colt was speechless for a moment. Carlie took a sip of her Pepsi as she waited for his response. Colt took Carlie's hands in his. "That is amazing! I can not believe Meghan found a buyer for you so soon!" Carlie beamed. "Yes. But we did check into their backgrounds and financials before accepting the offer. Meghan and I were both a little concerned when the offer was first made that they would not be able to keep up the payments and I did not want to be stuck in the position of having to resell the house." Colt nodded. "Makes sense."

He agreed noting just how intelligent this woman sitting across from him was. He had seen from the beginning that no one pulled the wool over the eyes of the smart and beautiful Carlie Michaels. "But," Carlie continued. "After an hour and half of looking at their finances and talking with them, I accepted the offer." She paused there as the waiter brought the food and sat it on the table. "Thank you." Carlie and Colt said in unison. After the waiter left them to eat, Colt turned his attention back to Carlie. "So when are you thinking about moving?" Carlie thought for a moment as she pulled a warm tortilla from the warmer and loaded it with the steak, onions and peppers, and sour cream. "I'm not sure. The Hanes' can't move in until after New Year's. I don't want to be packing during Christmas. So I am thinking that right after Thanksgiving would probably be best. I was going to celebrate one last Christmas here but then that would only leave a week to pack everything and move." Colt was studying her. Her expression was thoughtful. He could tell that Carlie had been thinking long and hard about moving and the right time to do so.

"Well, I think you are making the right decision. At least once you get moved, you and the kids can celebrate Christmas and you won't have all the stress of packing and being muddled." He paused there as he took a bite of the chilli releno. Carlie nodded, taking another bite of the fajita. Cheese dripped from her lip and she quickly grabbed a napkin to wipe her mouth. The fajitas tasted heavenly. She took a sip of her cold pop. "I agree. I called my Mom last night and told her that I was selling the house and moving. She was not too thrilled, but I told her I was doing what I feel is best for me and the kids." Colt could hear the frustration in her voice, even though he knew she was trying to be strong. He didn't know much about her relationship with her mother, but Colt could tell that Carlie was struggling with whatever the conversation had been with her Mom.

"Was she ok with your decision, your mom that is." Carlie nodded. "Yeah. I think it is just the fact that the house was her and Dad's and they gave it to me. It's never left the family and Mom is just nostalgic that way. She has a hard time letting go." Carlie paused and smiled. "She really had a hard time when I moved out and married Joe. I am the baby of the family and the only girl so it was really difficult for her. I think she cried for weeks." Carlie laughed out loud. "I love my Mom, but I need to move on and I think I finally got her to understand." She paused there as she finished off her last fajita and took a drink of Pepsi. Carlie set down her glass and wiped her mouth before continuing.

"At first I felt a little guilty about selling the house since it has always been in the family. I mean after all, it was where my brothers and I grew up. But then, the more I think about staying here, the more I know it is the right decision, selling the house and moving. Besides, there's this really hot guy in Colorado that I am dying to be closer to and to get know better."

Colt took notice of the teasing gleam in her eyes. He crossed his arms on the table. "Oh, is that so? Do I know him?" Carlie grinned. "You might. He is tall. Dark hair. Owns a furniture store in which he sells handcrafted furniture. He also owns a horse ranch and is very generous when it comes to rescuing damsels in distress." They both laughed out loud. "Well," Colt said, "It was quite a sight walking up on this beautiful woman who was kicking and screaming at her truck." Carlie laughed. "You will never know how embarrassed I was when I saw you walking up to me." Colt reached across the table and took her hands in his. "You were quite a sight, darlin'. Even at what seemed to be one of your weakest moments, you were still beautiful."

Carlie blushed. She didn't quite know how to respond to Colt's compliments. She was not used to the compliments and the kind gestures this man had been giving and showing to her. "I was a hot mess." She laughed. The waiter came and handed Colt the check. Carlie thought it was amazing how waiters and waitresses always assumed the man was the one paying for the meal. Sure, 99% of the time the man paid, but there was that one percent when the woman wanted to pay, or they split the check. However, today, Carlie didn't mind. She would let Colt pay for anything his big heart desired. Carlie was by no means a gold digger and she would never ask Colt for money, but if he wanted to buy things for her, she certainly was not going to turn him down.

Like this lunch for instance, if Colt insisted on paying, then she would let him. However, since she was the one who suggested they come here to eat lunch, Carlie felt obligated to at least offer to pay for her part of the meal. She started to take out her wallet, but Colt quickly stopped her by subtly shaking his head no. He winked at her as he handed the waiter his credit card. Carlie smiled and replaced her wallet back inside her purse. "Thank You." Was all Carlie could manage to say. "I would have paid for my half." Colt shook his head. "I wouldn't have it any other way." He said. Then, taking her hand in his, Colt Storm decided it was time to tell this woman exactly how he felt. There was no holding back now. No more waiting. Carlie was uprooting her life to move close to him and Colt knew it was time to say the words he had been dying to say to Carlie Michaels for some time now. Colt knew that Carlie had probably been thinking about moving out of this town anyway with everything that had happened to her. But, he also knew that she had made the decision to move to his state and his town to be with him.

"Carlie, I can't hold this in any longer. I flew up here because I wanted to see how you were getting along and how the house selling was going. I wanted to see you." He paused as he took her left hand in his. Then, reaching into the pocket of his jeans with his free hand, he took out a small black velvet box. He let the box sit on his lap as he wanted to tell Carlie how he felt and to see her reaction before actually presenting her with the object cradled carefully in the box. Colt continued to speak. "Umm I am not sure how to tell you this, but I......" Carlie squeezed his hand. *Oh boy.* Colt thought. *I love this woman! Now I Just gotta tell her. Come on, Colt, you can do this.* "I..um...." Carlie smiled, tears glistening in her eyes. "I know. I love you too."

Colt looked deep into her eyes. He saw it then. All the feelings she felt for him that she had held in were there in her deep brown love you-need you eyes. There was gratefulness, passion, and love. "Carlie, I love you. I know this is really fast since we've known each other for only a short time, but I can't help how I feel. I never just jump into a relationship, but since that first moment I saw you, I knew there was something there. Then, listening to your story, man girl, I just wanted to grab you up right then and kiss you." Carlie lowered her head just a little. "I know." She said softly.

"I really didn't mean to lay all that on a perfect stranger. It was just that it had been such an awful day and you were the first adult that happened to cross my path." She stopped there. Colt waited for her to continue. "And to be honest, I felt it too. I wasn't sure if it was because I felt vulnerable or because you were so darn handsome, caring and generous. I just felt like I could talk to you. To be honest, I thought for sure you would not call me after I practically dumped all my garbage in your lap." Now it was Colt who laughed. "Well darlin', I fell for you right then and there sitting in my truck waiting on Jack to come and tow yours." Carlie lifted her head and smiled. "Well, whatever happens, Colt Storm, I am glad that the good Lord above brought you into my life."

Colt grinned at that statement. Now he knew it was time. He took the velvet box and held it in his hand. He stood and walked over to Carlie where he knelt on one knee, taking her left hand in his. He opened the box revealing a heart shaped diamond surrounded by smaller, more delicate aqua colored stones with a sterling silver band. "Carlie Michaels, will you do the honor of being my bride and my partner for life and beyond?" Colt asked her. Carlie threw her arms sround his neck. "Yes! Yes, Colt Storm I will be your wife!" They stood together, embraced in each other's arms. The other patrons in the restaurant looked on as if the couple were putting on the latest love story off of *Broadway.* The audience cheered and clapped when Carlie said yes. Then just as quickly as they had cheered, the onlookers went back to thier lunches and thier conversations about their businesses and relationships and such.

Carlie let go of Colt and sat back down. She couldn't stopped staring at the ring. "It is so beautiful!" Colt beamed like a high school boy who had just given his class ring to the hot girl in school. "I knew you liked turquoise and silver so I had the jewelry store special order this ring." Carlie smiled at him. It was much more than a ring, she knew. Colt had taken the time to have one made just for her. He could have just picked out some nice big expensive rock to put on her finger, but he had put a lot of thought into this ring and had given her something that was her and just for her. She couldn't love anything more.

"I love you, Colt, and I can't wait to move to Colorado to be with you and to start our lives together." Colt nodded. "Me too, darlin'. I won't ask you to move in with me until we tie the knot. I know you and the kids will need to adjust, especially the kids." Carlie nodded in return. She knew that Colt respected her as well as her children and Carlie was grateful for that about him. "I agree. But it will be nice to start making wedding plans." Colt squeezed her hands in his. "Now in other news." Carlie's eyes grew big. "There's more?!" She said, surprised. She couldn't imagine there being much more news than Colt asking her to marry him. Nothing could top him putting a ring on her finger. The man she had only known for a month had just asked her to be his wife. What could possibly be better than that?

Colt nodded. "I know, but I wanted to let you know that I found a house for you to rent if you are interested. The local diner is hiring a part time cook if you are interested in that and like that kind of work. And I found a community college not too far from my town where you can take classes in whatever your little heart desires. I remember you mentioning maybe taking up culinary or creative writing classes so I made sure I found a school that offers you both." He took a deep breath as he watched the look of surprise and gratefulness settle on Carlie's face. Carlie could not be more in love with him than at this moment. She could not believe that with all the work he had to do on the ranch and running his business that Colt had taken the time to find her a place to live for her and her kids, let alone a job *and* a local school where she could start making her dreams come true. She wanted to hug him and cry.

Suddenly Carlie did not want to stay in Ohio for one day longer. She wanted to move now. Yet, she knew she would have to wait until she could contact the kids school and get their records so they could transfer. Carlie thought for a moment then decided it would be easy to obtain their school records. She could do that this afternoon. But, she would still need time to pack everything and get a trailer to move. She decided to wait until after Thanksgiving. That would give her a few days to get everything together and wrapped up. She had the check from the Hanes. She wondered if she should go ahead and deposit it or hang onto it until she could open a bank account in Colorado. She was opting for the latter, but she would run it by Colt. Carlie wasn't sure how much it would cost to rent a U-Haul truck.

"So this afternoon I am going to the kids' schools to get their school records so that they can transfer when we get to Colorado. I think that the Saturday after Thanksgiving would be a good day to start moving. I am not sure how much it would be to rent a U-Haul truck or something. Oh and I think I am going to wait to deposit the real estate check until we get to Colorado and open a bank account there. What do you think?" Colt nodded. "I think you have a plan. I can stay up here through Thanksgiving and help you pack. As far as a U-Haul truck, I can help you with that. We can pack most of the boxes in the back of my truck and you aren't taking a whole lot of furniture so we don't need a huge truck. And as far as a bank account, that's a smart idea. I would just withdraw all your money from your bank up here and close the account. That way you don't have to worry about any money getting lost by having it transferred to a new account, especially out of state." Carlie nodded. "That makes sense." She stated. "And Colt, thank you for staying and helping." Colt winked at her. "It was all a part of my plan when I decided to fly up here at the last minute." He grinned at her. "Shall we go then so we can get to the schools?" Carlie nodded, smiling back at him. "We shall." She said as she took his hand and exited the restaurant with the new love of her life.

Chapter 23

Carlie had no problems obtaining copies of the school records she needed for transferring the kids to what would soon to be their new school in Colorado. While visiting the middle school, Carlie was pleased to learn from the principle that Roxy's grades had come up and that she had been attending on a regular basis. Roxy had returned to being the student her teachers had admired and had known her to be. Carlie was relieved to find that her daughter had made such an amazing turn around. After the whole sign-his-kids off incident with Joe, Roxy had quieted down and her attitude had been more positive. Carlie attributed the change in her daughter to the fact that Roxy had come to realize that Joe was no longer a part of their lives. She also knew that Roxy could see her mother being more positive and was trying to make their lives more positive as well. Carlie was happy to see that their lives were starting to move towards a new and positive direction and she silently and sincerely thanked God above for sending Colt Storm into their lives.

"Anywhere else?" Colt inquired as they exited the middle school. Carlie studied him for a moment. "Well, I was planning on going to the store to get all the Thanksgiving fixings." Then added, "If that's not too boring for you." Colt pinched her arm teasingly. Carlie laughed as she jerked her arm away. "Nothing is too boring with you, darlin'." Colt grinned at her as Carlie hooked her arm back into his. The two climbed into Carlie's SUV and headed off to the store.

Once parked and inside, Carlie grabbed a cart and the couple began their first holiday meal shopping together. Turkey, potatoes and stuffing were on the list, of course. Then came the ingredients for homemade pumpkin and apple pies followed by ingredients for stuffed clams, asparagus, and antipasta salad. Carlie looked at Colt. "Is there anything special you eat or would like to have at Thanksgiving?" Colt thought for a moment. It had been a long time since he had had a woman cook him Thanksgiving. Heck, it had been a long time since a woman had cooked for him period. Jenna had not been much of a cook. Her idea of dinner was finding the most expensive restaurant around and eating out.

"Well now, I do like homemade mac and cheese or some shrimp cocktail." Carlie smiled. "We shall have both then." She added shrimp and cocktail sauce along with the makings of mac and cheese to the cart. "I think we have everything." She finally announced. Colt smiled at her as they headed to the check out lane. Carlie looked for Laura, but then remembered that her friend had gotten another job and no longer worked in the grocery store. Once everything was bagged, paid for, and loaded in the cart, the couple headed out to load the car up and then to Carlie's house to put the groceries away. Carlie would start baking pies and cookies on Monday. As Colt pulled into the drive, Carlie wondered if he had gotten a hotel room. She thought about offering him her sofa bed. It was downstairs in the living room far away from the bedroom and any temptation.

Once the groceries had been brought in and put away, the couple relaxed on the sofa in Carlie's living room. "You have some really nice pieces in here. Are you sure you want to get rid of it?" Colt asked. Carlie nodded. "Nothing in here is worth keeping. It is all pieces Joe and I bought together. I just want new stuff that doesn't remind me of him. The kids love their bedroom sets so I am keeping them. I was going to keep mine, but I think now that I don't want to keep it. Too much past history. When I said I wanted to start over, that meant with everything. I don't want the memories of Joe following me." She replied. Colt drew her closer. He could definitely understand where Carlie was coming from. Besides, he could help her with new furniture once she settled into her new place in Colorado.

"Besides," Carlie continued, "I got a really good deal on all this furniture." She smiled at him, snuggling into the crook of his arm. As she did, Colt got a wif of her freshly washed hair and her perfume. It had been too long since he had held a woman this close and Carlie was making him feel things he had not felt in a long time. He knew he had to be careful. It would be too easy to fall into the temptation he knew had to wait until they were married. He took a deep breath. "I understand that, darlin'." He smiled down at her. "So where are you staying while you are in town?" Colt shifted slightly. "I booked a room at the hotel I stayed in last time I was here." He answered. Carlie nodded. "If it's too much for you, you are welcome to crash on the couch." The words came out before Carlie could stop them. She tried to quickly recover by stating that she wasn't trying to seduce him or anything like that. She knew that both of them wanted to wait until they were married. Colt grinned."Darlin, as heavenly as that sounds, I think the hotel will be fine. Better to avoid any temptation don't you think?" Carlie nodded in agreement. "Of course. Besides, the kids might not understand." She smiled up at him again. "I guess the kids and I have a lot to talk about tonight."

Carlie sounded a little nervous and Colt knew that she was wondering how Roxy and Josh would react to the news of their mother getting married again; to a man that was not thier father. However, Colt was willing to bet that neither Roxy or Josh would have too much of a problem with it being that their dad had basically written them off. Carlie had informed him that Joe was going to pay her child support every month. Colt could not understand how a man could just dump his children and decide that he never wanted to see them or be a a part of their lives again. It just didn't make sense. Was the man really that selfish about his own life and new relationship? Colt just could not wrap his mind around it. He was, however, grateful that Carlie belonged to him now. He at least had Joe to thank for that.

Colt knew Joe had hurt Carlie and her children more than he could ever imagine and Colt vowed that he would try and be the father figure and husband that Roxy, Josh, and Carlie needed. He knew it was a lot of responsibility to take on a whole new family, but he also knew without a shadow of a doubt that this was where God had led him. He would prove to Carlie and her children what true love was. He knew it would be an adjustment, but Colt also knew that God would knit them all together.

Colt relaxed as he planted a soft kiss on Carlie's forehead. "Don't worry sweetheart. I am sure Roxy and Josh will understand and accept this. They need a real man in their lives and I will do all I can to be that man for them and for you." Colt assured her as he squeezed Carlie a little tighter. She sighed. "I love you, Colt. Thank you for that and I know God will bring us together and knit us together to be a real family and the kids will be just fine. I think they will be happy once we get settled and they get adjusted."

Carlie responded with tears in her eyes. She had never felt so in love as she did right now. Sure. She had loved Joe, but now as she looked back, she wondered just how much Joe had loved her. She wondered if it had been love on her part or if her and the kids had just been a way to gain stature in the community. Joe had strived to become a pillar of society and Carlie was convinced that the perfect wife and two children had pushed him to that level. She was certain that since he had gained his status, Joe had signed his family off. He had no longer needed them once he was established in the community. He had sought out a new life with a younger woman. Carlie knew she had to let all that go. She had found an amazing man with whom she could start a completely new life with. A man who would love her and her children unconditionally. Colt was everything Carlie had hoped and prayed and wished for. She knew her kids would accept him and she could not wait to start their new lives together in a new home and a new state. Carlie turned and kissed Colt softly. She smiled at him Everything was going to be just fine now. Colt kissed her back. *Barkis is willin.* He thought to himself smiling.

Chapter 24

After a couple of hours of coffee, cuddling, and talking, Colt stood to leave. He knew that Carlie's kids would be coming home from school soon and that she would need the time to sit and talk with them. Carlie had told Colt of her dreams of being a writer or a culinary chef, or both. She had told him all of this when they had first met, but he did not mind hearing it again. She informed him that she longed to go to Italy someday, specifically to Venice and Rome. Colt smiled. He wanted to make all of her dreams come true and told her so. Carlie could not believe how much this man loved her. She could not believe how much she had fallen in love with him over the short period of time they had known each other. She was more convinced than ever that this was God's will. His way of healing her and showing her real love. Colt kissed Carlie before leaving. He promised her that he would be back later for dinner and a movie with her and the kids. Colt knew and understood that Carlie needed some time to talk with Roxy and Josh about the events that had taken place with the house selling and spending Christmas in Colorado instead of here in Ohio where they had spent it all of their childhoods. He reassured Carlie that the kids would be accepting. After all, Roxy and Josh already knew that they were going to be moving and according to their mother, neither of the kids had any problems with the decision to leave Ohio. According to Carlie, both Roxy and Josh were excited about the move and had no issues with her dating Colt. Colt was glad for that. He knew this is what God was giving him; this family, this opportunity. God was working and Colt knew that Carlie and her kids would be healed and be able to move on with their lives and with him.

After Colt left, Carlie prepared after school snacks for Roxy and Josh. She heated a pepperoni hot pocket for Roxy. Roxy would be home in just a few short minutes and would be wanting a snack. She put ice in a glass and filled it with Dr. Pepper, Roxy's favorite pop. Carlie smiled as she put out a plate of cookies that would wait for Josh to arrive 45 minutes behind his sister. She was excited and nervous about telling the kids how quickly the house had sold and that they would be moving right after Thanksgiving.

She was hoping that Colt was right and the kids would be as excited as she was. What was that old saying she read once in a play? Oh yes. *Barkis is willin.* She smiled again. She only hoped Roxy and Josh were willing. Forget Barkis, her children were who mattered. And as long as her children were happy, Carlie was happy.

Roxy came through the door just as Carlie finished pouring the Dr Pepper. "Hey Mom." Roxy said as she slumped down in a chair and dropped her book bag on the floor. "Hi Honey. How was school?" Carlie greeted her daughter. "Ugh. Don't ask!" Roxy answered as she took a drink of the cold pop. Carlie set the hot pocket in front of Roxy. "That good, huh?" Roxy took a bite of the pocket and swallowed. "Classes are fine. I aced my history and English exams. I just can't wait to get out of this town! I hate trying to dodge questions and looks from the other kids. It's been a year, Mom. Why can't everyone just get over it already?!" Carlie understood her daughter's frustrations. "Well, honey, I have some news, but it has to wait until your brother comes home." That seemed to spark Roxy's interest. "Please tell me we can move like tomorrow!" Carlie smiled. "Not quite that soon. I'll explain when your brother gets home." Roxy nodded as she finished off her snack. She could live with the fact she had to wait another half hour or so to hear the news. Judging from her Mother's tone of voice, Roxy knew the news had to be good. Her Mom never sounded happy when there was bad news and she certainly was never as excited as Roxy could tell she was. So, Roxy concluded that she and Josh were about to recieve some really awesome news. Maybe they could finally leave this town and move to Colorado.

Roxy had decided that she liked Colt. He seemed to be good for her Mom. Her mom seemed to always be happy whenever she got off the phone with Colt. And in Roxy's eyes that was a good thing. Plus he had a horse ranch and Roxy *loved* horses. She could not wait to go riding on one of Colt's horses. She knew that her brother would love it too. He could be a boy and do guy things with Colt. Josh needed that, Roxy knew. She put her plate in the sink and sat and chatted with her Mom until Josh finally came bursting through the door.

Carlie turned to give her son a hug. Josh threw his bag on the floor. "I hate school!" He exclaimed without warning.

"Everyone is so mean! It's not our fault Dad's a loser!" He ran into Carlie's arms and cried. Carlie held him tight and kissed the top of his head. After a couple of minutes, she gently pulled her son off her and bent down to look him in the eyes. She gently wiped away the tears that were running down his face. "Honey, I'm so sorry." Carlie said in a quiet voice. "Listen, I have something to tell you and Roxy. Go sit down and I'll pour you some ice cold milk and we will all talk." Josh nodded and took a seat next to his sister who smiled at him.

Carlie sat the promised glass of milk in front of Josh. She poured herself a Pepsi in a glass and joined her kids at the table. "As you guys know," Carlie began. " We have been talking about moving to Colorado. Well I have some news. We may be moving quicker than what I thought we would be." She stopped there to watch the expressions on her kids' faces. Roxy's eyes widened. Josh dropped his cookie and stared hopefully at his mother. She kept them in suspense just a few seconds longer. "I sold the house this morning along with most of the furniture. Just the pieces I don't want to keep. Colt is here in town and he is going to help us with the moving arrangements." Carlie studied her children once more as she waited for their responses.

Roxy jumped up and hugged her mother. A few moments later, Josh was in his mother's arms as well. "About time, Mom!" Roxy exclaimed. "When? When can we move?" Josh chimed in. "When can we see Colt? I really like him!" Roxy added. Josh nodded in agreement. Carlie hugged her kids tight and smiled. "Well, I figured we could have one last Thanksgiving here with Grandma,Grandpa, your uncles and cousins. Then the Saturday after Thanksgiving we can start packing and be moved in a week." Carlie paused. "We can still go to the Holidazzle parade in town Saturday night if you guys want to and then we can start moving to Colorado on Sunday. I already pulled you out of school and have all your records. Colt found us a place out there and some job leads for me. So we are pretty much set to move."

Roxy and Josh both smiled. "Sounds great, Mom! Really!" Roxy said as they sat back down at the table. "I'm glad. As far as when you can see Colt, he would like to come over tonight for dinner and a movie if that is ok with you two." Josh grinned his boyish grin. Roxy's face was beaming like Carlie had never seen it before. She knew her children were genuinely happy about the changes that were taking place. She knew now that this was God's plan for her and her children. He had brought Colt into her life and everything was falling into place. Josh and Roxy were thrilled at the fact that Colt was coming over. After their snacks were finished, Carlie shooed them into the living room so she could clean up the dishes and decide what to make for dinner.

Two hours later, Colt was standing in the kitchen with Carlie as she set the table. Chicken cordon bleu was the special for the night, with asparagus tips and fried potatoes. She had manged to make a cheesecake for desert. As she put the glasses out, Carlie caught Colt popping an asparagus tip in his mouth. She teasingly smacked his hand, finding herself being pulled into his arms when she did. He smiled down at her and kissed her. "So, Miss Michaels, did you tell the kids the news?" He inquired.b"I did." She anwered.b"And?"bhe asked.b"Well, I don't think they are happy about it." She teased, wrinkling her nose at him. Colt laughed. "I know you are lying Miss Michaels. Why I just saw Roxy dragging a suitcase up to her room when I came in." Carlie laughed. "You got me. They couldn't be more thrilled." Colt let go and looked her in the eyes. "I am glad." Carlie nodded. "Me too. It's been a long time coming." She acknowledged as she placed the last glass in front of a plate. The table was set and ready for dinner. As Carlie went to call for Roxy and Josh, Colt stopped her and pulled her in for one more private kiss. Carlie kissed him deeply as she let him hold her close. Once they let go, Carlie smiled at Colt. She knew that everything from now on was going to be perfectOK.Ok, so she knew nothing was absolutely perfect, but this was pretty close to perfection.

Supper was full of laughter and chatter about the holidays and the big move to Colorado .Carlie could not help but to feel emotional at the thought that Thanksgiving would be the last time she would ever be in this house. This was where she and her two brothers had grown up. This was where she had lived and had her children. There were a lot of memories in this old place, both good and bad. Carlie knew however, that the future was going to be bright. It was time to pack up the old and move on with the new.

She smiled at Colt and her children as she took a sip of sweet tea. Right now, in this moment, she could not be happier. Colt looked across the table at his fiancee. He saw the tears she was fighting. He knew the cause for those tears were both happy and a little sad. He knew it was not easy for her to just give up the very house she had lived in all her life and had her own children in. Yet, he also knew that she was glowing with joy at the prospect of being with him and starting a new life with him and her children in Colorado. The latter made Colt overwhelmed with joy himself; joy and gratefulness for God bringing this amazing, strong woman into his life. And Colt Storm would not have had it any other way. Carlie's eyes met Colt's. She smiled at him as her eyes sparkled. The struggle was over. Carlie knew that she and her children were going to be very happy with Colt in Colorado. She silently thanked the good Lord for bringing this man into her life. She looked at Roxy and Josh who were laughing with Colt and each other. Yes. They were going to very happy in their new life. The struggle was over. True love and real peace had finally made their way into Carlie Michaels' heart, life, and family.

Synopsis

When Carlie Michaels finds out that her husband is having an affair with a much younger woman, everything changes. After the divorce, she finds herself struggling to raise her two children, Roxy and Josh on her own while holding down a job which barely meets her bills. On top of all the usual struggles of being thrown into single mom status, her trusty blue truck breaks down and Carlie is left trying to figure out how to keep everything going. When Carlie's estranged husband decides to write off their kids forever, the news throws the family into another world of hurt, pain, and confusion. Carlie finds herself finally turning back to the One she knows who can heal herself and her children. Carlie Micahels finds herself once again struggling to trust God, who she knows loves her, yet she can not comprehend why Joe Welsh left her and the kids not once, but twice. She is left to wonder if the struggle and pain will ever end.

Colt Storm, a rancher and furniture maker from Colorado, enters into Carlie's life at the most awkward moment. Unexpectedly, he helps Carlie in more ways than Carlie could ever expect or dream about. But is it enough for Carlie and her two children who are also struggling with the hurt of the divorce? Colt does not want to jump into anything with Carlie Michaels, but leaves everything in God's hands and prays for God's will in both his life and Carlie's life. Colt can only trust God to work in Carlie's life as he watches her struggle and sees the hurt and pain in her and her children. Will God bring them together as a couple or was Colt just in the right place at the right time to be a small miracle in Carlie's life when she needed it?